POTLUCK AND POWERS

MIXING UP MAGIC, BOOK 4

ROSIE PEASE

PAISLEY PRESS BOOKS
WEST WARWICK, RHODE ISLAND

For all the grandmothers out there.
Thank you for all the love you provide.

With special love and thanks to Jackie, Gertrude, Bertha, Julie, Dorothy, Mary P, Mary R, Barbara, Meg, and Doreen. The grandmas, gammas, nans, nanas, grams, gramas, and great-grandmas in my family, the ones I have, the ones I miss, and the ones I wish I got to meet.

ABOUT THIS BOOK

An anticipated visit brings about unexpected revelations.

And the implications could change Joanie's life forever.

Gram's quick trip promised to teach Joanie how to protect her house from ghosts, a crash course in how to be a witch, and a bit of fun during the full moon. Instead, the two find themselves dealing with more than they bargained for when surprises keep showing up at Joanie's front door.

Now at the center of several mysteries involving all aspects of her paranormal powers, will Joanie be able discover the truth? Or will Gram's antics and embarrassing stories derail her friendships when Joanie needs to trust them the most?

AUTHOR'S NOTE

Dear Reader,

Thank you so much for picking *Potluck and Powers* as your next read. I hope you enjoy the direction Joanie's story takes as Gram comes to visit.

This book contains a few of my favorite scenes out of the series thus far, including the opening with Saffy. The tortie calico has been great fun to write, and it's fun to insert a bit of my soul kitty Zoe's personality into her.

At times throughout the book, the plot even surprised me. There was one twist I did not see coming until the truth was out of the character's mouth. I had to write that scene twice, once with the way it surprised me and once again the way I had planned it to see what I really liked better. And the surprise stuck. Sometimes one's characters know better than I do what's going to happen. But that's all I'm going to say about that for now.

I love hearing from readers. If you'd like to reach out to me, you can do so across social media @WriteRosiePease.

Happy reading!

Cheers,
Rosie

CHAPTER I

S affy chased me through the living room.

"No, you silly thing. You can't have this yet."

It was all a game to her.

It was anything but a game to me. Gram was coming, and I had to be ready.

I stopped at the mantel over the fireplace that I'd turned into a bookshelf shortly after moving here, knowing I wouldn't use it for a fire. The dark wood mantel and my various knickknacks were coated in a fine layer of dust.

Saffy slid to a stop against my legs before turning to scramble up the chair next to the fireplace.

There were mere seconds left to dust before she'd strike.

I swished the feather duster I had in my hand over and around all the trinkets I'd collected over the years. Pretty shells I'd found on the beach near where I went to culinary school, a stone with a hole through it that I'd found on a family vacation to Florida when I was a kid, an empty tin of saffron, the hairbrush Ashley had let me keep after freeing her grandmother's spirit from it. All that and more were up there, and I didn't want my pudgy calico to send everything flying by jumping up here.

It was the feather duster she wanted. She was nearly as crazy about it as she was about catnip.

Saffy stood on her hind legs and braced herself against the mantel with one paw as she batted my hand and the duster with the other.

"Let me finish. She'll be here soon. I'm running out of time."

Saffy did not let me finish.

With one good swipe, she grabbed on to the feather portion of the duster with her claws and yanked it right out of my hand.

The duster popped up into the air, and Saffy lunged after it as I reached for it.

She won.

Saffy knocked it to the ground and landed on top of it before grabbing the feather end with her mouth. She ran off with it.

Now I was chasing her. "I still need that!"

She didn't listen and instead scrambled up her cat tree and onto her favorite perch. She dove her face into the feathered end, then flopped to her side to kick at the stick end with her hind paws.

This was why I didn't dust often.

"All right, you win this time, Saf." She always did.

Drats. It really *was* a game.

At least I had gotten the mantel done. Mostly.

Saffy's head popped up, and a few moments later, I heard it. The rumble of Gram's car engine as it entered the neighborhood. It was an older model something or other, but that's not why it was loud. It had been that way for as long as I could remember. She'd done something to it to make it that way. When I was a kid, Gram's neighbor had a deaf dog, and he liked to lounge in her driveway. Gram claimed the louder noise gave her engine a stronger vibration that the dog could feel and know to move out of the way before Gram got to her driveway. The dog was long gone, but Gram said the noise now benefited all the animals along the roads she drove. It also gave me a last-minute opportunity to make sure I'd not missed anything in getting ready for her.

"Oh, the tea!" I scooted into the kitchen, then turned on the burner below the already full teapot.

As the noise from Gram's car engine grew louder with her approach, I grabbed out two teacups and saucers, then placed them on the countertop. I'd let Gram choose what tea she wanted to drink.

Finally, when I thought it could get no louder, Gram's car went silent. She'd made it to my driveway. Less than a minute later, the car door slammed shut, and I scurried to the living room to open the front door for Gram and, no doubt, her many bags. I'd never seen the woman travel lightly. Years ago, when she helped me move into my apartment while I was still in culinary school, at least a quarter of what we'd packed up was dedicated to Gram's bags. Sometimes not all the bags would come out of the car, but she liked to be prepared. That was Gram, though. I didn't question it then, and I didn't question it now as I pushed the storm door open and stepped out onto the porch to let her in.

"There's one more bag in the trunk if you wouldn't mind grabbing that for me," Gram said as she shuffled past me.

"Hey, Gram. Mind the step up," I warned her.

When I saw that she was safely clear of the small step and in the house, I let go of the screen door and headed for the classic convertible, its top down in this gorgeous but hot summer weather. The trunk was still open, and I reached to pull out the medium-sized suitcase. Under the impression it was going to be lighter, I nearly lost my balance as my hand slipped off the handle while trying to lift it. It was a two-handed job, for sure.

With one hand on the top handle and the other on the side handle, I heaved the bag up and out of the trunk. It smacked my right hip with each step as I walked back into the house. I'd carried bags of flour and sugar for the bakery that were heavier than this, but the suitcase was awkward.

I plopped it down in the middle of my living room floor. "You know you're only here for two nights, right? Why do you need all this?"

"One can never be too prepared, especially when we have a cleansing to do, wards to reestablish, and who knows what else. The energy in here is all out of whack. No wonder ghosts are popping up in here at will."

"What do you have in here, bricks?"

Gram laughed. "No, but you're close. Books. And a set of crystals for you."

Of course. I should have guessed. Books and rocks. So very Gram.

I eyed my staircase. "It's going to be a little heavy carrying this to your room."

She waved me off as she approached Saffy. "It will be perfectly fine down here." She leaned forward to scratch Saffy behind the ears, her bracelets clinking together with the movement. "And how are you, sassy cat?"

Saffy popped her head up from the feather duster she'd gone back to picking apart after she'd identified the noise from Gram's car. I'd need to replace it before dusting again. It was a goner. Part of a feather was stuck to her tongue, and she twitched her head as she repeatedly stuck her tongue out and back in to work the feather off. I could hear the tongue-smacking noise from five feet away.

Gram giggled. "Feather got your tongue? Maybe that's been the problem all these years as to why you never say anything."

"She's a cat, Gram."

"Well, that could be it too. I know Sterling isn't always in the mood. Oh, that reminds me. I should let him know I've made it safely." She straightened, then turned back toward me with her arms wide open. "But first, come here."

We each took a few steps toward one another and wrapped each other up in a big hug. As great as Libby's hugs were, they had nothing on Gram's. Gram was warm, and her patchouli perfume reminded me of childhood.

I breathed in the scent. "It's so good to see you again. Thank you for coming."

"I'm sorry it took this long. And your mom is sorry that she couldn't make it, but she's still dealing with the insurance company and has an emergency board meeting tonight because of the damage."

"It's all right. She couldn't have predicted the storm the other night would cause one of the library's trees to go crashing into the building."

Gram nodded. "She looks forward to coming to visit soon, but if I'd realized how much the energies in here had shifted, I'd have come sooner. I'm sure she would have too. I can call and have her come after the board meeting if—"

"No, it's okay. That's a lot of driving if she's just going to have to turn right back around for another meeting tomorrow morning. I'm just glad you're here."

Gram gave me a final big squeeze before we ended our hug. We stepped back a foot but remained holding on to one another by our forearms.

I took in my grandmother. Her long silver hair was braided, the tail coming over her right shoulder. I was used to it being loose and a bit unkempt, but this kept her hair more manageable on long car rides with the top down. She called it her "driving look." Her mauve silk blouse was accented by several long necklaces and pendants. Some bearing crystals and gems, others metal charms, and one, a small glass vial, had who knows what in it. Some sand for sure, and maybe a few sprinklings of herbs, but the rest was a mystery to me. She wore ankle-length leggings, also part of her driving look, and finished her outfit with sneakers. Preferring to go bare-foot when she could, she'd never fussed over footwear, choosing comfort over style, usually in the form of sandals. No doubt she'd be changing once she had a moment to settle in.

"You were especially busy these last couple of months, so don't worry about it. You're here now. How are you and all your friends doing?" I asked. At that moment, the kettle on the stove whistled. "Come. You can tell me all about it over tea."

Gram smiled. "That is exactly what this old lady needs."

"Gram, you'll never be old," I replied as I passed her and headed into the kitchen

Laughing, she followed me into the room, and I pulled out my supply of loose-leaf teas. "I'm running low on a few"—I pushed the box toward her—"so if you don't see something you want, we can go to Leafs and Grounds later to restock. Gary has a great assortment, even more than he did the last time you were here."

She searched through the box of teas. "I have a few for you from Susan's shop, too, in one of my bags. I know how much you liked hers."

I turned off the burner but left the kettle on it. "What's going to happen to her shop?"

Gram pulled out a bag of black tea with hints of grapefruit. One of my summer favorites. "Well, her sister's taken it over for now, but we'll see what happens. It will most likely stay a tea shop since it does well, but it won't be the same without her, that's for sure."

Miss Susan had died a few months ago, sending Gram's circle of friends—her coven—into a tizzy. I'd found out about Miss Susan's death from her ghost when she'd come to visit me in my living room to pass along a message about my skills being cursed blessings. She hadn't said she'd been murdered, although that's what had happened.

Gram proved to be instrumental in catching who'd done it, even receiving a special commendation from the mayor, but it would have saved her a lot of time had Miss Susan told me who'd killed her.

I handed Gram an infuser basket and a spoon, and she scooped out a hefty teaspoon of leaves before putting it into the infuser. We swapped places at the counter so I could choose my tea, and she settled the infuser basket on top of her cup before pouring the near-boiling water over it until she had enough for tea. I did the same, then followed her to the kitchen table where she'd sat down.

"Things have calmed down now since the commendation ceremony," Gram began. "The coven has really come together, and one of the girls who Susan was mentoring in the ways has taken over her garden, and as I said, her sister is running the store now. She's got good business sense, but her skills are not the same as Susan's."

I thought back to wandering in Miss Susan's expansive garden as a kid. The flowers were bright and colorful, and the smells intoxicating. Yet somehow, it never got disturbed by bugs or other critters who would typically raid a garden like that. "I'd be sad to see that garden go. I'm glad someone will be tending it. But what about her house? Once that sells—"

"She donated it to the coven. Well, to some trustees who are in the coven, myself included. I don't know what we're going to do with it, but both it and the garden will stay in our hands."

"Oh, wow. She thought of everything."

"Well, she wasn't expecting to be killed, but when you get to a certain age and you have no younger family members to pass things down to, you need to come up with a plan before something happens."

I nodded. I'd be twenty-eight in a couple months. Not old by any stretch of the imagination, but right now, it was just me. Maybe it was time to create a contingency plan for the bakery just in case. The events with Bruce Malloy last month still weighed heavily on me. What if he had done more than go after my bakery to try to sink the business? What if he had come after me?

I shook the thought away. Things had worked out between the merrows and the selkies. The real killer had been caught. Even Bruce was being kinder now that his own secret had come to light. I caught sight of him every once in a while around town with Greta and Celia. He and I would never be friends, not by a longshot, but maybe someday we could be cordial if we ran into one another. For now, I avoided him as best I could, even forgoing a marshmallow rice treat when I saw he was at Leafs and Grounds.

"What are we doing today?" Gram asked, drawing me from my thoughts.

"I wanted to stop by the bakery today to show you all of the updates, and I invited some friends over for a potluck dinner tonight. It's Monday. I always have people over for dinner, even if it's just Matt." I blew across my teacup to cool it down. It was still too hot for me. "But I thought we were going to reestablish the wards around the house today."

"Ah, well, not all of that can happen today." Gram took a small sip from her cup before taking a larger second one. "We need to charge up all the crystals tonight during the full moon."

"Oh, okay. I hadn't thought of that. So how about, once you get settled, we head out to the cider mill and have lunch up there?"

"I like that idea. Maybe I can even find something to make for your potluck."

I sipped my tea, blinking at her. Was she serious? Gram did not cook. Not well anyway.

Gram cracked a smile. "I'm kidding, I'm kidding. You didn't get your kitchen witchery from me, that's for sure, but I'm positive I can contribute something to your get-together tonight." She winked.

What was I getting myself into?

CHAPTER 2

When we reached the walkway after stepping off my porch, Gram tossed her keys at me. "You're driving."

"We can take my car, Gram."

"Nope." She continued walking toward her car.

"You want me to drive your convertible?"

She jumped, literally, into the passenger seat, never having opened the door. "You know how I love the route out there."

"All right . . ." I opened the driver's side door, then got in. In all my years of driving, I'd never been allowed to drive her convertible. "There are no tricks to this thing, right?"

She laughed. "No. It's loud, but I promise you, there's nothing different about it than any other car. She patted the dashboard. Probably runs better than yours."

My station wagon was getting up there in age, although years newer than Gram's car. It had its moments, but I'd worked so hard to get the trunk set up to make deliveries that I hesitated to think about the car's eventual replacement.

After buckling in, I turned the key in the ignition, and the engine roared to life. Between the noise of the car and the air whipping around us with the top down, there'd be no talking on the way to the cider mill. And I needed to talk to Gram. There was so much I had to learn about all this witch stuff. I'd been reading what I could from the library, but I was having trouble putting it all together. What applied to me?

As I drove out of the neighborhood and across the main road into Heartwood Hollow's rural outskirts, I repeatedly glanced at Gram. She had large purple sunglasses on that covered nearly half her face. She'd kept her hair in a braid— that should have been my first clue that we'd be taking her car wherever we went today—but she'd changed out of her sneakers and leggings for cushy leather sandals and a pair of pants made that flared in such a way it looked like a skirt. I liked it. They were a subdued paisley pattern that slightly reminded me of Kate's pants the night she had appeared in my bedroom while I was trying to free her from her hairbrush.

We curved around the first hill, then ascended the second before coming up on the crossroads right before the big hill crested. This was one of my favorite views around. Farmlands dotted the landscape below, and the hamlet of Bug's Creek lay just ahead, the actual Bug Creek flowing somewhere out of sight behind the trees to the northeast. The whole sight was so picturesque it almost saddened me that there was a road here because I could never take it all in and capture it in the short moment before whatever car I was in began its descent. I only ever got bits and pieces that eventually formed the whole image in my mind.

I took my foot off the accelerator as we started our downhill journey. We'd coast until the terrain leveled out at the bottom of the long hill.

Gram raised her arms straight up and over her head, standing as she did. When had she unbuckled her seat belt?

"Gram!" I yelled, but I doubted she'd heard me. Either that or she was ignoring me, not wanting me to tell her to sit down.

"Whoohoo!" she shouted at the top of her lungs, her voice carrying in the wind.

As we coasted down the hill, past the big red barn that had been converted into housing for med students doing a rotation at the hospital and further past one of the local motels that catered to summer tourists on a budget, I looked at my grandmother. Her hands up in the air, still yelling, she seemed so free. At that moment, I envied her a little.

Maybe I just needed to follow her lead. I was still figuring myself out, but she seemed to know who she was in the world.

As the road leveled, Gram plopped back into her seat, then relatched her seat belt. "That was great. I've always wanted to do that. Thank you."

And then I saw the flashing lights turning onto the road behind us from the motel parking lot.

"Drats."

Gram looked behind her as I pulled to the side of the road, the police cruiser doing the same right behind me. "I'm so sorry. I'll pay the cost of whatever ticket you get."

A moment later, the police officer walked up to the driver's side of the car.

"Joanie?"

I knew that voice, and it wasn't just because the officer was one of Heartwood Hollow's finest.

I glanced up at my best friend's boyfriend, warmth flooding my face. "Hi, Seth."

After handing him my license and registration, he asked, "When did you get a convertible?"

"I didn't. It's—"

Gram leaned forward and lifted her sunglasses onto her head. "It's mine," she said with a slight finger wave.

"Seth, Gram. Gram, Seth." I turned my head to get a better look at my grandmother. "Seth is Courtney's boyfriend. You remember meeting her the last time you were here, right?"

"Oh, I do. Lovely girl. Great laugh. Hullo, Seth. So nice to meet you." Gram leaned across me to shake Seth's hand.

"Likewise. So, um, were you just standing up in your car?"

Gram tilted her head to one side in a sheepish look. "I was. I don't know what came over me. It's such a good hill, and it's a gorgeous day, and I really couldn't help myself. I'm sorry. Please don't give my granddaughter a ticket. She didn't know what I was doing until it was too late. Look. I have my seat belt back on now."

"I see that." He sighed. "Well, can you promise me you won't do it again?"

Gram crossed her heart. "I promise."

"All right. I'm going to give you a warning this time. I don't want to hear it from Courtney if I give her best friend's grandmother a ticket, especially on the same day that we're due to go over her house for dinner." He glanced at me. "I'm looking forward to it very much."

I breathed a sigh of relief. "Thanks, Seth. I really appreciate it. I'll keep a better watch over her from now on."

Seth barked out a laugh. "Somehow I think she's not going to make that easy for you."

I laughed along with him, hoping he was wrong.

He handed me back my license and registration. "Okay, I'm going to let you go. I'll see you later."

"See you later."

"And thank you," Gram added. "Please tell Courtney I'm looking forward to seeing her again."

"She'll be excited to see you, I'm sure." Seth turned on his heels and strode away, allowing me to put my things away. After he got back into his patrol car, he waved us back onto the street, then the lights on the cruiser turned off.

I gave him a wave over my shoulder as we drove away, and I watched in the rearview mirror as he made a U-turn and headed back toward town.

"That was exciting," Gram said loud enough so I could hear her. She chuckled.

"You're lucky it was Seth who pulled us over. I don't know any of the other officers as well as I do him."

"You should probably fix that. You never know when you might need them to do a favor for you or apologize for getting too close to a crime scene even if you were right about it all along. It helps smooth things over."

Gram was speaking from experience, knowing all about getting involved with police investigations after Miss Susan's murder. I hoped to never be in her shoes, but after making the claims I had about Bruce Malloy last month that proved to be false, it probably wouldn't hurt to try and win some of the officers over. Even though I hadn't accused Bruce formally, thank goodness, I'd have to bring some cookies over to the police station soon.

As we reached the hamlet of Bug Creek, I turned right at the intersection and drove about a mile until we hit Cider Road, where Bug Creek Cider Mill was situated, at least the storefront anyway. The entire operation spread out for acres around with its groves of various types of apples.

The mill store was busy, unsurprising for a Monday afternoon at the height of the summer at lunchtime. The store was a destination unto itself along with its resident geese, ducks, and chickens, and the fact they made delicious food in addition to having yummy samples throughout their shop certainly contributed to their popularity. I parked the convertible in the large dirt parking lot across the street from the store, and then we made our way into the main lot.

"Food or samples first?" I asked Gram, whose gaze was darting between the store building and the smaller structure where their cider mill's food stand was situated.

"Food. Then I won't fill up on samples first. I want to make sure I eat my entire lunch this time."

I laughed. She'd learned since the last time we'd been here. It was a mistake I'd made myself a time or two as well.

We wove through the line behind several others still waiting to order from the woman at the window. It gave me time to figure out what I wanted. Unlike at Olde Templeton or Leafs and Grounds where I almost always ordered the same thing every time I stayed for lunch, I liked to vary things up a bit here. Did I want the pulled pork with apple barbeque sauce, the chili mac and cheese where the chili had chunks of apple in it, or a pot roast sandwich that had slow cooked in the mill store's apple cider?

Decisions, decisions.

I was still trying to decide as Gram and I stepped up to the window.

"I'll have the pot roast sandwich with a side of apple fries," Gram said to the woman working the window.

That took the pot roast out of the running for me. I never liked to order the same thing as the other person I was eating with. And this way, I could order something else and still have a bite of the sandwich when Gram offered me a bite to try. She may not have been a good cook herself, but she had always made sure to expose me to a variety of foods when I was growing up, even if that meant me having a piece of whatever she was having to see if I liked it. I may have grown up, but Gram hadn't stopped the practice.

"And how about you, hun?" the woman asked me.

"I'll have the pulled pork sandwich and a cider doughnut." The likelihood that someone would be bringing mac and cheese to the potluck tonight was pretty good, and Courtney made a fabulous chili that I wouldn't be surprised to see either.

"Anything to drink?"

"A cider float," I answered.

"And I'll have the apple wine," Gram said. Gram had always appreciated good wine, and the mill's was some of the freshest I'd ever had.

After we paid for our meal, we chose a seat under the extended roof of the building, where the mill had set up several picnic tables, and waited for our order number to be called. There were so many things I wanted to ask Gram, so much I wanted to know about being a witch, but I knew it was best to not rush her. Both of us worked better with a full stomach anyway, although for me it was so that I wouldn't eat everything I baked.

"Number twenty-seven!" someone called from the kitchen after a few minutes.

I stood from the table. "That's us."

I walked the several feet to pick up our lunch, and when I turned back around, I found Gram standing next to the table we'd been sitting at.

"I thought it would do us some good to sit in the sunshine for a while. It's good for my old bones too."

"Gram, you're not old," I said, repeating my earlier statement to her. She'd barely aged a day since my childhood. Her hair had turned silvery white, but she still looked the same to me beyond that. She'd had my mother young, and my mom had me young, too, so Gram was younger than most grand-parents of people my age.

Then again, maybe that was part of Gram's magic.

"I'm older than you. Now humor your grandmother and come sit in the sun." She walked out to one of the picnic tables in the side yard where a small playground had also been built. I'd regularly seen parents sit out here as their children played.

As soon as she sat down, Gram bent over and pulled off her sandals. She placed them on the seat next to her as she let her feet drop to the ground and then dug her toes into the grass. I hadn't even placed our tray of food on the table yet.

"Twenty-seven," she said as I sat across from her, setting the tray down as I did.

I removed my food from the tray, then slid it over to her. "Yeah, that was our order number."

"It's fitting, that's all." She reached for her wine glass, then put it up to her mouth.

"What do you mean?"

Gram took a small sip, then set the wine back on the table with a small *aah*. "Numerology. The two and the seven. But first, take off your shoes."

I lifted an eyebrow at her. She knew I preferred keeping my feet covered.

She returned the look, not breaking it even as she took a bite of her pot roast sandwich.

"All right. You know best." I slid off my flats, grateful I wasn't wearing socks, then set my feet down on the grass. Shaded by the table, the grass was cool, and a chill spread up my back.

"Good. You're grounding yourself. Now let that energy fill your spirit as you fill your belly." She popped an apple fry into her mouth. "In numerology, the study of numbers, the two represents duality, partnerships, connections in relation-ships . . . be it person, job, anything really. It's a good one for you as a matchmaker. You seek to find these connections for people and work to make them whole."

Munching on my sandwich, I nodded. That made sense to me.

"Now the seven. The seven draws lunar energy, and as you know, it's a full moon tonight. You see this number pop up in intuition-related workings. Maybe you never noticed it before, but I'm sure it's been around you often in your work. Your matchmaking draws from intuition as well, that feeling of people being right for one another."

"But this was just the number we were given," I said finally before taking a sip of my float. The vanilla ice cream, ginger ale, and apple cider combination was one of my favorites. I rarely drank soda-based drinks, but I made excep-tions to those that involved ice cream, like this float and the Brown Cow at Double Aitch.

"Based on a lot of different factors right down to me taking a moment to choose to eat first. Eat after and we're many numbers after this one. Take a few seconds less deciding and we get in line ahead of that other couple, and we're order twenty-six. Not get pulled over on the way here and we end up in front of everyone eating right now. There are no—"

"Coincidences," I finished for her. "I know."

"And two plus seven is nine, which among other things is for the humanitarian, which is also you."

I nearly choked on my bite of sandwich. "Gram, I hardly think I'm a humanitarian."

"Oh, no? You are. Look at all that hullabaloo you went through to keep your last couple together, the compassion you had for that fellow who pulled the knife out in your store, the generosity and selflessness as you help the ghosts who have come to you through one way or another. The nine also represents growth, and you've been doing a lot of that lately in your personal sphere. Ken and Ivy, for sure, but also in your acceptance of who you are and could be. You'd never have believed you were a witch years ago."

"Well, that's certainly true." I took another sip of my float. "Why didn't you ever just come out and tell me?"

Gram barked out a laugh. "We tried! It was all around you."

She had a point. Since I moved to college, they'd been cleansing wherever I lived with smudge sticks. When I was a kid, we'd opened and closed doors at the New Year to let the energy flow, the old out and the new in. Gram worked with crystals. Aside from being a librarian, Mom was a matchmaker. And before I'd accepted all this witchery, I saw ghosts and had become a matchmaker too. Not to mention my aunt, cousin, and my family's friends who also had special gifts now that I thought about it. Like Miss Susan and her tea.

"How do you manage it all? The moon phases, the crystals, the recipes." Recipes were what I called spells. It was easier for me to wrap my head around and allowed me to talk about some of this out in the open without drawing attention to myself the way using witchy words could. I'd accepted what I was, but I wasn't ready for the wider world to know yet. The paranormal support group was enough for now.

"It all comes with time. This has been my whole life. This has been yours too, but you've only been embracing it for a few months. You'll get it. Don't worry. You've been studying. Casting your own spells. It will come."

"It's all a lot to take in."

"And you have me to help when you need it. And your mom." She grinned as if she weren't telling me something, but I knew it was better to leave it alone. She'd tell me when the time was right.

A short while later, we finished our meal and then headed back around to the front of the store building. It was time to shop and get some inspiration for new dishes at the bakery.

CHAPTER 3

"There's my favorite customer!" a familiar voice called, putting a smile on my face.

Standing on the front porch of the mill store was Cindy Bug, the owner of the cider mill and one of my favorite people here. The older woman stood waving at me in her green cider mill store shirt and khaki pants.

"It's so good to see you again. Let me get the door for you," she said as Gram and I climbed the three steps to the porch. She grabbed the door handle and pushed in at the same time an employee on the inside pulled it open. "Whoops!"

"Thank you," I replied. "It's good to see you too."

Both women gave me a big smile, and Cindy followed me in as I grabbed a shopping cart from the other employee.

The store was set up so you almost had to follow a path to try all the samples, but Gram never was one for following the crowd. She took off toward the cheese and wine as I started along the wall of sauces, dipping a pretzel stick or tortilla chip into each sample to try.

"We've had a lot of new products come in since the last time you were here," Cindy said.

"Oh, I can't wait to try them." I hadn't been here since taking Ken and Ivy before the tourist season picked up. Before that, it hadn't been since sometime between Thanksgiving and Christmas. I mostly came here during the late summer and throughout the fall because this was where I bought all my apples for anything I baked in my shop.

As I went down the wall of samples, Cindy pointed out the new products, giving me her opinion on them. Occasionally she'd stop to tidy up one of the shelves, but for the most part, when Cindy was working, it was like having a personal shopping assistant. Maybe it had something to do with just how many apples I bought each year. Whatever the reason, it was one of the things I liked about coming here. I could always tell how much everyone cared about their customers.

As I turned the corner to start trying the salsas and hot sauces, my shopping cart already a third of the way full with products I had loved the samples of, I spotted Gram approaching me from the corner of my eye.

So did Cindy. "Oh, well, I should be getting back now. You don't need me following you around when you're here for fun shopping with your grandmother."

"Really? I'm sure she won't mind. I always enjoy your company when I shop."

She smiled. "You two enjoy yourselves. I'll see you next time. Wave to me before you go." She turned and headed back down the way we came, nodding and saying hello to two couples who had come in after Gram and me.

I eyed Gram's shopping cart full of cheese, wine, a half peck of apples, and a pound of fudge. "I did tell you I make fudge at the shop now, right?"

"You did, but you also told me you haven't expanded much beyond chocolate yet." She pointed at the box. "That has orange cream, penuchi, and apple pie."

"All right, I'll let it slide . . . this time." I laughed.

So did Gram. "But I do want to try some of your fudge once we get to your shop."

"I think we can do that." I grabbed the front of her shopping cart. "Now come on, you have to try this one sauce that Cindy recommended. I think you're going to love it."

Gram was no kitchen witch, but she could pour sauce over pasta. We returned to the front of the store to start the wall of samples over. I only retried my favorites, but Gram had everything. We then continued through the salsas and hot sauces, although Gram skipped most of the hot sauces. I quickly grabbed a peck of apples to try out some new recipes before rolling them out for the fall, then chose some wine for the potluck tonight. Steph loved the wine from here. When I first moved to Heartwood Hollow and across the hall from her and her brother, Alex, we came here regularly. And every time, Cindy greeted me from the porch.

"You don't need cheese for tonight," Gram told me as I approached the cheese case. "I plan on cutting up a lot of this to make a cheese and apple platter for the potluck. It's the least I can do."

"You're my guest, Gram. You don't have to make anything."

She raised an eyebrow at me in an incredulous look. "I most certainly do."

I quickly surveyed what kinds she had in her cart before grabbing a cave-aged cheddar and dropping it into mine. "This one is not for the potluck," I assured her. Although it would be backup just in case. If it wasn't needed, I'd be perfectly happy eating it with one of Zeke's focaccia rolls dipped in oil for the next couple of days. After trying the rolls, I understood why he'd had a line out the door for them. They were delicious, and now I made sure to keep a regular supply around the house when he made them for the first time in several years. Since going back to my shop after using his kitchen while Suncraft Bakery was going through renovations—never mind the reason why they'd been needed—we'd been trading baked goods. My scones and muffins for his rolls and breads.

As Gram and I headed for the checkout, I grabbed a bag of baked catnip treats for Saffy. I was running low on the tuna catnip treats I made for her and figured these would do nicely to appease her for the potluck tonight. With so many people coming over, including Ivy, she deserved the treat. In truth, Ivy had been much better around Saffy lately. She'd told me that she was trying to prove to her dad that she could have a cat. Ken wasn't fully convinced yet, but I predicted he'd break soon.

I let Gram check out first, giving me time to glance around for Cindy to say goodbye, but I didn't see her anywhere. She was probably back on the porch greeting customers. The mill store liked having someone stationed there "to make every guest feel welcome" she once told me. On busy weekends in the fall, they regularly had two people on the porch. During fall festival weekends, which happened monthly at the mill, they had more because of how long the line was to get in the store.

Once we were done, Gram and I headed back outside and toward the parking lot across the street. I cast one last look at the store as the front door opened and Cindy stepped back out onto the porch. I must have missed her when I'd first looked for her.

She caught my gaze and waved, shouting, "Come back soon!"

I waved back before weaving through the parked cars to get to the convertible.

"I really do love coming here," Gram said, setting her bags in the trunk. "I know we just ate, but I'm already looking forward to eating all of this."

Placing my bags next to hers, I laughed. "And if you think that about here, just wait until you see everything we have going on in the bakery too."

CHAPTER 4

As the car crested the large hill once more, this time leaving Bug Creek, I realized we couldn't go straight to the bakery.

"We need to make a pit stop at home first," I said loudly so Gram would hear me over the noise of the air moving around us.

She turned and gave me a quizzical look. "Is everything okay?"

"Yeah, but only if we head home to put our stuff in the fridge. We don't want to leave cheese sitting in the hot car, even one with the top down."

She nodded but said nothing. Instead, she leaned her head back to take in more of the sun. I couldn't see them behind her sunglasses, but I would have bet her eyes were closed.

A few minutes later, we were back in Heartwood Hollow proper, and a minute after that, I pulled onto my street.

As I turned into the driveway, a purple piece of fabric caught my eye. I cut the engine and then pointed toward the porch steps. "Looks like we might have dropped something carrying your stuff in."

Gram perked up at that. "Hmm . . . Don't know how we would have missed that coming out."

I opened the car door, then stepped out, shutting the door behind me. She had a point. Part of me wanted to go investigate, but it could wait the minute it took to grab our bags.

Gram got out of the car and reached into the back for her things. I took my two bags, and together we made our way back up the flagstone path. I couldn't stop to grab the fabric bundle with my hands full and Gram behind me, but as I passed by, I saw pretty embroidering of suns, moons in various states of fullness, and stars all in a lighter shade than the main cloth. The pattern screamed Gram.

Bracing a bag between me and the wall of my house, I dug my key out of my purse, then unlocked the front door. Saffy, who had been asleep in the window, raced to the end of the couch as soon as I pushed the door open. I took both bags and headed straight into the kitchen to start putting things away, Saffy following close behind.

The screen door opened and shut twice moments apart, followed by Gram saying, "It sure is a pretty altar cloth, but it's not mine."

Curious, I returned to the living room to find Gram inspecting the fabric. It was completely unfolded in her arms, which were spread out to look at the whole thing.

"Did you say altar cloth?"

Gram nodded, although I could only see the top of her head from the way she was holding the cloth.

"And you're sure it's not yours?"

I could practically feel the raise of Gram's eyebrow over my question. She lowered the purple fabric. Yep. Her eyebrow was up. "Positive. I do travel with an altar cloth just in case, but this is not it. I'd never randomly leave it somewhere

where it could fall out of my suitcase, and besides, mine is a burgundy color."

"But then how did this get out there?"

"My guess," Gram said, folding the cloth once and then a second time, "is that it's for you."

"Me?"

She handed the celestial-patterned cloth to me. "We never would have missed this when we left given where it was placed. Must be for you. No one here would be leaving me presents."

Maybe that was it. "It wouldn't be the first time someone left me fabric on my doorstep, although last time, there was at least a note to let me know who it was." I looked at the paisley pillows on my couch that I'd finally made. The fabric for them had been left to me by Kate and Daniel, two ghosts I had helped a few months ago. They had spent decades apart waiting for one another, and I got them back together. The design on the fabric had been the same as that on a pair of Kate's pants. I'd complimented them the first night she appeared to me. I glanced at the brush she had been bound to on my mantel and smiled fondly with the memory.

"Well, this is more than just any old fabric, but we can get into that later."

I pinched my lips to the side as I studied the cloth. It was pretty. I traced my fingers over the lavender design. "Is it possible someone found it and thought it was mine so they put it here? Like if it were on the sidewalk in front of my house? I don't know why someone would give me an altar cloth. Few people know I'm actually a witch."

Gram raised an eyebrow at me once more. "I doubt someone randomly picked it up off the sidewalk, but I'd be more likely to believe that a note blew away. Someone probably left it for you once they realized you weren't home after ringing the bell. Either way, there are no coincidences, so no matter how it got here, that cloth was meant for you."

"Did you see anyone drop it off, Saf?" I turned with the cloth in hand, expecting her to have followed me back into the living room especially once Gram and I got talking. "Saffy?"

Her dish rattled in the kitchen.

A smirk appeared on my face, and I shook my head slightly as I returned to the kitchen to find her tapping her food bowl.

Tap. Rattle. Tap. Rattle.

I placed the purple cloth on top of my bags from the mill, then walked over to her bowl. "So sorry for making you wait. I know. You wanted something, and you thought you weren't going to get anything." Only the center of her bowl was bare. "It's not even empty, you silly thing."

She cast a look over her shoulder as if to say I was crazy. She could see the bottom of her bowl. Thus, it was empty.

"Well, you're in luck. I have a surprise for you."

Saffy perked up at this, stood, and then turned around to watch me as I reached over into the second bag from the cider mill. I pulled out the tiny white paper bag of catnip sticks, then turned back to my cat. I opened the top, and her tail shook with excitement, nearly vibrating.

"I was going to save these for tonight, but I'll keep the others for later instead." I took two of the tiny sticks out of the bag, but before I put them in her bowl, I picked it up, then gave it a shake to re-cover the center with crunchies.

No sooner had I placed the bowl back down than Saffy's head was inside it, munching away at her treats.

"Such a sassy cat," Gram said, a look of amusement on her face.

After putting away anything that we needed to, and giving one more treat to my spoiled cat, Gram and I headed back outside. There were no mysterious presents this time. As Gram continued toward the driveway, I looked around the porch and behind my bushes against the house.

Gram stopped. "What are you doing?"

"Looking for a note," I said from my kneeling position. I lifted a few branches off the ground—nothing underneath them—then shook a few more branches to see if something had gotten stuck inside the bushes.

"Anything?"

I shook my head as I stood. "Who would just leave something like that without one?

"Can't tell you, but I don't think we're going to find the answer in the bushes." She took another couple steps but turned around once she reached the driveway. "How about we walk? It's a nice day, and maybe something will come to you on the way."

I agreed and quickly caught up with Gram. Even with the top down on her convertible, it was too nice of a day to not make the short walk to the bakery.

As we passed Leafs and Grounds, Gram stopped to look at the sign in the window.

"That's new," she said. When I didn't respond, she added, "The logo. It's more dynamic now. Before it was too similar to that chain coffee place. Is it a dancing tree?"

"Oh, yeah. A leaping dryad." I'd never realized it until Gary had pointed it out to me, but the logos on his cups were still of his originally stoic logo that I'd previously overlooked, making the dryad connection less obvious. Since the tree planting in the north woods and the dryads being more open about who they were, Gary had decided to redo the logo for Leafs and Grounds to reflect what he and some of his staff were. I'd also learned that the building the coffee shop was in had once been home to a small dance and gymnastics studio called Leaps and Bounds. All along he'd been paying homage to the studio and the building's history with the name of the coffee shop, but the new logo took it a step further.

"I like it," she said with an approving nod.

"We can go in if you want."

"Maybe on the way back. I don't want to spill anything in the bakery."

I took a step toward the door. "It's all right. There are tables. And if we get something now, mine will be cool enough to drink that much sooner."

"All right. You and your taste buds know best." Gram knew I didn't drink or eat anything while it was overly hot. Burning one's tongue was one thing, but as a chef, doing so made work difficult." She followed me into the coffee shop, where Gary was at one of the tables wiping it down.

He lifted his head at the sound of the bell. "Joanie! Good to see you. And who is this with you?"

"It's good to see you again, Gary. It's been some time," Gram said.

Gary smiled. "I hardly recognized you with your hair in a braid." To me, he added, "No way is she your grandmother."

"Such a charmer," Gram said, pretending to be embarrassed, but she was eating it up. "You sure you aren't part witch?"

"No, ma'am. I'm one hundred percent dryad."

My mouth dropped. I'd never expected him to be so open about what he was with someone he barely knew. And the coffee shop wasn't empty either. But as I surveyed the front room, I realized the couple in the corner were dryads. As was the woman by the window. This was as safe a place as any.

Gary barked out a laugh as he walked back around the counter. "Now, what can I get you both?"

I gave him my order for his herbal tea special, a tasty rooibos tea with peaches that almost had me convinced to try it iced. Almost. I preferred most of my drinks hot—well, hottish.

After Gram perused the tea blends listed on the wall, she ordered a lavender Earl Grey. It was a delightful blend that I regularly had in the morning.

"Good choice," I told her.

She nodded before turning back to Gary. "I like what you did with the logo."

His smile brightened. "Thanks. It was time for an update after everything that's happened recently. Joanie, have you figured out who the model is yet?" He pointed to a painting on the wall that was a full-color version of his logo.

I walked up to the art to examine it, something I rarely had time to do whenever I came in here. The dryad's black hair was twisted up into the branches, and her floral tattoos were incorporated into the bark as well as a floral vine that wound up the one leg that was touching the ground. I didn't think I had ever seen her in shorts to see that the cherry blossom tattoo on her arm ran down to her leg, especially not in Leafs and Grounds, but I would recognize the dryad anywhere.

"It's Holly!"

"Sure is," Holly said as she made her way into the main part of the shop from the back room where she must have been cleaning up after the lunch rush. She held a rag and a spray bottle in her hands. "I've modeled for the art club in town several times before, so when Gary told me what he was thinking about doing, I talked to one of my art friends and posed for it. Gary owes her a lot of coffee now for the use of it as the logo, but we paid her too for the art. She's a . . . friend, so she was happy to do it."

I wasn't sure if by *friend* she meant another dryad or something more, but it didn't matter. "It's a beautiful piece. Truly." I pointed at the flowers on Holly's arm. "Does your tattoo really go all the way to your leg?"

"In outline only. I'd like it to be full color like it is here"—she rubbed her upper arm—"but I'm still saving up."

Gram approached Holly's side to take a closer look. "I've always thought about getting one of these. Does it hurt?"

"Parts of it did, but not everywhere. It all depends on where you decided to get one done. They say getting it on bone hurts more, and it did right on my hip, but for me right on the muscle was worse."

"Oh, wow." Gram got even closer to Holly's arm as she examined the body art.

"What were you thinking of getting?"

"Oh, a few symbols here and there that mean a lot to me. It would take a while to explain them all."

Holly nodded. "I totally understand. Well, if they mean a lot to you, you should go for it."

Gram, get a tattoo? I'd never really thought about it before, but it didn't surprise me in the least. I could see her rocking some ink, as some might say. Me, I didn't like needles, so I'd never get one.

Gram turned to me. "Didn't you say one of your friends was a tattoo artist?"

David. "I did. He and Chelsea got married last month." I didn't say more than that. Gram could fill in the blanks from there with what I'd told her during our weekly phone calls. She knew they were one of the first couples I'd matched upon moving here, although I'd done my best to avoid telling her more than the ghost's involvement in their situation and the fact their families hadn't gotten along. It wasn't my place to say—then or now—that either one was more than human. That was one of the biggest rules of the PSG. No revealing what you knew of others. It had to be a safe place for all paranormals or else, what was the point of it?

"Hmm . . ." she said, placing her finger on her cheek, the rest in a loose fist under her chin. "I don't suppose he takes walk-ins?"

"You want to get a tattoo today?"

"Well, I *could* get it tomorrow too."

"All right. I mean, it doesn't hurt to ask. His shop isn't too far away. We can stop there after the bakery."

Gary slid our two teas across the pick-up counter. He'd been packaging our tea selections into little bags so we could steep them on the go.

I looked at the steam rising from the drinks. "Or now. We can do that first. Then by the time we get to the bakery, these will be ready to drink and we can sit down for a few."

"Sounds good to me." Gram removed her wallet from her purse and walked back over to the counter to pay Gary. I grabbed two lids, then popped them onto our cups.

As Gary handed her back her change, he plunked a marshmallow rice treat onto the counter next to one of the cups. "Now, do you like these as much as your granddaughter does?"

"I sure do."

Gary pulled another treat from behind him, then set it down on the counter on top of the first. "Well then, here you go."

She tried to pay Gary for them.

"Nope, these are on the house. You only came in here for tea."

She turned to me. "A charmer, I tell you."

After a quick see you later to Holly and Gary since they were both coming to the potluck, Gram and I left Leafs and Grounds, and instead of crossing the road toward the bakery, we turned down Main Street and headed to the tiny tattoo parlor.

The bell above the door chimed as we opened it.

"This isn't what I expected," Gram said. "It's bright."

I'd had a similar reaction the first time I'd come to the shop too.

David stepped into the room from somewhere in the back, and once we said our hellos, I let Gram take the lead to explain what she wanted to have done. I didn't know what the symbols she was referring to were, but David seemed to understand.

"I don't have anything available today"—he clicked a few things on the computer sitting on the counter—"but if you come tomorrow before lunch, I can squeeze you in for something that size."

Gram nodded. "Let's do it."

Wow. Gram was going to a tattoo. Although it didn't seem all that out of character for my free-spirit grandmother, part of me wondered if she would be doing this if Mom had come with her. Mom had learned much of what she knew about witchcraft from Gram, but Mom was more reserved. She always had been. She'd even tried to tell me that keeping Saffy when she showed up on my doorstep wasn't a good idea. Gram put a quick stop to that. She was constantly trying to get Mom to loosen up a bit.

With an appointment booked, Gram and I left the tattoo

parlor. I'd invited the three couples I'd recently helped to the potluck, so we'd be seeing David and Chelsea soon.

Drinks in hand, we headed back up Main Street toward the bakery. I couldn't wait to see Gram's reaction to the updates.

CHAPTER 5

"All right, prepare yourself for a brand-new bakery," I warned Gram as we reached the shop. Beyond the overall pink, yellow, and purple color scheme, little in the shop looked the same. Even the cases had been refreshed with a new coat of paint.

"I've been looking forward to this since you told me about all the work being done," she answered. "Now can we please go in? All of the smells coming out are making me hungry."

"You just ate!" I laughed, leading the way through the open doorway and into the bakery. Although I made deliveries that regularly took me out of the shop, and had lately been taking an afternoon off here and there as needed to deal with ghosts or matchmaking issues, the bakery smell had never affected me as much as it was right now. It seemed so much stronger today. Even I was getting hungry.

Sarah and Lauren were busy behind the counter, helping real customers, but they smiled and waved as I walked in and ushered Gram beside me.

Her gaze swept across the room, her head slowly turning from one side to the next as she took in all the changes.

"Wow," she mouthed before saying, "You weren't kidding." She walked over to the tables I had set up on the side of the room. Lily and her boyfriend, John, had made them and the chairs that went with them, and Lily had painted the daisies that graced the tabletops before they were sealed to make the wood food safe.

"If you like these, you should see the counter up close."

As the customers left, Gram scooted toward the counter. She ran her fingers over the pink epoxy resin. "This is gorgeous!"

"They picked a beautiful piece to use," I said of the trunk slab that had come from the north woods as I smiled at my friends behind the counter. "Hello, ladies. You remember my gram, Carol, right?"

"So good to see you again," Sarah gushed. Since Sarah had been working for me since the bakery opened, she and Gram had seen each other several times over the years.

Momentarily I wondered if Sarah's knowing Gram had played into her belief I was a witch. Sarah started making comments about my witchiness before the rumors that swirled through town about me ever reached my ears and long before I ever admitted the truth to myself. Gram never hid that she practiced witchcraft, although I never realized that's what it was growing up. I'd thought she and Mom were new-agey with their beliefs, all the sage burning, the candles, the incense, and more. Now I knew better.

Gram reached over the counter and took one of Sarah's hands between both of hers. "Likewise, Sarah." Dropping Sarah's hand, she then went over to Lauren and greeted her the same way. "And, Lauren, how are you?"

"I'm good, how about yourself?" Lauren glanced toward me. "Have you been enjoying your day together?"

We quickly told them about going to the cider mill, skipping the part where we got pulled over. I didn't want that to become part of the gossip that flew around town. With the way stories twisted sometimes, and I'd experienced that myself when the bakery had been wrongfully closed down, I wouldn't have been surprised to hear that both Gram and I had been arrested or something equally ridiculous.

I turned to Gram, who'd been perusing what was left in the bakery cases. "Do you want to see the kitchen and basement?"

She straightened. "Sure. And then I want some of this." She pointed at the case in front of her, her forearm moving in tight circles.

I led Gram into and through the kitchen, pointing out some of the upgrades, but I knew most were over her head. The kitchen had never been her domain, and that was all right by me. As she told me during one of our phone calls, she was happy that I was happy about the changes.

Gram followed me into the basement, an area that had received significant updates since the last time she was down here, the week I signed the lease to the lower half of the building. I thought back to the spontaneous road trip that had led me to Heartwood Hollow for the first time. It would be five years next month for that. A couple months later, I signed the lease on not only the bakery but also my apartment, making me a Heartwood Hollow resident.

"It's a lot cleaner down here, that's for sure," Gram said.

I couldn't help but laugh. Nothing but dust and cobwebs had been down here five years ago. Today I was able to show her the new refrigeration units, the shelves, and my favorite, the washer and dryer, which allowed me to clean the aprons and cleaning rags here instead of at my house.

Gram looked down as she headed toward an unoccupied corner of the basement. "The floor is beautiful."

"That's new too. It's epoxy like the countertop but with a different design. Much easier to keep clean."

"This would make a great space for an altar," Gram said once she reached the far corner. "You spend so much time here. It only makes sense that you would have one here as well as at home."

I raised an eyebrow at her. "But I don't have an altar at home."

Gram raised an eyebrow right back at me. "Yet. We'll get you started on that as part of what we do while I'm here. Then you can incorporate what you learn there, here, with a few tweaks for the fact this is a business, of course."

"But not everyone here knows what I am. And any one of them can come down here to grab something. How am I going to explain an altar to them?"

She crossed her arms. "Well, you could just tell them. You must trust them since they work for you. And haven't you started to tell people in the group that you helped form? They don't look at you any differently now, do they?"

"Well, no, but everyone in that group is different too. They get it. Not everyone on my staff is paranormal, and I can't expect them to treat me the same after I tell them."

"You most certainly can. And if not, you fire them. You're the boss. They have to respect you. And what you are is a witch. If they can't handle that, that says more about them than it does about you."

She had a point, but still, something was holding me back. "I know but—"

Gram sighed. "Look. I'm not saying you have to run up there and tell them right now, but think about it." She walked back over toward me and then held my forearms. I grabbed hers in return. She smiled at me warmly. "And in the meantime, you can create an altar in an unassuming cabinet in the corner that no one will bother with or question you about."

I nodded. That I could do. "All right."

She put her hands on her hips. "Now, we should probably go back upstairs. We've spent enough time down here."

"They're going to think you're fascinated by basements."

Gram winked at me and said, "Maybe I am," before spinning around toward the stairs. She led the way back into the bakeshop, where Sarah was ringing out a customer. Once he had gone, Gram rubbed her hands together. "All right, ready for my big order?"

"Now remember, you already got something for the potluck tonight. The cheese platter and apples will be plenty. And the girls are bringing a cake with them when they come." I glanced back at them quickly. "That's all set, right?"

"Sure is," Sarah replied.

Gram broke into a boisterous laugh. "Who said anything about these being for the potluck? I'll bring these back to the ladies in my circle. We're meeting tomorrow when I get home."

"Oh, like a knitting circle?" Lauren asked.

Gram smiled, holding back more laughter. "Something like that. Only a bit witchier." She winked. I'd grown up with Gram calling her friends *the ladies in her circle*. Only recently did I realize that her *circle* meant her *coven*.

Lauren chuckled good-naturedly, but I wasn't sure if she understood that Gram was serious.

Sarah, on the other hand, looked like she could burst with excitement. It was as if this were confirmation of all her comments telling me to embrace my witchiness. Although I'd stopped being so defensive about those comments and had accepted it on a personal level, I'd never confirmed with her what I was. Gram was right. Maybe it was time I told Sarah.

She didn't come to the paranormal support group meetings, and as far as I knew, she wasn't paranormal. Part of me had been waiting to make sure she'd be fully okay with it if I told her the truth. So far it looked like she'd come undone with happiness.

I glanced at Lauren, who was still standing there smiling.

Maybe right now wasn't the time, but I promised myself to tell Sarah later when we were alone.

"So what can we get for you?" Lauren asked as she plopped a bakery box on top of one of the cases.

For the next few minutes, Gram picked out two boxes of baked goods, keeping both Sarah and Lauren busy. Meanwhile, I sat down at one of the chairs to have my tea, which had finally hit a drinkable temperature. Still warm but no longer at a point where I had to worry about burning my tongue.

This was only the third time I'd been in one of these chairs since John had delivered them. It was rare for me to ever get the chance to sit down when I was at the shop. I could always find something that needed doing. But today I was off, and Lauren and Sarah had things—Gram—under control.

Sitting there, I thought about what Gram said, both about the altar in the basement and about telling my team I was a witch. Maybe I'd start by telling them the matchmaking was real, that it was more than me having good luck with getting people together. They'd all been with me long enough to see many of my matches happen, and I was sure they knew about the others with the way people talked in this town. If they could accept the matchmaking as truth, then maybe they would be more open to the witch stuff after that. They'd all heard about the now-true rumors about the spells I put in my baked goods, even teased me about it before I realized what I could do. But I wouldn't mention the ghosts. I hadn't even told the paranormal support group that I could see them. Lily knew, but she'd seen it. That ability was a hard truth to swallow when I couldn't offer proof on demand. And that was one thing people always wanted proof about.

I could start with Sam. He'd believed me about the spells in the food, no questions asked, no proof needed. He'd asked me about the matchmaking, too, if I'd felt something between him and his boyfriend, Todd. So adding the witch element on top of that wouldn't be difficult.

As for an altar at the bakery, well, we'd see how things went with having one at home. But maybe it wouldn't hurt to find a cabinet somewhere, maybe an antique one with doors that I could put down in the basement. If it sat there a while, everyone would get used to it and maybe I could turn it into an altar without them noticing. Then again, if they knew I was a witch, an altar wouldn't be a big deal. At least I hoped.

"And there you go," Sarah said, putting one box of baked goods on top of the other. "You are all set. The *ladies* are all going to be thrilled by this."

"You're telling me. Joanie used to bake me cookies to bring to the meetings." Gram turned to me. "Do you remember that?"

"Wow. I haven't thought about that in forever." I took one last sip of my tea for now, then stood.

"I'm sure they miss it. They liked seeing you a couple weeks back, granted the circumstances could have been better," Gram said, referring to the commendation ceremony in her honor for solving Miss Susan's murder. All the ladies had been there. "You should come back and have a regular visit sometime. Come see the whole circle and what we've been up to."

"And bring cookies," I said quickly, hoping to put a stop to this topic for now before Gram told me to join her coven in plain language right in front of Sarah and Lauren.

Sarah was smart, though, and had already picked up on the veiled offer. "Maybe those little witch hat cookies you do for Halloween." She was getting way too much enjoyment out of all this witchy talk.

I rolled my eyes with a slight shake of my head.

Lauren, once again, however, hadn't realized what we were talking about and changed the subject for me. "Do you have a lot of stories about little Joanie?"

Gram let out a burst of laughter. "Oh, do I ever!"

"And you can talk all about them at the potluck," I said as I walked over to the case with the boxes on it. Picking up the two eighteen-inch boxes, I added, "You know, when I don't have to stand right here and listen to all of them."

Gram's smile grew mischievous. "Why? Worried about what I might say?"

"A little. I fully intend to be on the other side of the yard when you all get to talking to save myself from the embarrassment."

"All right, all right. I won't say anything . . . now." Gram started to walk toward the door but spun back to face Sarah and Lauren for a moment. "I will see you two later."

"I'm looking forward to it. Bye, Carol. Bye, Joanie!" Sarah sounded so excited she had practically sung my name.

I turned to follow Gram out the door. "See you both later, and thanks for taking care of the cake."

"See you later!" Lauren called after us.

Pulling the shop door closed behind me, I sighed internally. There was nothing I could do about Gram's promise to the girls right now. And at least it was just Sarah and Lauren. Whatever embarrassing story Gram told wouldn't come back to haunt me. I hoped.

CHAPTER 6

"I forgot how fun that Sarah was," Gram said as we walked up Founder Street toward home. "She's just so excitable."

"And she's one of the biggest town gossips, so please be careful about what you tell her tonight."

"Oh, don't worry about that. I won't say anything too scandalous." Gram took a sip of her tea. "You weren't like that as a kid."

"No, but she is fascinated with the idea that I could be a witch. She's been making comments about it almost since the day I hired her."

"Considering you are a witch"—Gram took another sip of her tea, longer this time—"she's a smart girl."

"She is that. I'll be sad to lose her someday."

"Who says you're going to lose her?"

"I do. She's meant for more than the bakery."

"Bah! I don't see her stepping out of your life anytime soon even if she does leave the bakery. Haven't you been thinking about expanding more than you have already?"

Gram had just seen the tables that had been set up to

allow people to eat and drink in the shop, which was one part of that expansion. As we turned the corner onto my street, I told her more about my recent partnership with Lucy at the ice cream shop and my needing to hire someone to focus on making candy. Problem was, I didn't know how Sarah would fit into those elements more than she already did.

"You'll find something," Gram said. "You always do."

We walked up to the house, chatting about what we—or really, I—needed to get done for the potluck in the hour and a half we had before people would start to arrive. I handed Gram the two boxes of baked goods I'd been carrying, freeing up my hands to dig out my house keys from my bag. "We should probably put these in the side room so that no one mistakes them for something they can eat tonight."

"Good point," she said as I unlocked the door and held it open so she could step through.

I followed her into the house, greeting Saffy, whose head had popped up as she likely tried to figure out who was hidden behind the two boxes Gram was holding. "Just us, Saffy, but people are coming soon, so how about I give you an early dinner."

Saffy took off so fast her back feet went out from under her as she curved into the kitchen, and she scrambled to find purchase on the floor so she wouldn't hit the doorframe in the process.

"Silly cat," I muttered, letting the storm door fall closed behind me. It clicked securely shut, and I proceeded to walk into the living room, leaving the wooden door open, both to let the fresh air in and so I could shout for early arrivals to let themselves in.

Gram had disappeared into the side room and now reemerged without the bakery boxes. She followed me into the kitchen where Saffy sat tapping her empty food bowl.

"Later I'll give you a couple of treats up in my room so you'll have something to occupy yourself while company is here." Saffy had never been a fan of lots of people, although she hadn't been hiding during my recent smaller get-togethers. Instead, she'd been staying up on the highest perch of her cat tree where she could keep an eye on us all. Tonight's potluck, even with us mainly staying outside, would likely push her limits.

I scooped out some crunchies for her, then dropped them into her dish. When she was about half done with those, I opened a can of wet food to give her part of. She always had to eat some of the dry first or else she'd only want the can and ignore the rest until later, which tonight she couldn't do.

"There you go," I said, straightening. I popped a cover onto her canned cat food, then put it into the fridge for tomorrow. "All right, now, where was I?"

"You need to cook your dish," Gram reminded me. "Where are your cutting boards? And I'll need a knife for the apples too."

I grabbed her a cutting board, passed it to her over my shoulder, then pointed to my knife block.

She got to work washing the apples as I pulled out a casserole pan from under my oven and set it aside. I reached into the freezer, then pulled out a gallon-sized bag of pierogies. I could have done a similar recipe in the slow cooker, but in trying to get everything prepared for Gram's arrival this morning, I hadn't had the time to get it ready.

"What are you making?"

After setting the oven to preheat, I turned around and smiled. "Pierogi lasagna."

"Are they homemade pierogies?" Gram asked excitedly. "I remember when you used to make them."

"Sometimes I cheat and use a box, but I made a batch a

while back and froze them." I grabbed a pot hanging off a hook on the wall, then filled it with water before setting it on the stove. "Would you mind cutting up an apple into thin slices for me while you're doing the others?"

"Can do? What do you need it for?"

After I turned on the burner to bring the water to a boil, I looked back at my grandmother and winked at her like she usually did at me. "You'll see."

She smiled knowingly at me, then got back to cutting her apples as I turned the burner on under the pot.

"I'll be right back," I told her, heading toward the door to the basement.

She didn't respond, and I walked downstairs to my unfinished basement where I kept a shelf of foods that served as my root cellar.

Once I was back in the kitchen with the onion I'd grabbed, I dropped my pierogies into the now-boiling water to let them cook most of the way through. It wouldn't take long. Next, I buttered the baking dish to prep that for when the pierogies were done.

"Here's you go," Gram said, pushing thin slices of apple toward me on her cutting board.

"Thanks. Could I bother you to chop the onion for me too?" I reached for a pan, then put that on the burner next to the pot.

She nodded and as I took the sliced apple from her, I told her to give me half-inch wide sections of onion and to separate the layers when she was done.

I put the apple to the side, then grabbed spinach out from the fridge. I plopped the spinach into the pan, then turned on the burner beneath. As the spinach cooked down, I went back to the refrigerator and dug through it to find kielbasa I'd picked up from the deli down the street from the bakery. Locating the link, I plopped it on the counter.

A few of the pierogies had risen, letting me know they were done. I skimmed them out from the pot, then spread them in a single layer on the bottom of the baking tray. Next came a layer of the paper-thin apple slices. I topped that with some of the spinach, which was also ready.

"Onion is done," Gram announced.

"Great. One sec." I moved the remaining spinach out of the pan into a small bowl, then grabbed the cutting board full of onion from Gram. The onion sizzled as soon as it fell into the pan, and I stirred it around. I passed Gram a new cutting board and knife for the rest of her apples so they wouldn't be oniony, then used the first cutting board to slice the kielbasa into coins. Those got added to the pan of onion. When all of that was done after a few minutes, the onions having taken on a brownish translucence, I added all of it on top of the spinach, followed by another layer of pierogies, apples, spinach, and finally one last layer of pierogies. I capped the baking dish with its lid, then slid the whole thing into the oven.

"Anything I can help you with?"

Gram pointed to the fridge. "Cheese."

After grabbing the cheese, I settled down next to Gram, and together we worked on making her cheese and apple platter.

"I remember doing this when you were a kid," Gram said, "only these apples were for pie instead of a cheese platter."

I leaned my head on her shoulder. "Pie baking starts soon enough. You're welcome to come back at any time."

"I might just have to. I've missed this. I've missed you." She rested her head against mine. "It really had been too long between visits, and I'm not counting you coming for the commendation ceremony since that was out of the norm for what we would have done on a regular visit."

I sighed. "It would be nice to go home sometime. I just don't feel like I can up and take off with the bakery. Did you know that today was the first real day that I've had off since opening? Even with all the ghost stuff lately, I've always been in at least half the day. The team says I need a vacation. But I'm still learning candies, I need to hire someone to teach that to and someone to replace Sam . . . There's just so much."

Gram wrapped her inside arm around my shoulder and made a motion like she was going to touch my head before stopping, her hand an inch away from me. She chuckled. "This would be where I'd stroke your hair like I'd do when you were little, but I don't think you want all of the sticky apple mess in it right now."

"A lot of people here are used to seeing me covered in flour and batter, so they'd probably not bat an eye at apple in my hair, but you're right." I chuckled alongside her.

Gram turned and kissed the top of my head. "You should listen to your team sometime. Take a vacation. Even if it isn't to go home. Maybe something with your man friend."

Speaking of my man friend . . .

I straightened, then looked at the clock on the stove. The timer was running, so it was hiding what time it was, but based on how long the lasagna had left, he'd be here soon. "I should go warn Saffy that Ivy will be arriving in a few minutes."

"That reminds me. I need to check in with Sterling before we get started on your wards later. I want to make sure he's eating."

Gathering some of the cheese wrappers to help clean up as I stood, I asked, "Do you have cameras going inside your house aimed at his food bowl or something?"

"Something like that," Gram answered cryptically but said no more.

"Is it one of the new kinds with a speaker so he can hear you?" I was surprised that Gram, who disliked technology would ever have gotten something like that, but she was crazy about her cat. After I dropped the wrappers into the trash, I walked over to the cabinet where I kept Saffy's treats. "I heard you talking to him as you were getting ready to go earlier. I think that would drive Saffy crazy. Maybe it's a good thing she pretty much stays on the couch or up on her perch."

"She might surprise you," Gram replied. "But you don't need one of those systems until you start contemplating a vacation. You're just down the road during the day." Yet Gram had one, and she barely left her hometown. This trip was an exception, although I didn't point that out.

I opened the cupboard and then reached in for the treat container. After finishing her dinner, Saffy had left the kitchen, but as the lid popped off, there was a thud from the living room followed by a scurrying of kitty paws on the wood floor.

"That didn't take long," I told my cat as she slid to a stop at my feet.

She looked up at me as if she'd been waiting forever for the treats, pawing my leg for effect.

Gram snorted back a laugh. "Such as sassy cat."

"Just two right now and we're taking them upstairs." I reached in and grabbed the baked tuna and catnip treats.

Saffy threw her head to the side dramatically as if to tell me upstairs was so far away.

"Ivy's coming," I told her.

She lost her theatrical guise and scooted out of the room. Although they'd been getting along better, Saffy could only handle Ivy in small doses, and there was no guarantee of that tonight.

I glanced over at my gram, who was stifling her laughter, her shoulders shaking. "Be right back."

Gram quickly waved me off. By the time I'd reached the stairs, she let out a cackle, likely unable to contain it any longer. She'd always been amused by Saffy's antics, and now she was getting to see them again firsthand.

Saffy was sitting in the middle of my bed when I entered my bedroom. Upon seeing me, she stood, then turned in a few circles, kneading the duvet I'd thrown on top of the bed this morning to give it a more made-looking appearance. It was a good day when I pulled up my covers, never mind straightening them. But Gram was a stickler for these things, something about the intent of one's day and starting the morning with one thing already checked off the to-do list, so I'd wanted the bed to look good in case she saw it.

I placed the treats by Saffy's feet. "Don't get used to this. You're only eating up here because of all the people coming over. You know how I feel about crumbs in my bed." I didn't even snack up here. "This is a one-time thing." At least with the duvet, there was a smaller chance of anything ending up in my sheets.

Saffy tilted her head at me. If she could raise an eyebrow, she probably would have.

"I know, I know. Like you're going to leave any crumbs."

She dove toward the first treat, biting a chunk off with a crunch.

I spun on my heels. "Enjoy."

Now that Saffy was all set, I could concentrate on the impending arrival of my guests.

CHAPTER 7

The oven timer went off just as I reentered the kitchen. Gram had mostly calmed down since witnessing Saffy's actions but was still chuckling to herself.

I pressed the cancel button on the oven, stopping both the baking and the timer at the same time. After placing a trivet on the counter and grabbing potholders, I opened the oven door, then slid the baking dish out to place it on the trivet. Glass baking dishes couldn't sit on the stovetop, especially when either the burners or the oven was still warm. They could explode. I'd seen that happen at a Friendsgiving celebration I'd been invited to one year. Glass everywhere. We couldn't eat the stuffing because of shrapnel, but a brave few strained the gravy so they could still have some. Even though they didn't find any shards of glass when they did, I stayed far away from it myself. Thankfully the mashed potatoes and turkey had been covered and were safe.

"There." I put the potholders to the side in case I needed to use them as extra trivets at the potluck. "All set."

"And I'm done too," Gram said, standing up from the

chair. She held her arms out in a showcasing fashion toward the platter at the center of the table. "Ta-da!"

"It looks great. And once the guys get here, they can move the tables so we can get these outside."

The front doorbell rang at the same time there was a knock on the kitchen door. Glancing at one, then the other, I was happy to see my setup crew had arrived.

"Come on in," I called to them both from where I was standing.

"Perfect timing once again," Gram commented.

"That has a way of happening around here," Nathan said as he stepped into the kitchen and the front door closed shut.

His comment surprised me. How had he picked up on that? Oh well, I couldn't think about that now. "Hey, Nathan, you remember my gram, right?"

"So good to see you again, Nathan," Gram said, taking his offered hand between hers.

"Likewise, Miss Carol."

Footsteps thumped through the living room, then abruptly stopped at the entrance to the kitchen.

"Nate!" Ivy chirped excitedly. She rushed over to him, giving him a big hug as she reached him.

Ken was a few feet behind her. Coming to a stop at my side, he leaned forward and kissed me on the cheek, then let his arm wrap around my waist. "How are you?"

I smiled warmly, excited two of my favorite people were finally getting to meet. "Good. I'm good. I'd like you to meet my grandmother, Carol. Gram, this is my boyfriend, Ken."

Ken and Gram both stepped forward and shook hands. She took his hand in the same way she'd taken Nathan's. I couldn't see Ken's face, but even Gram's eyes were smiling, the very few wrinkles she had deepening at the outer corners of her eyes.

"It is wonderful to meet you," Gram said. "I've heard so much about you."

"Joanie talks of you fondly. I know how much she was looking forward to having you out here so we could meet."

"I'm glad the timing finally worked out." Gram turned to Ivy. "And you must be Ivy. I hear you like to bake like my Joanie does."

Ivy stood a little taller and tried puffing out her chest. "I sure do! Joanie's been teaching me. Oh! Daddy, the brownies!"

"They're right on the coat-tree next to the door where you put them," he answered, looking at his panicked daughter. Ivy sped out of the kitchen, and Ken turned back toward the rest of us. "She saw Nathan and tried to take off, but I stopped her and made her put them down first."

We all laughed as Nathan said, "No doubt you saved me from a shirt full of smooshed brownies. I appreciate it."

Since the day Nathan had helped me in calming Ivy down the first time I watched her by myself, or rather calmed her down for me since I was completely useless during that tantrum, Ivy had developed a fondness for him. It was almost as strong as the one she had for—

"Mattie!" Ivy squealed.

"Let me go," Ken offered. He took two steps toward the living room to go help my elderly neighbor, but Ivy had it handled. She was out on the porch holding the screen door open for Matt so he could walk inside.

"Why, thank you, Miss Ivy," Matt said in his polite, soft voice. "That's very kind of you."

"You're welcome, Mattie," Ivy replied, her voice equally soft and sweet, a tone I only heard her use with him.

Gram glanced at Nathan. "Looks like you have some competition."

That sent me off into another bout of laughter. "You have no idea. But just wait. She'll get that way with you too."

Matt entered the room, holding Ivy's hand with one of his and using the other to hold a large bouquet of flowers. "You know I'm no good at cooking, so I thought I could fancy up a table with this instead."

"They're beautiful! Thank you." Matt handed me a bouquet of zinnias, Gerber daisies, and other colorful flowers I didn't know the names of, and that's when I realized he was still holding a smaller bouquet of six peach-colored carnations.

"And these," Matt said, turning to Ivy, "are for you."

Ivy hopped repeatedly, her mouth dropping open. "Thank you, thank you, thank you!" She threw her arms around Matt's middle in a big bear hug.

"Did you forget something?" Ken asked Ivy after she let Matt go.

"I said thank you," she responded quickly. When Ken arched an eyebrow at her, she gasped. "I forgot the brownies again!"

Ken brought his hands out from behind him, revealing a batch of brownies on a princess-themed plastic platter. "Fortunately, I did not."

"Thank you, Daddy!" After taking the platter from Ken, trading him for the bouquet, she turned to me. "I made brownies!"

"That's awesome. I can't wait to try one. How about you put them next to the cheese and apples for now." I pointed to a spot on the table. "Your dad and Nathan are going to help move tables so we can bring everything outside."

Ivy set the brownies down. "Okay. Can I go outside too?"

"Of course you can," I answered. "You know where my little shed is, right?"

She'd been in my backyard several times over the last few months, so she nodded. I told her to open the shed door and supervise the guys in moving the tables. She loved the idea.

"I'll be outside as soon as I put these in water." I spun around on my tiptoes to reach one of my empty vases up there.

The three headed outside, leaving me with Gram and Matt.

"Pardon me," Matt said behind me. "In all the commotion with Miss Ivy, we have yet to be properly introduced. I'm Matt Hoffman. I live across the street."

"Oh my goodness, I'm so sorry." I turned back to them, a vase in hand. "Matt, this is my grandmother, Carol. Gram, Matt."

"So lovely to meet you, Matt. You come over to have dinner with Joanie sometimes, right?"

"Sure do. Just about once a week. She's a wonderful cook, although you know all about that. As I said when I got here, I'm no good at cooking myself. I even burn things in my microwave."

Somehow, Gram managed to stop herself from wrinkling her nose at Matt's mention of using a microwave. It was the reaction she had whenever anyone mentioned them. She had never liked them and didn't have one in her house. "I'm glad she's taking care of you."

"Good care of me," Matt confirmed. "Always sends me home with leftovers." A thought struck me then, and I hoped he hadn't been burning whatever I gave him in the microwave later on. The thought was quickly pushed aside, however, as I remembered his admitting that he used microwave mishaps as an excuse to come over.

Still holding the bouquet, I placed the vase in the sink, then turned the water on. Once the vase was full, I grabbed a pair of utility shears and cut the bottoms of the flower stems under the running faucet. Miss Susan had taught me that one time after she let me pick flowers in her garden. It refreshed the ends of the stems and was especially needed for store-bought flowers, although these seemed fresher than most. After each cut, I placed the flower into the vase, arranging them as I went along.

Gram and Matt continued talking the whole time, but I could only make out a word or two of their conversation over the water.

Finally I was done with the big bouquet. I left the stuffed vase sitting on the counter for now, certain they'd be safe if they had to go unattended for a minute or two since Saffy was upstairs. Had she been down here, all bets would be off. I'd end up with either chewed flowers or a vase on the floor. That's why I kept any flowers I did get on top of the refriger-ator where she couldn't reach.

When there seemed to be a pause in the conversation, I turned to my neighbor. "You didn't see anyone drop some-thing off at my house earlier, did you?"

He thought a moment. "Can't say that I did. Was some-thing the matter with it?"

I shook my head. "There was no note. Wanted to be able to thank whoever it was." Really, I wanted to know who left it so I could ask them why, but I wasn't about to go explaining the mysterious altar cloth to Matt. Who knew what he'd make of me being a witch. I was sure Gram would tell me to trust him and tell him the truth, but I'd be so sad if he didn't approve.

"Sorry I can't be of help," he said.

"That's all right." I gave him a small smile. "I'm sure I'll figure it out eventually."

Just then, Ken popped his head back inside. "We're all set out here, so whenever you're ready."

"Great." I grabbed the brownies off the table, then handed them to him. "Will you let Ivy do the honors?"

He winked at me. "Sure thing." He disappeared from sight as the doorbell rang.

Part of me had worried no one would show, and I grinned that my fears hadn't come to pass. "I'll get it. Matt, would you mind bringing the flowers outside?"

"I'd be happy to," Matt said, already taking a step toward the counter.

I walked to the front door, where the smiling faces of Holly, Lily, and John greeted me. "Come on in and head through the kitchen to the backyard."

Holly led the way, carrying some wine, followed by Lily who held a few bags of chips—she'd helped make the cake this morning that Sarah and Lauren were bringing—and John, who had a baking dish in his hands.

"Seven-layer dip," he explained as he passed by me.

"Fabulous." That was perfect potluck food.

"Don't close the door," a familiar voice called as I started to turn away.

I peeked out the screen door. Sam and Todd had just reached the driveway along with a girl their age who I didn't recognize.

"This is Brittni," Sam said once they were on the porch. "She's a friend of ours from school. I hope it's okay I brought her."

"Absolutely. Like they say, the more the merrier." I studied the girl. She was wearing cut-off jean shorts, a white short-sleeve button-up blouse with red hearts scattered about it like polka dots over a tight band t-shirt, and her blond hair had been pulled back in a ponytail with two hair sticks running through it. Along with her hair, brown eyes, and smattering of freckles, she reminded me of someone. "It's nice to meet you. You look familiar."

She blushed. "Maybe you know my dad. Pete. He works at the circulation desk at the library if you go there at all."

Sam stifled a chuckle as I exclaimed, "I know Pete! I'm there all the time. I invited him and a couple of the other library staff tonight." I'd hoped they'd have given my mom someone to talk to, but that was before she had to cancel her trip here. But I was happy to have them come, Mom or no Mom.

Her eyes widened. "He had mentioned going out with friends, but I had no idea he meant *this*. I can't believe I'm going to the same party as my dad." She scrunched up her face but quickly tried to hide her reaction. "Oh! I didn't mean for that to sound like I don't want to be here. I actually think this is pretty cool, just the whole party with your dad thing is . . ."

"It's okay. I get it. The backyard is plenty big enough that you can pretend you don't know him if you'd like."

She laughed. "No, it's okay. He's not that bad." She thrust her arms forward, which were holding a plate of cookies. "Here. I know you're a baker and everything, but this is my signature dish, so that's what I brought."

"Thank you. All the food's out back on tables, so just head on through the kitchen and out the door." I pointed to the open doorway across the living room.

She and Todd did as I said, but Sam hung back a minute. He inclined his head toward the cookies. "They're really good. That's who I was talking about for the shop as my replacement."

I led Sam toward the kitchen. "Think she'd be a good fit?"

"Absolutely."

"Then I guess I have a cookie to try." I smiled as Sam continued out to the backyard without me. With more and more people showing up, I wanted to make a quick sign to tell people where to go. If I had to get the door every time someone got here, that would be all I'd do. I ducked into the side room where my rarely used desk was, then grabbed a piece of computer paper from my even less-used printer and a pen.

Come On In
Backyard Is Through The Kitchen

Thank goodness people could see the kitchen from the front door. I left my side room, headed for the front door, then stepped out onto the porch. Courtney and Seth were just arriving as I slid the sheet of paper into the corner of the screen.

"I'm so glad to see you!" Courtney said, holding two grocery bags. Next to her, Seth held a slow cooker.

I leaned in toward her and gave her a quick hug. "You too. Chili?"

"Of course! Gram already out back?"

"Sure is. Please stop her from telling anything too embarrassing about me."

She pressed her lips together in a tight line. "I can make no such promises. You know how much I like your gram's stories."

I turned my attention to Seth. "Good to see you too. Did you tell her?"

Courtney spun on her heels to look at her boyfriend. "Tell me what?"

That answered that question. "You can get Gram to tell you instead." I was curious to know how she'd spin the story myself. "Probably more interesting if she tells it anyway."

Courtney looked confused, but then eager resolve settled across her face. "Oh, I'm going to go find out right now. It's gotta be good." She marched through the house and out the back door, Seth following.

After ensuring my sign stayed where I put it once the screen door banged shut behind me, I headed back into the house, grabbed the pierogi lasagna and several serving utensils for any dish that needed them, then walked into the backyard.

There were several more people back here than had come through the front door. I glanced toward the gate at the side of the yard and watched it pop open as Chelsea and David approached it with Rachael and Mark. They hadn't yet touched the gate and were still a few steps away, and no one had opened it for them from the other side. It was just as Ashley had said that time she had knocked on my back door after she had a ghost-involved disagreement with Rich—it just popped open for her. Had that happened with everyone else who hadn't come through the house? It was like the house knew who was coming here and had invited them in on its own. It reminded me of the bakery with its lights that brightened and dimmed depending on a person's mood.

David pushed through the gate, holding it open for the others. Chelsea and Rachael were holding hands, chatting away. I hadn't realized until Chelsea's wedding that they were cousins. I assumed the now obviously pregnant Rachael was also a merrow, but she hadn't told me herself. Maybe she wasn't. I didn't know if her husband, Mark, was anything either. Not that it mattered if they were or not, but the question now lingered in the back of my mind about nearly everyone I'd ever met in Heartwood Hollow.

I descended the two steps from the back door to the yard, heading toward the tables where an already overwhelming amount of food had been set out. It was hard finding a space for my dish, but I managed, squeezing it between some baked ziti and a tater tot casserole. I placed the serving utensils wherever it looked like they were needed, leaving some at the beginning of the table for anyone still bringing something.

"I have something for you," Rachael said in a sing-song voice. She held an envelope out for me to grab.

A huge grin broke out across my face as I took it from her. "Is this what I think it is?"

She nodded in quick little motions. The excitement radiated off her. "I'm sorry to be getting it to you so late."

"Don't even worry about it. I won't be starting it until Friday, so now is perfect."

She let out a hard breath. "Okay, good. I've been worried."

"No need to be doing that. You take care of you and that little one inside you."

"That's exactly what I'm doing now." She giggled and grabbed a plate.

As Mark came up behind her, wrapping his arms around her middle so that his hands rested gently on her bump, I thanked them both for coming, then excused myself to go say hello to the others who were already here. Mark's proximity to Rachael had set the matchmaking tingle I felt whenever a perfect couple was nearby into a tizzy. Even once a couple was matched, the feeling I got never really went away. Sometimes it stayed down by my feet, but other times it rushed through me, especially when the couple was exceedingly happy.

Never having had so many of my matches together in one place, my system soon went into overdrive. Some couples hummed softly, but others like Rachael and Mark, excited over their growing family, and Chelsea and David, recently married, were loud like the cicadas that came around every several years. Lily and John, and Rich and Ashley, all matched within the last few months were also louder than the others. Drew and Megan, new parents who I'd matched my first year here, were similarly noisy. I could also sense the perfect matches between existing couples who had found each other all on their own, but unfamiliar with those specific matches, I couldn't pinpoint them without getting closer or staying too long in one spot.

I hadn't expected to be so affected by everyone. I just had to keep moving, going from one group to another so as not to be overwhelmed by dueling and battling tingles and vibrations, but even in the open air of my backyard with plenty of space to mingle, that wasn't going to be easy.

CHAPTER 8

The backyard gate opened once more, falling open wide enough for Sarah and Lauren to walk in carrying a giant sheet cake.

"We're here," Sarah called, her gaze searching the crowd until we made eye contact. Then she looked behind her to the gate. A look of confusion crossed her face before saying, "Can someone close that for us?"

It seemed to me she had been expecting someone to be standing there holding the gate open and was surprised to find it unmanned. So she hadn't kicked it open. Nathan, who'd been standing nearby talking with his father and several of the other older partygoers, headed toward the gate to close it. Just before he placed his hand on the gate, it started to swing closed. The gate wasn't weighted to do it on its own, but maybe it had settled in just a way that it could swing back after a short time by itself. If not, it was a strange coincidence.

But after these last few months, I had a hard time believing in coincidences. And if it were like the bakery lights, as I was starting to think, could I have been causing both all along? I was the only thing the two places had in common.

I met Sarah and Lauren down by the dessert table. Others had already begun to clear off a spot for them to put the cake down. Never one to skimp on food, I'd planned for a larger cake than needed. But this was massive. Easily enough for everyone to have a heaping serving and maybe a second slice on top of that. I'd likely be sending people home with cake too. Good thing I bought containers for the occasion.

Sarah took one end of the box lid, and Lauren the other. Together they lifted it off the base. A chorus of oohs and aahs sang out through the backyard as everyone came nearer for a better look at the beautiful cake.

"You all did a wonderful job," I said loud enough for all to hear, then searched for the faces of Gina, Bryan, Lily, and Sam so I could make sure to acknowledge them specifically for having made this cake. Delicate fondant flowers ran along the perimeter, alternating with actual cookies, and inside, Gina's scrolling letters of *Summer Potluck* were interwoven with a scene of the Main Street and the bakery. "Does anyone have a camera?"

Ken passed me his cellphone, the camera app already running. I hadn't even considered my phone, but it was somewhere in my bag inside the house. When I was home, I never had it on me. It didn't work.

I took a step back to make sure I could get it all in the photo, then called my entire team over to pose in front of it so I could get a shot with all of them too.

As they hammed it up for the photo, Ken pulled the camera from my hands. "You get in there too."

"But I didn't make the cake."

"Come on, Joanie," Sam called. "It wouldn't be a bakery family photo without you in it."

Once the others backed Sam up, I relented, joining them all and squeezing into the middle of the group. It struck me then that, with Sam leaving for school in a matter of weeks, this could be one of the last times we'd all be together. I fully believed that I'd lose Lily sometime soon too. Her woodworking skills were great, and it only made sense she'd eventually go to work at John's furniture shop. Lauren had a year of college left to go, but I didn't know what her plans were after graduation. And although I didn't know when it would happen, I knew Sarah was meant for more than the shop, despite what Gram had said.

At that moment, Sarah gave me a side hug, as if knowing I needed to be brought back into the present moment. I couldn't control the future, and I shouldn't dwell on it as a result.

I glanced at her and smiled. "Thanks," I mouthed.

"All right, everyone, say cheese . . . cake?" Ken snapped the photos as we laughed and smiled for the camera. After a moment or two, he announced, "Okay, I think I got it."

The bakery team unfolded from the close huddle, me nearly tripping and falling on my face as Sam and Bryan shifted away, causing me to lose my balance. Bryan turned and grabbed me before I could make contact with the ground, then helped haul me to my feet.

"Thanks."

"Careful there." He looked me over. "All good?"

I nodded once.

He smiled. "Thanks for a great party. This food is delicious."

"Glad you're enjoying it. Thanks for coming."

"So are you going to cut the cake? It's only fair that you should do the honors."

Nearby, someone started a chant. "Cut the cake, cut the cake."

Soon the entire backyard was repeating the phrase in one loud chorus.

I pivoted on my heels to find something I could use but then realized I'd be better off getting a knife from the house. It was the one thing I, of all people, hadn't thought to grab earlier.

The chant followed me as I rushed inside and back, careful to not do anything that would hurt myself in the process now that I was holding a sharp object. Paper dessert plates had materialized next to the cake in the minute I'd been gone, and Sam was at the ready. As I cut, Sam passed out slices, handing them to whoever was close and letting them distribute the pieces to those who were farther back in the crowd.

Once it looked like everyone who wanted one right now had a piece of cake, I stopped cutting so that there would be less air getting at the remaining portion. We hadn't even come close to eating half of it yet.

"Have you eaten anything yet?" Sam asked.

"I've picked here and there but haven't had what I'd say is a full meal."

"Go get some food but start with one of Brittni's cookies before they're all gone." He reached back and grabbed one from the table.

"Would you get me a brownie too? I promised Ivy I'd have one."

He shifted his hand over to get a square for me, then reached for a napkin. "You'll probably want one of these too," he said, handing it to me before giving me the cookie and the brownie.

"Thanks. Having a good time?"

"Yeah. You should have been doing these regularly the last few years."

I nodded but didn't smile, instead quirking my lips to the side. "You're absolutely right." It was a shame I hadn't been. There'd been the occasional dinner party with the girls, and Monday dinners with Matt, but I hadn't ever done something like this before. It had taken reconnecting with Steph and Alex to remind myself how fun larger gatherings could be. They'd been the ones to throw parties at their apartment when we lived across the hall from one another, not me. Although, none of them had ever been this big. Our apartments wouldn't have held everyone. That was probably a good thing given how I was handling so many matches being nearby right now.

"Promise me we can do something like this again when I come back to visit from school."

"Not sure the weather will cooperate for a potluck, but we can put together a dinner or something. You can show off all your new skills." I bumped my elbow into his side, hoping that by next time, I'd have figured out how to manage the overwhelming tingling sensation or at least be better prepared for it.

He chuckled. "I'd like that."

"I've been thinking," Ken said, coming up next to me, "your backyard would be a great place to have a fire pit. My yard is too small and has all that tree cover everywhere. Great for having Ivy's swing set, but not for fires."

"Oh, that could be fun," Sam agreed. He smiled at me. "I look forward to having one at next summer's potluck." He turned away and stopped to shake hands with Matt before heading back to Todd, Brittni, and a couple other people they knew.

"I'd never really thought about it," I told Ken. "I'm

thinking a garden might be good out here, though. Maybe try making some of my own teas." I had a small herb garden in a window box, but maybe it was time for something bigger. I'd first thought about it after Miss Susan died, but Gram and I talking about her earlier had made the memories of her beautiful garden float back to the surface of my mind once more.

"That sounds perfect for you." Ken kissed me on my forehead.

I surveyed the yard, trying to figure out where a garden could go, wondering where it could fit if I was going to keep having gatherings like this. I'd have to look more when the lighting was better.

Libby caught my attention from a few feet away, a big smile on her face. "Did I hear you say something about a garden?"

"You did." Then I told her about my thoughts. Her excitement grew with every sentence.

"Feel free to come over anytime," she said. "You know I'm always in that garden of mine between having fresh flowers for the public rooms of the inn, gathering herbs for whatever I need to make, and sometimes even Veronica at the florist's calls me to see if I have anything special for her bouquets."

"I'd like that."

"Good. We can talk more about it sometime when you make a delivery. But for now"—she looked to Billy—"we gotta get going. We have a few rooms booked at the inn tonight, so we have to be there to see to them. Thank you so much for having us. It was delightful."

I loaded each of them up with a cake slice for later, and they went on their way. A moment later, they were followed by Drew and Megan, who were eager to get home to their three-month-old daughter. It was the first time they'd left her with a babysitter. The two left hand in hand, their specific frequency of tingling fading away from my core with each step. Just having one couple gone was an improvement for me.

Ken returned after another minute, a plate of food in hand. I hadn't realized he'd even walked away during my goodbyes with the two couples.

"Here. Eat something. Brownies and cookies can't be the only thing you have tonight, not that you've even tried what's in your hand yet."

I looked down. "Oh, that's right! I completely forgot once Libby mentioned the garden. I do need to try these." I broke off a piece of Ivy's brownie. It was richer than her last effort but had just enough chew, and the remains of chocolate chips gave it an extra layer of texture. Her baking skills were improving each time. I glanced around the yard, hoping I could give Ivy a thumbs-up, but she was busy talking with Matt and everyone else in that group. Gram had been with them earlier in the evening, but she was no longer there.

Right then, she cackled, and I located her across the yard over with my baking team, Courtney, Seth, and a few others. No doubt a few stories from my childhood had already been told. Either Sarah or Courtney would tell me later.

I broke a chunk off the cookie—toffee, chocolate chips, and coconut from the looks of it—then popped it in my mouth. "Oh, wow. You need to try this." Based on its creamy texture, I believed Brittni had used cream cheese instead of butter. Either way, it was delightful, and I wanted another one.

Ken looked at me as if he were expecting me to give him a piece of mine.

"Oh, no," I said, my mouth already full with the next bite. "You need to grab your own. Trust me on this."

He turned toward the table for a cookie. Before he had

even come back around to face me, he'd had a bite. "You need to get the recipe."

"I'm going to do one better," I replied with a smile. "I'm going to go hire the girl who made them." I started across the yard toward the large group, where Brittni stood talking with my bakers, the librarians—including her father—and several others.

Suddenly, the matchmaking tingle swelled, surging through my body and sending the butterflies into a tizzy with a new flight pattern. Someone had just found their match right here at my potluck. Being a matchmaker, I was used to that happening in my presence. It had happened over a dozen times since I'd moved to Heartwood Hollow. But mixed with all the other matches, some already in overdrive, this new match overwhelmed me.

Instead of heading toward Brittni, I pivoted toward the steps leading up to the back door and my kitchen just beyond.

I needed to leave.

CHAPTER 9

Inside, the sensation was dulled but still stronger than I wanted it to be.

Maybe upstairs would be better.

Leaving my plate of food on the counter, I hoped no one would come in and think it was trash. It was a risk I had to take. Even given the situation, there was no way I could break my own rule about food upstairs or else Saffy would expect treats there all the time. I retreated up into my bedroom, where I flopped onto my bed.

Saffy was on top of me in an instant. Not her usual settling in between my knees and not her backup spot by my head in the crook of my neck. No, she sat squarely on my chest, leaning forward, her head taking up my entire field of vision.

I rubbed her ears with both hands.

She didn't move but just kept staring at me as I focused on her, unable to look at anything else. With her on my chest, I was forced to take long slow breaths.

And it was helping.

"All right, I think I can sit up now." I tapped the side of the bed next to me.

Saffy stood, her paws transforming into instruments of pain as she slowly stepped on every pressure point, then hopped off me. But instead of sitting next to me, she walked out of reach.

I rolled to my side. Saffy was over by my nightstand where I kept my landline. She bonked it with her head, then rubbed against it before hitting it once more with her head, making the phone fall off its cradle. It thwacked onto the wood nightstand.

Sighing, I pushed myself onto all fours, then crawled across the bed to reach for the phone. As I knelt with the phone in my hand, I wondered if Mom had ever been overwhelmed by her matchmaking ability. We'd once talked about how our abilities felt similar, and if that were the case, then maybe she'd have tips for me now.

I glanced at the clock next to the phone's cradle on the nightstand. Maybe I could catch her in time.

"Joanie, is everything all right? Shouldn't you be with Gram? Is she okay?" The worry was clear in her voice. I needed to call her more so this wouldn't be her normal reaction when she answered the phone.

"Gram's fine, Mom. She's out in the backyard making friends at the potluck I'm throwing."

"Why aren't you out there?"

I sprawled back out on the bed, and Saffy immediately joined me up by my head. "I was hoping you could maybe give me a little advice. I didn't catch you at a bad time, did I? I know you've been dealing with the incident at your library, so if you're busy, I get it."

"I was just wrapping up dinner before the board meeting reconvenes. I have a few minutes. What's going on?"

"You know how you can feel your matches, right?"

"Yeah, mine starts in my fingers."

That was one thing I was glad we differed on. I wouldn't have been able to handle having my fingers tingle all the time as I worked. I needed them fully functional for my work at the bakery.

I slid my pillow under my head. "Well, do you feel all of them all the time?"

"If they're close enough, I can."

"Okay. There are multiple matches at my potluck tonight—"

"How many?"

"Six? Seven?"

"And you're overwhelmed because everyone's so close together."

"I was managing by staying moving, but one couple is newly married and another is expecting a baby, so those are wicked strong, and then all of a sudden there was a brand-new match made right in the backyard." I let out an exhausted sigh. "And it was all just too much."

"So now you're hiding," she said sympathetically as if she understood.

I nodded even though she couldn't see me. "Do you have any advice? Anything I can do to tamp it down a bit?"

"You had the right idea by moving around earlier. It's probably why you've never gotten too overwhelmed at any of the festivals your town has. Everyone else is moving around too, so the tingles ebb and flow. But that doesn't help you now with everyone right there in your backyard hanging out."

"Not at all, especially with this new one."

"Did you stick around long enough to figure out who it was?"

"No. I felt it and bolted."

"Joanie!" Mom's disappointment was evident.

I groaned. "I know!" Never once had I ever fled from a match. I placed my palm against my forehead and pressed hard, my whole face pinching with frustration.

"What if they leave before you find out who they are? What if they need a push?"

"That's why I'm calling. Is there anything I can do?"

She sighed. It was more a tired sound, one that made me feel guilty for calling with everything else she had going on. "Have you gone over any of the crystals with Gram yet?"

"No, we were going to . . . charge them tonight by the full moon? Is that right?"

"Okay, right. Then we won't do anything with those right now, although we can talk again later about that. I don't want you to take anything that will make you sleepy and too relaxed tea-wise either since you'll need to be on top of things tonight. How about this." She paused a moment. Just when I wondered if her call cut out and was about to ask if she was still there, she continued. "Go make a sandwich."

"A sandwich? But I'm at a potluck. There's plenty of food here."

"Then sandwich whatever you want together. Two cookies with something in the middle, two pieces of lettuce with a cucumber. I want you to try to spell your way out of this."

"But I only made the pierogi lasagna."

"Oh, I do miss your pierogies . . . Ah, Melissa, stop thinking about it." I smiled at her chiding herself. "I'm curious to see how much of your spell work is in the making of something."

Now it made sense. "So maybe I can reduce this over-whelming feeling down enough by making myself something to eat. Are you sure a sandwich is going to work? It seems too simple."

Mom chuckled. "I don't know anything when it comes to you sometimes, Joanie. It's been that way ever since you were little and started seeing ghosts. A sandwich just seemed like the quickest thing you could make, but maybe it's too easy of a recipe . . . if you could even call it one."

Willing to give it a try, I sat up, then swung my legs off the side of the bed, disturbing Saffy, who had fallen asleep next to me.

She looked up at me, one eye open, before stretching into the spot where my head had been. I gave her a quick pet in thanks for helping me overcome my anxiety tonight, wondering if she realized what she had done for me, both in making me focus and by going to the phone.

"Thanks, Mom. I'm going to see what happens."

"Good luck. Let me know how it goes. Probably tomorrow, though. I have no idea how long this meeting is going to go."

"Then I'll say good luck to you too. I love you. Come visit soon, okay?"

"I will. Love you too."

The line disconnected, and I turned the phone off before setting it back into its cradle. I stretched, touching my toes, letting out a big puff of air as I did, then held my breath for four seconds before I stood back up. The tingling was still there in full force, but at least I felt calmer. Maybe I should start taking classes at the yoga studio. I bet Kim would have some other breathing techniques that would prove beneficial to calming me down if this ever happened again.

"All right, Saffy. I'm going to go make a sandwich." I left my bedroom, my cat following close behind, her concern outweighing her dislike of large gatherings. When we were halfway down the stairs, someone who could only be Ivy screeched with excitement, and even though the noise had come from outside, Saffy hightailed it back toward my room. I couldn't blame her. No doubt she was overwhelmed like I was right now, but at least no one minded her not being present at the potluck.

In the kitchen, I was relieved to see my plate still on the counter. Nothing else had been disturbed either. Likely no one had come inside while I'd been gone. Had anyone realized I was missing?

"Okay, a sandwich," I mumbled to myself, studying what was on my plate that I could use. The thing about a potluck was the food had such a variety that the dishes didn't necessarily mix well for a single bite. Some things would go well, like the cookie and the brownie, but my options for a sandwich filling were limited. I took my fork and pulled apart my pierogi lasagna to investigate.

Apples! They were flimsy from being cooked, but I could stick the brownie between two slices.

"Calm," I whispered as I positioned the first piece of apple on my fingers. I placed the brownie on top of it. "Allow me to feel the matches but not be overwhelmed by them in number or strength." For good measure, I closed my eyes and repeated my intentions as I placed the second apple slice on top. At the bakery, all I had to do was think about something. Spelling my baked goods came so easily that I'd been doing it for years without ever realizing. It had likely been happening longer than I'd been in Heartwood Hollow. Colds cured the day after I'd brought food over even if it wasn't soup. No-bake breakfast bars curing my friends' hangovers in college within minutes. Snacks during cramming sessions that my friends swore helped them to remember things better. We'd chalked up anything that had happened to coincidence when it was likely a result of my food. I should have known better. Gram sure did. She'd been calling me a kitchen witch since I was a kid, but had she expected all of this?

Keeping my eyes closed, I brought the apple brownie sandwich to my mouth, then took a bite, effectively half of the sandwich. Since I couldn't be too careful, I chewed with the thought of *calm* repeating in my head, being mindful of my breathing throughout. I popped the last bite into my mouth, continuing the focused breathing and thoughts.

"There you are," Sarah said. "You disappeared from your own party. Just poof! You okay?"

I swallowed the bite in my mouth, then turned to face her. "I will be."

"You kinda looked a little pained there. You were squinting even with your eyes closed."

"Nope, just thinking." How much had she seen?

She raised an eyebrow at me. "Thinking really hard, I guess. So how was the apple brownie combination?"

"You saw that?"

Nodding, she sighed. "I saw the whole thing, but I know you don't like me always bringing up the witchy stuff you do, and I was being nice since we are in your house, after all."

I smiled at her, appreciating her honesty. "I think it would have been better without all of the oils from the sausage and onion." I'd have to give apple cinnamon brownies a try. I think they could be a great fall treat at the bakery.

She wrinkled her nose. "So why were you eating it?"

Maybe now was the time to come clean like Gram had suggested. "You know how I'm kind of a matchmaker?"

"Kind of?" She raised an eyebrow at me.

"Okay, more than kind of."

"Sure I do . . . but what does that have to do with brownies and apples?"

"Well, it's not just a knack I have."

"You don't have to tell me that. I've seen you do that magic."

"No, I probably didn't, did I? But it's true. I don't guess either. It's a feeling I get. A real feeling. Tingles and everything."

"You tingle?" I nodded. "So is it just when you first realize a couple belongs together, or is it all the time?"

"All the time."

Sarah glanced out the kitchen window. "You have a lot of matches out there."

I blew out a hard breath. "You're telling me."

Her face softened as she faced me once more. "How are you even able to function?"

I shrugged. "Usually it's not so bad. I'm rarely around so many at once."

"But tonight it's bad?"

Leaning back against the counter, I nodded.

"So exactly how does that tie into you eating an oily apple brownie sandwich?"

"I was seeing if I could spell it like I do the baked goods to help myself calm down or maybe lessen the feeling for the night while everyone is still here."

"I see." She was quiet a moment. "And *that* was what you decided to make?"

"It was what I had available. I didn't think anyone would catch me doing it."

Sarah laughed. "I catch more than you realize."

"I don't doubt it. You saw that I was a witch even before I did."

"That's true," she said, my admission seemingly not fazing her in the slightest. "For years I've seen you do your magic. No one would just randomly try to get a dryad and the son of a lumberjack together if they didn't know it was meant to be.

They're like cats and dogs. You don't expect them to be friends."

I nodded letting what she said sink in. And then it hit me. "Wait, go back. You know about the dryads?"

"Of course I do. And the merpeople, the selkies, fairies, trolls, and more."

"But you've never said anything."

Sarah put her hands on her hips. "Were you ready to talk about it? I've been trying to get you to admit that you're a witch for over four years, and the best I've gotten out of you until tonight is you've stopped being so defensive when I bring up the topic. You've accepted it, and I'm sure you've said it in the paranormal support group, but you've never said it to me."

"You have a point. A few of them actually. Okay." I took in a deep breath and released it in a controlled exhale. "I'm a witch."

"Good. Now you won't have to be so cagey when other people who know come in and you need to talk about them. Don't get me wrong, I've been enjoying the coffee breaks and seeing Gary—don't tell him that—but the extra shots of syrup have not been helping my waistline." She patted her love handles. Her smile warmed. "Doesn't that feel better now that you've told me?"

"You know? It does."

"So, why did you run off?"

"My matchmaking—which I guess is one of my powers—comes with a physical feeling."

"The tingling. You mentioned that."

"It starts in my toes, and when a match is made, it courses through me, usually coming to a rest in my stomach. Most days it stays in my feet, even when I'm around matches."

"But it's not right now."

I shook my head. "Between newlyweds, a pregnant couple, and the brand-new match in the backyard, it's overwhelming."

Her eyes went wide. "I pride myself on knowing what I do, but I had no idea that you continue to feel your matches after you've made them."

"I feel *all* matches," I clarified. "Not just the ones I've made. Walter and his wife, Martie, out there? Found each other on their own."

"Or there was a matchmaker here way back when."

"Do you know that for a fact?"

"No. Before my time, that's for sure. Just assuming it's a possibility. It's Heartwood Hollow after all. Guess I could ask my aunt about it. She might know more, but she would have been a kid when they got together. Could ask my grandpa too." She shrugged nonchalantly. "So back to what you said just before that. About this new match. One just happened in the backyard? Who?"

Avoiding her gaze, I cast mine to the floor. "I don't know. It happened so quickly, and the feeling was so strong I came in here before figuring it out."

"Well, how are you feeling now? How's the tingling? Is the sandwich working?"

For a moment, we were silent as I assessed the tingling sensation running through my body. It was still there, but it was as if a blanket had been thrown over it, muffling the intensity.

"I think I'm good," I told her.

"Ready to go back outside?" She turned toward the door.

"Not yet. I have so many questions for you. For starters, how do you know about all this?"

She raised her hand, displaying a one-minute gesture. "There will be plenty of time to talk about all that later.

People are going to start to notice if you aren't back out there soon."

She had a point, and I took a step forward to follow her.

"Don't forget the rest of your food."

I quickly backtracked to grab my plate off the counter before heading outside.

"There you are," Ken said at the bottom of the stairs. He searched my face. "I was just coming in to find you. I'd assumed you went to the bathroom, but you were gone awhile. You feeling okay?"

I gave him a genuine smile. "Yeah, I ended up talking to my mom for a few. She was supposed to come but couldn't."

"You said something happened at her library?"

"Yeah, a pipe broke. She has to deal with all the damage and the insurance and whatnot. She was getting ready for another board meeting to discuss it all."

"Ah, well, I hope she'll be able to visit soon. I'd love to meet her."

I reached for his hand with my free one and gave it a slight squeeze. "I'd like that too. I know she was looking forward to it as well."

"So you're sure everything is good? One minute, you were getting ready to hire someone over a cookie, and the next, you're not out here enjoying the party."

Ah, right. Brittni. That's what I'd been doing. "It's all good. And now I am going to go do what I said I was going to do and hire that girl."

"Daddy!" Ivy called from somewhere in the yard.

Ken kissed the top of my head, then chuckled. "I'm being summoned. Good luck with your hiring."

"I'll come find you once I talk to Brittni."

With a nod, Ken walked toward the back fence close to the open gate between my yard and Nathan and George's.

Nathan had figured leaving it open would allow his father an easy retreat if the crowd got to be too much for his father. George was getting older and sometimes grew confused, especially in the evenings. A couple of months ago, I'd found him in my backyard, wearing absolutely nothing, looking for his hot tub. He seemed to be doing well tonight and was happily chatting in the same group I'd seen him with earlier, the same one Ken was heading to.

I scanned the backyard, searching for who would hopefully become my next baker.

CHAPTER 10

I located Brittni still over with Sam, Todd, her father, and the other librarians. It looked like she'd gotten over the slight disappointment of attending the same party as her father.

"Hey everyone," I said as I wiggled my way into the circle between Sam and Brittni. "Everyone having a good time?" I looked at all their faces, but inside I was concentrating on the dull tingle. Was the match here? Nothing seemed stronger than any other match I was feeling, including John and Lily who were also a part of the circle. I believed Emily liked Pete, but it didn't seem like them. And I couldn't pick up on anything from Sam and Todd either, unfortunately.

"There is so much food," John remarked. "And it's all really good."

"That's the nice thing about potlucks," Emily said. "Everyone brings that one dish they know they can make well."

"Well, I hope you've all been getting your fill." I pointed back to the table. "There are containers if you want to bring home slices of the cake or anything else. There's plenty."

Pete's eyes lit up, and he patted his stomach. "I will definitely take some cake home."

"And speaking of good food," I said a bit quieter as I turned to Brittni, "can I talk to you for a minute?"

A surprised but worried look flashed across her face. "Me?"

Behind me, Sam shifted, and I was hit with a wave of excitement as he stifled a squeaky gasp.

He must have given Brittni some sort of assurance I couldn't see, maybe a quick thumbs-up, because with more confidence, she replied, "Sure."

We stepped out of the circle and walked a few feet away toward my shed to get some semblance of privacy. I didn't want her to feel like she had to take the job because all eyes—especially her father's—would have been on her had we stayed with everyone.

"Those cookies were amazing," I began, a smile on my face.

"Really? You think so?" All worry that she'd had faded away and was replaced with a small look of pride. "I can give you the recipe if you'd like."

"I would like that, yes, but Sam tells me you like to bake more than just the cookies. What else do you make?"

"A little bit of everything really, although those cookies are my standouts. I make these brookies that I do with a blondie instead of a brownie. I still call them brookies, though, because the other name options weren't appealing." She scrunched her nose.

I chuckled.

She let out a steadying breath. "Sorry, I'm rambling, aren't I?"

"It's all good, no worries. I was going to ask you if maybe you'd consider coming to work for me. At least for the rest of the summer to see if you like it. Then maybe we can figure out something for school, similar to what Sam did, if you want to continue. And I hope you do. I think you have talent."

"You do?" Her eyes widened as the corners of her mouth turned upward in the start of a smile she seemed to be holding back as if not to seem too eager.

"Uh-huh. We were able to make it an official internship for credit. And he gets paid too, of course, as would you."

"I'm honored. I don't know what to say. I mean, I do know what I want to say, but it's all just, wow, I wasn't expecting this, you know? I thought I was just coming to a party, and now here I am talking about a job and getting high school course credit and a paycheck!"

"Should I take that as a yes?"

Her smile finally broke across her face. "Oh, yes! I was rambling again, wasn't I? Yes, please take that as a yes."

"Great! The bakery is closed tomorrow, as we are every Tuesday, but stop by sometime on Wednesday once the shop opens. With Sam leaving for school soon, I'd love to get you trained while he's still here. Have you learn a bit of everything from everyone on the team."

"Oh my gosh, really? You're serious?"

"Sure am! You're hired."

She jumped up and down. "Thank you, thank you, thank you!" She settled back into place, but her smile remained. "I'd hug you, but I don't know if that's appropriate, so I'm going to go hug Sam and tell my dad." She let out a small *eep* before half-skipping away to rejoin the circle of people she'd been with. I watched as she took Sam's and Todd's hands, and then the three of them jumped up and down. Amused, I wondered if there was going to be enough space for all that jumping in the bakery. Pete had stepped toward his daughter, a wide grin across his face, no doubt waiting for his hug. He caught my gaze and nodded slightly in acknowledgment.

I returned the gesture, then made my way over toward Courtney and Steph. The circle they were in was by far the largest group that had formed in the backyard, the majority of everyone being the same age and having grown up here. They'd likely all been classmates—Heartwood Hollow wasn't large, and the junior high and high school complex of seventh to twelfth graders only boasted a population of five hundred in a crowded year.

As I looked around the circle, I smiled. Here, humans, merrows, selkies, dryads, fairies, and who knows what else were enjoying their time with one another, some aware of what the others were through the trust of the paranormal support group and others not knowing at all. After last month's incidents between the merrows and the selkies, it was nice to see that everyone could get along.

"Have you eaten anything?" Courtney asked, breaking me from my thoughts. "I swear that's the same plate you've been carrying around all night.

"I had a brownie, a cookie, and a few bites of things here and there, but not a whole lot."

"Well, you are going to stand here and eat that with us," Rachael said from a chair that had been set out for people to use. Or maybe it was one they had brought. Didn't matter. She was off her feet. "Unless you want to get a fresh plate. I can send Mark to get something since he's going to go get me more right now."

"I am?" Mark asked, looking confused at his pregnant wife. She handed him her plate, and he stood. "I mean, I am. So if you want something, Joanie . . ."

"It's all right. This is all still fine." To prove my point, I dug into a pile of tater tot casserole. The surface had cooled, but the interior was still warm.

"Another brownie please," Rachael called to Mark as he crossed the yard. She turned back to us, giggling. "Potlucks are wonderful options for pregnant people. So much food to satisfy my cravings, and now that I can eat, it's all I want to do."

We all laughed at that, and together we chatted and ate, and I finally got to finish a plate of food.

"Well, we best get going," Rachael said, patting her stomach before lovingly placing her hand on top of her bump. "I'm stuffed . . . in more ways than one. And if I'm not eating, I'm sleeping, so it is time for bed."

She and Mark made the rounds as they said their good-byes before leaving. That started a wave of departures, many citing early mornings. I completely understood. Had tomorrow not been Tuesday, I'd have been saying goodnight to everyone, too, so I could get to bed. Bakery mornings started early. Too early for this natural night owl, but I'd adjusted, and it wasn't that bad considering I got to go to the bakery every day, something I'd wanted to do since I was a child.

About childhood . . .

I turned to Courtney. "Okay, so how bad were the stories Gram was telling earlier?"

"Oh, they weren't that bad. Little Joanie was so cute!" she said with a teasing squeal to her voice. "I love when she starts talking about how you would make mud pies in the yard, and I can totally see you trying to figure out a way to make them actual pies by bringing mud into the house to bake."

Bringing my hand up to my face to hide my embarrassment, I asked, "Did she tell you I tasted that one?"

Courtney barked out a laugh. "And that you made your cousin try it too."

"I did not *make* her," I stated with a chuckle of my own. "She helped me. We were in it together and had to try our creation."

"I ate dirt once," Ivy said from behind me, startling me in my seat. "It wasn't that good. But some grass and flowers are good to eat, did you know that?"

Ken sat in the empty camping chair next to mine, and Ivy crawled up into his lap almost immediately.

"No, I don't remember dirt being that good either," I told her, "but yes, I did know there are flowers that are good to eat. Would you like to try some in a cookie soon or maybe a candy?"

"Okay." She rubbed her eyes.

"I think someone is crashing from a sugar high thanks to all of the desserts. We'll have to get going soon."

"All right. I hope you had a good time. I didn't get to see much of you." I gave him an apologetic smile.

He dropped his arm closest to me off the side of his chair and opened his hand, waiting for mine. "You had a lot of people here you needed to talk to. We'll have time for just the two of us again soon. Ivy's got another sleepover this weekend."

I gladly took his hand. "Sounds good to me."

"How did the hiring go, by the way."

Courtney's eyes widened. "Oh, you hired someone new?"

"Yeah, Brittni. She's one of Sam's friends. She made the cookies. Try one if you haven't."

With a small yawn, Ivy softly said, "They're all gone."

Ken closed his eyes and shook his head slowly. "Someone

tricked all her friends into giving her cookies when they went to get more food." By friends, he meant Nathan, George, and Matt. Probably himself too. "Somehow she managed to convince them that she'd only had one or two cookies. And it's not like this is the first time either. I don't know how she does it."

I chuckled lightly. "Maybe they just like spoiling her. She's everyone's adopted grandchild." I wondered if she had Gram wrapped around her finger yet. I searched the yard and found Gram still over by the fence, now sitting in a chair at a circle full of people, the remaining half of the partygoers. More would be leaving soon. The sun was well on its decline, and it would soon get too dark in the backyard. The spotlights on the house only did so much.

As if knowing what I was thinking, Ken patted Ivy's back, and she slid off his lap. "What do you say we get going?"

"Okay, Daddy." She then took a few steps over to me and gave me a hug. "Thanks for having us."

"Well, thank you for coming and bringing the brownies. They were really good."

She perked up a little at that. Good. Maybe it meant that Ken wouldn't end up carrying her halfway home. She'd probably need the extra bit of energy the walk would provide just to get ready for bed.

"Come on, kiddo. Let's go say goodbye to your friends," Ken said.

As Ivy turned away, letting me out of her hug, I held my hand out to Ken. Nathan and George were standing, no doubt ready to step through the opening between our yards to head back to their house. Matt, too, stood as Ivy started to cross the yard.

Ken helped pull me out of the chair.

I smiled. "Thanks. I want to make sure to say goodbye to

them before they leave." To the others in my circle, I promised I'd be right back.

Courtney stood. "We're actually going to go too." She looked back at Seth, one eyebrow raised. "Despite working all day and pulling over certain individuals on their way out of town, he likes to be available should anything happen on account of the full moon. You know how Heartwood Hollow can be."

I grinned at her reference to Seth letting Gram and I go with a warning earlier today. "It was so good to see you both. Let's do dinner soon. Maybe a double date this time."

Courtney nodded as Seth said, "Speaking of dinner . . ." He took off toward the food.

Ken wrapped his arm behind my back as he, Courtney, and I crossed the yard.

It didn't hit me until then that the matchmaking tingle had lessened so much that I'd been able to stay in one spot for nearly an hour among several matches. I barely felt the magical sensation, all the different strands dulling to a monotone hum. Except now, I realized, as the evening wound down, I hadn't figured out who the new match was. There was no way for me to tell who they were with my senses like this. Despite how overwhelmed I had been, I wasn't sure I liked the feeling.

As Courtney diverted toward the food tables a few feet away to help Seth pack up a few leftovers and grab her slow cooker, I tried to reach out to my tingles and trace the threads between matches, but it was all a jumble. Had the new match already left? Would I get another chance to find out who they were? The town was small, but unless I ended up in the same close area as the couple again, I wouldn't feel the match again.

That settled it. I was inviting everyone who had been here to another potluck.

As Ken and I reached the circle, Nathan said, "We're going to head home." An amused smile formed on his face. "Long walk and all that."

I matched his grin with one of my own. "Yes, I sometimes worry if you'll make it home safely. Be sure to wave from your back deck to let me know you've survived the trek."

"We're going to take a dip in the hot tub. I'd extend the offer of having you all join us, but your grandmother said you have other plans for the evening."

Ah, right, the full moon and the crystals. After all the food and conversation, I'd almost forgotten that we still had more to do.

Matt clapped Nathan on the shoulder. "I, however, have no other plans, and Nathan assures me they have extra trunks for me to wear. I've never been in a hot tub, so why not try it?"

Ivy seemed to have gotten a second wind and looked up at her father with puppy-dog eyes. "I've never been in a hot tub either, Daddy."

Usually that did the trick, but Ken smiled warmly at Ivy. "Another time, kiddo. By the time we'd get back after going home to get your swimsuit, it would be time to leave so you could go to bed."

Ivy sighed dramatically. "Okay . . ." She hugged each of the three men goodnight, then gave a hug to Gram. "It was nice to meet you."

Gram returned the little girl's embrace. "It was nice to meet you too, Ivy. I'm sure I'll see you again sometime."

Ivy looked back up at Ken and said, "I'm going to get the brownie plate," before trudging off to the now deserted tables.

Ken quickly said his goodbyes to everyone, then turned to

me. Softly, so no one else could hear, he said, "Enjoy your time with your grandmother. I hope what she can teach you helps." He may not have fully understood what Gram and I were planning, but he supported whatever it was that I needed to do to keep me and my house ghost-free unless I purposefully brought one home.

Standing on my toes, I kissed his cheek. "I'll call you tomorrow."

He met up with Ivy over at the dessert table, where she was trying to pack up a couple cake slices that were just out of her reach. Providing containers had been a great idea. I had less than a quarter of the cake left now.

"Could I interest you gentlemen in any cake to bring home?"

To George, *cake* was a magic word. He had quite the sweet tooth. His smile grew mischievous. "Cake? Can I have cake?" He turned to Nathan.

"You had cake already, Dad."

"No, I didn't."

For a moment, I worried George had overdone it and was becoming confused. There'd been a lot of activity out in the backyard tonight, and he'd talked to a lot of people.

He shrugged. "Well, it worked for the little girl. I had to try."

Nathan pressed his eyes closed before opening them and directing his gaze toward the sky, but a smile crossed his face. "Dad . . ."

I quirked an eyebrow. "Is that all Ivy had to do? Just say she hadn't had a cookie?"

"Pretty much," Nathan replied, his cheeks reddening.

Matt shrugged. "Well, who wouldn't believe a face like that. Such a sweet girl."

Gram chuckled, then said, "She is rather enchanting" in a

way that made me think she had fallen for Ivy's words too.

"Can I have cake?" George repeated. "I know I already had some, but that doesn't stop me from wanting more."

We all turned toward Nathan.

"Fine," Nathan started, "but it is for tomorrow, you hear me? Tomorrow."

I took a step toward the table. "I'll go grab it for you."

"Two pieces if you don't mind," Nathan said, the color continuing across his cheeks. "It is good cake."

"Of course." I stepped away from the group to go to the desserts, then returned a moment later with three containers in hand. I gave two to Nathan. "I could only fit one per container. They're really big slices."

"Thanks, Joanie. If you finish up whatever you're doing and feel like coming over if we're still out on the deck, feel free."

As I fumbled for a reply, George reached for one of the containers, but Nathan pulled both out of his father's reach.

"Had to try," George mumbled.

I pivoted to face Matt and handed him the third container. "And this is for you. You know I can't let you leave without sending you home with something."

"Thank you, Joanie."

Standing next to Matt, George looked up at the sky. "You have a good night, dear. Full moon tonight."

"That it is, darling," I replied with a small smile to my elderly neighbor. Hopefully it would be the only moon I saw this evening. "You all have a goodnight too. Enjoy the hot tub."

Gram quickly echoed the sentiments, and we waved to the men as they exited my backyard and crossed into George and Nathan's. I closed the gate behind them, ensuring it was properly latched.

"They're such sweethearts," Gram said, turning toward the tables still covered with food and forgotten serving dishes. I'd send things through my dishwasher tomorrow and leave everything on my porch for people to collect.

"I got really lucky with my neighbors. That's for sure."

There were only a few people left in the backyard as I started to condense everything with food still in it to part of one table. Gram brought as many of the empty dishes and dirty utensils as she could carry inside. She returned a moment later with some cleaning spray to wipe down the now-empty dessert table.

"What are you going to do about the tables now that you don't have the Ken and Nathan here to help move them back into the shed?"

I was fully capable of doing it without help, and I was about to tell Gram that when Bryan, Alex, and John walked over.

"We can do it."

If they were offering, then I wasn't going to argue. I smiled at them and then at Gram. "They can do it. Thanks, guys."

"And we can help clear the rest of this," Sarah offered, swinging her finger around to point at herself, Jill, Gina, Steph, and Lily. They were already carrying a couple of my chairs.

"Thanks, everyone. That's a big help."

"Don't mention it. That's what we do for family," Sarah said.

"Speaking of family, where did Sam go?"

"He went with Todd and his friend for ice cream," Gina replied, handing Sarah the chair she had so she could consolidate a few plates of food. "Something about a celebration over a new job?"

Ah, right. Since everyone else from the bakery was here, now was a good time to tell them the news. "Yes, starting soon, we'll be adding a new face to the kitchen. Brittni. Sam's friend. As you know, Sam's leaving in a few weeks for school, and he recommended her. She made the cookies tonight if you had any of those."

Bryan's eyes grew wide with the mention of cookies. "Oh, those were good!"

"I thought so too," I answered. "She's going to train for a little bit and be full-time like all of you at least through school starting. If she likes it, we'll do something like what we'd been doing with Sam."

"She seemed nice," Lily said, grabbing the dish of remaining tater tot casserole.

I was happy they were all in agreement. They'd known I was looking for someone, but tonight's hiring had been unconventional. Usually they would have met Brittni under more formal circumstances. It probably helped they'd tried her cookies. They made everything better.

Together, we made quick work of the rest of the backyard, and soon Gram and I were saying goodbye to the rest of our potluck guests amid promises that we'd have more potlucks before summer ended and that Gram would visit again soon.

I closed the door after watching Sarah and Jill turn onto the sidewalk, giving them a quick wave. Saffy was already in the window. It hadn't taken her long to come out at all once she heard the goodbyes. People-watching was one of her favorite activities, but I believed she liked watching people leave the best.

I spun back around to face Gram. Now it was time for the real work to begin.

Gram smiled excitedly. "Are you ready?"

CHAPTER 11

"As ready as I ever will be, I think." I shook my head. "No, it's time. No more questioning this. Yes. Let's do it."

Gram clasped her hands together in front of her, looking at me with a warm expression on her face. I rushed over to her and hugged her, wrapping her tightly in my arms. I said nothing, letting my unspoken thanks come out in the embrace. It was good to make her feel happy like this. Had she been waiting for this my entire life?

"You're ready," she said proudly, no hint of a question in her voice.

Releasing her, I whispered, "Thanks for coming and helping me fix this."

"Anytime, although with what I'm about to teach you, you might not need me to come all the way to help if these wards break again. You could do it yourself." She waved me into the side room where I'd stored her heavy suitcase earlier in the day.

"You don't need two people? But you and Mom always did it together for me."

"It certainly helps it all go faster, but it isn't necessary. I'm more than capable of doing this on my own, but the whole point is to teach you. There are plenty of solitary witches who carry out these sorts of things on their own all the time."

"Am I a solitary witch?" I asked, pointing to myself.

"You aren't right now. I'm here."

"And when you're not? I'm the only witch who attends the paranormal support group meetings."

"There's a chance that you might be the only one who can work your type of magic around here, but that doesn't mean you are the only witch around. You could try finding a coven. You'd learn a lot from them, paranormal magic or not."

"But where would I find them?" I thought for a moment as Gram unzipped her suitcase and dug through it.

"You're always welcome to join mine, but I know it's a drive. I could see if any of the ladies in my circle have friends or relatives out this way that might be in something a bit more local." She glanced up at me, then winked. "Or you could ask around. Pretend it's another investigation that you've gotten so good at. There might be more around you than you might think."

"Well, I guess I could try Emily. She once said something to me that you regularly say. 'Thank the Goddess.'"

"I agree. It sounds like she might be a good place to start."

"I could probably ask Sarah too."

Gram seemed surprised as she pulled a wooden box out of the main compartment of her case. "Sarah? Your assistant?"

I nodded. "Sarah claims to know a lot about the paranormal world, including everything I can do."

"But at the bakery today, she didn't even know for sure that you were a witch."

A huff of a laugh escaped me. She had a point. "A lot has happened since then. We talked during the potluck. Apparently, she's known all along and has been waiting for me to admit it to myself and others. She didn't want to force it on me by confronting me directly but hoped her side comments all these years would have made me think about the possibility that I was." I explained to her the conversation we had over the apple brownie sandwich and then what had led up to my eating said sandwich.

"Huh. That was good of your mother to suggest you make yourself something to eat." She passed me the box she was holding. "Well, these should start to help once we give them a bath and charge them by the full moon."

I opened the box to reveal an array of crystals in a gorgeous rainbow of color. Most kinds I recognized from their having been around my house growing up, not that I knew the names of them.

"You wash crystals?"

"Some you do. Some can't get wet, so you cleanse them with other crystals. Some just need the moon. Some barely need any help from us at all."

"So should I go fill up the sink?" I pursed my lips. It was full of everything from the potluck.

Gram shook her head. "A big bowl of saltwater will do."

That I could take care of. After closing the box to prevent a disaster should I have a klutzy moment, I headed into the kitchen, then set the box on the table.

Saffy was right behind me as she usually was whenever I came into this room. Only this time, instead of running to her food bowl, she jumped onto the kitchen chair closest to the wooden box. Putting both front paws on the table, she leaned in as close as she could to sniff the delicately carved box.

"Something new, huh, Saffy? It's pretty, isn't it?" I traced the knotwork carved into the box.

"It's the crystals inside she's after," Gram explained as she entered the kitchen. "She can feel the energy coming off them already. Sterling likes to play with some of my spheres. Just you wait until they are cleansed and charged. She'll be rolling the spheres across the floor."

Considering the games she played with the feather duster this morning, I could picture her doing something similar with the spheres with crystal-clear clarity—pun intended.

The sink was too full, so I pulled the spray nozzle from the corner to fill the bowl I'd grabbed out of the cupboard, then turned the water on. Not being given any parameters aside from *a bowl,* I'd chosen a medium-sized mixing bowl that seemed large enough to hold all the stones at once if need be. I glanced back at Gram as I waited for the bowl to fill. "Does this need a special kind of salt? I have regular table, sea salt, pink, black . . ." I probably had more than that too.

"There may be times that you'll want something like the black salt, but no, sea salt is fine. Table would do in a pinch, but generally, the less processed something is the better."

With the bowl full, I returned the spray nozzle to its spot, then grabbed the sea salt from the spice cupboard above Saffy's dishes. The little built-in cubby had likely held an ironing board at one point, but someone had installed small shelves at varying heights throughout it, making it perfect for my vast collection of spices and sweeteners.

"Tell me when," I said to Gram, a hint of question in my voice as I tipped the saltshaker over and began twisting the grinder.

After a few moments, Gram said to stop. I put the salt away before carrying the bowl to the kitchen table, setting it next to the box. Saffy hadn't moved, even with the threat of a big bowl of water coming close to her head.

"All right, so now what do I do?" I opened the box again to

reveal the stones. Saffy nosed a large purple one. Amethyst if I recalled correctly. "Just drop these in here?"

"Ah, well, not all of them. Some of them can't get wet at all, remember, so let's pull those to the side." Gram sidled up next to me, then began removing a few of the stones, telling me their names as she went. "Amber, turquoise, hematite, labradorite, calcite, pyrite, and often fluorite. Better to be safe than sorry with that one. Then we should take out the black tourmaline too. It doesn't care for the salt, although you could rinse it with water if you wanted."

That still left me with several crystals. "How will I remember all of this?"

"Well it does take time to remember it all, but it gets easier. Besides, I'm more doing it this way with you now so you can get a feel for working with them. All of these that I'm giving you are perfectly fine to set out in the moonlight from here on out to cleanse or charge."

"But what if it's cloudy during the full moon?"

Gram raised her hand to stop me from asking more questions. "We'll get to that. Let's work on this first, shall we?"

I took a deep breath, then nodded.

"Okay. The first thing I want you to do is to take that amethyst, that's the purple one"—ah-ha, I had been right—"into your hands."

Doing as asked, I waited for more instructions.

"Now, clear your mind of all thought and dip the stone into the water while you picture a white light around it and yourself."

Eyes closed, I submerged my hands and the amethyst, doing my best to conjure the white light. It was there. Kind of.

"This should be similar to what you do when you spell your baked goods. Think about your intent for yourself and the stone. Amethysts, and the reason I chose for you to grab it first, are known for helping to purify your aura, banishing negative energies, and opening your spiritual and psychic sides. With your ability to see ghosts, you have an open conduit with your psychic self, but we should give it a cleanse, too, after all that's been going on. But we want to extend this beyond you. So now picture that white light so that it surrounds your house as well. All the while, think about purifying and cleansing your abilities. This stone will protect your house and you when you're inside from any negative energies wishing to interact with you."

I repeated the words in my head. *Purify, cleanse, protect* as I moved my hands around the chunky purple crystal.

"When you feel ready, remove the amethyst from the water, rinse it with tap water, and put it back in the box."

Another moment longer, I did as Gram instructed. "What's next?"

"What one is calling to you?"

I perused the box, staring at each one for a moment before picking up an orangey chunk of crystal that reminded me of the amethyst in form. "This one."

Gram's sliver of a smile widened, and she rubbed the knuckle of her index finger beneath her nose as if to distract herself from giggling.

"What?"

"That's citrine. It started as amethyst, only it was heat treated by nature, changing its composition slightly and obviously its color. It's a great stone for you, both here and in the bakery. It's used for asserting yourself in leadership and business, but it can also help create a healthy boundary between your home and everything that isn't welcome. Since it is staying here, concentrate on the boundary aspect. We can always get you another crystal for the shop if you feel it would help."

Like with the amethyst, I repeated Gram's keyword in my head. *Boundaries*, asserting *boundaries*.

This time, I didn't need to ask Gram when to put the crystal down. It was as if the citrine told me after I swirled it through the water.

I repeated the process with the other stones Gram had said could get wet. When finally we were done, I put the last crystal in the box, shut the top, then fingered the intricate design. Two crescent moons facing opposite directions flanked a brilliant sun. Within the sun was a grand tree, its root system crisscrossing and knotting together as were its branches that spread out overhead. One end of the tree was nothing but bare branches with only a hint of leaves and buds. The other had only a few stray leaves hanging from empty branches. It was easy to tell that those were spring and winter. The summer section featured a portion of the tree full of leaves and blooming flowers. In autumn's section, the flowers had been replaced by apples. At the middle of the tree, the branches cleared, revealing a sun starting to be eclipsed by the moon.

"Why do I know this symbol?"

"I have a painting of it in my living room, then a line drawing just like this in my altar room. It's the symbol of the Suncraft Coven, the main coven in Sunny Valley, silly. You've grown up seeing it your entire life. You know, for someone who named her bakery after it, I thought you'd have known that right away."

"I named my bakery Suncraft to carry a piece of home with me. I never really gave it much thought before to what it stood for."

Gram tsk-tsked before continuing to explain the symbols behind the design. The apples were there not just for fall or for how many orchards existed up by her but also for the idea that apples represented so much to so many from fertility to knowledge to Wicca itself with the hidden five-pointed star inside, revealed only when you cut them open from side to side. The knots ran the gamut of meaning. Some for prosperity, others—like the triquetra—representing the mother, maiden, and crone, and still more for setting spells into motion.

"Then this overall design is the triple moon symbol," Gram explained, "which also represents the Goddess, although for our coven, we've added the rays of the sun around the central portion to pay homage to our home. Never forget that you can make tiny changes to symbols as well as spells so that they are tailored to you and your needs at the moment."

"You mean like when I had to burn the sage from a spice jar?"

Gram cackled. "Yes, I mean exactly that. There aren't hard absolutes for that sort of thing. There are some rules, of course. To know yourself is a big one." She assessed me with a smile. "You're getting there. But also to do no harm, and that what you send out will come back to you. Those sorts of things you'll pick up via your books or in a coven. Tonight, though, let's focus on what you'll learn best by doing it in person."

"So what's next?"

"Well, we're going to take everything that you just washed as well as the ones you couldn't outside in the moonlight."

"You can't just do it in the window?"

"Why waste the beautiful night by staying inside? It's more powerful out there anyway." She picked up the box and handed it to me. It felt almost as if she were passing me a torch. "These are your crystals, meant to be yours. Only you can touch them without their needing to be cleansed again. And Saffy too, but cats are different."

So much for getting help doing this whenever I needed to if no one else could touch them.

"Now, now. No need to give me that look. This will be much easier to do by yourself after you've done it once. Remember what I said about there being solitary witches?" She carefully spun toward the living room without waiting for an answer.

I followed. "But how was Mom able to help you all that time?"

"Did you see her with any crystals?"

I thought back on all the times they had cleansed the places I'd lived. Gram had said she'd put crystals in each one, too, but I'd never seen her do it. It had been a complete surprise when she said there were stones above all my door jambs and windows, wherever there was a ledge to hold them. Since I'd never even noticed the stones here, it was possible Mom never touched them. Maybe she had only taken part in the smudging.

"That reminds me," I said, not answering Gram's question out loud, as I placed the box of crystals on my coffee table. "I gathered all the crystals I could find in the house to cleanse tonight like you asked me to."

"Wonderful," Gram answered. "They'll be happy to finally get a charge after all these years."

Leaning forward to open the drawer on the coffee table, I paused. "Is it okay that I touched them?"

"Absolutely. They were always meant to be yours someday. They've gone with you everywhere since your dorm. They've grown in number, of course. You need more here than you did back in your dorm or even your last apartment."

It warmed me that Gram had been on top of this for

years as a way of protecting me. Before, I'd been skeptical, thinking Mom and Gram were into all of this because it was new-agey, that it didn't do anything but make them feel better. After the last few months and accepting I was a witch who could bake spells into foods, I had to believe the stones had helped me with my ghost problems. At least until I broke the wards by unknowingly inviting a ghost inside my house.

I pulled out the bag of crystals from the coffee table drawer, then placed the bag on top of the box before picking everything up. "Did you do this at Mom's house too?"

"Your mom has crystals throughout the house. When things started happening with you, we fortified your room with several more. Those are still there, though. For all the times you were home on break or if you had to go there now for some reason, like when you came to the ceremony and stayed overnight." Gram looked at the stones in the bag. "Where's the selenite?"

"Selling what?"

"The selenite slab. Hang on." Gram scooted toward the door. No, not the door. My coat-tree. She lifted the lid to the small storage compartment at its base, then dug inside it, removing several of the things I had stored in there. After a moment, she pulled out a large opaque white crystal. *Slab* was definitely the right word for it. Flat and thick like a classic brownie, it had to be nearly ten inches wide and at least that long. She lifted the bag of crystals I'd collected, then placed the slab on top of the box, nearly covering it entirely. It had to weigh a few pounds. "This is a selenite slab. You can find them in other shapes, but I like the slabs so you can put crystals on top of it." To illustrate her point, she set the bag back down.

"How long has that been in there?"

"Oh, since you moved into your first apartment," she said matter of factly.

I'd moved into my own apartment during my junior year of college. "That was years ago. I never knew it was in there."

Gram winked. "Shows you how often you clean that spot out."

"Why didn't you tell me?"

"You didn't believe in any of this then."

"I believed in some of it," I argued.

She gave me a look. "Not enough, but I appreciate you having humored us all that time with the smudging."

"Well, I believed that you believed it was helping me with stuff. But now that the ghosts have been coming back, I know all of this had been working."

She seemed to accept my answer. "Regarding your question, I didn't tell you because I didn't want you taking it out and not realizing what you were doing."

I took a step toward the door, wanting to move this along. All of this was getting heavy in my arms. "So what has it been doing in there all this time?"

"It's a charger, a crystal that doesn't always need to be charged itself. People place other crystals that need charging on selenite, just like what we're going to do using the moon. I'd put it in there with the hope of proximity charging for the crystals that had been above your front door."

"If it doesn't need to be charged, why did you take it out?"

"I said doesn't always, not never. It still can benefit from some moonlight." She put her hand on the doorknob, then turned it.

Still facing me, she pulled the door open and was unable to see who was standing there.

But I could.

"Sarah?"

CHAPTER 12

Gram spun around to see my bakery shop assistant standing at the front door, her hand still up as if about to knock.

"That was some timing," Sarah said, a sheepish smile on her face.

Looking at her quizzically, I asked, "What are you doing here? Did you forget a dish or something? You could have called. I would have cleaned it and taken it to the bakery on Wednesday."

Sarah shook her head. "That's not it. Actually, I was hoping to talk to you, but it's the full moon. I should have figured that you'd be doing crystal work with your gram. I can come back." She pointed a thumb over her shoulder.

I glanced at Gram, and she shrugged. "We have time. And you were just talking about finding someone to help you with this sort of stuff if I'm not here."

At Gram's statement, Sarah began bouncing on her heels. "Help? Me? I'd love that!" She seemed so excited she was practically vibrating. "That's actually what I wanted to talk to you about."

"Would you like to come in for some tea?" I had a feeling this was not something I wanted to discuss on the front porch.

She let out a shuddered breath, almost as if it, too, vibrated. "Yes, tea would be good."

Was she nervous? I don't think I'd ever seen her like this. I put the box of stones, the slab, and the bag of crystals on the end table next to the couch as Gram opened the screen door for Sarah and said, "Come on in."

Sarah stepped into the house, passing Gram as she followed me into the kitchen.

I turned the burner under the kettle on to make tea as Gram closed the front door. She came into the kitchen, then sat at the table, motioning for Sarah to take a seat as well. She took the spot across from Gram and intertwined her fingers, but she tapped her thumbs together repeatedly.

After switching the burner on, I opened the cupboard where I stored my tea. I glanced over my shoulder at Sarah. She was a coffee drinker so hadn't had a lot of my teas. But she looked like she needed something to calm her down a bit. Something with peppermint that would calm her but not necessarily put her to sleep. "Gram, do you have a preference?"

"I'll have whatever you are having."

All right, three peppermints. With as much as we still had to do, I couldn't fall asleep from the tea either, but I was feeling a bit nervous myself. After Sarah had revealed that she'd known all about the paranormal world at the potluck, what she wanted to tell me now had to be bigger than that. Was she a paranormal being too?

"Please, help yourself to any of the leftovers from tonight if you're hungry," I told Sarah as I packed three infuser balls with the loose-leaf tea. "It's all wrapped up in the fridge, and there's plenty of it. Just not the stuff in our bakery boxes or the Bug Creek fudge."

She waved her hand in a no fashion with short deliberate strokes. "I am still so full, but thank you."

I didn't want to push her too much before we could all sit down, but one question was at the forefront of my mind. "I know you said we'd talk later about how you know what you know, but I wasn't expecting it to be tonight. Especially after you left."

"Once I told you as much as I did, I knew I'd have to tell you the rest soon. I've been waiting for this since I first met you. Before that, actually." The excited energy from earlier seemed to take over her nerves once more. "It would have been weird to have Jill stick around. She would have heard things about you and others that aren't for me to tell. I may be a gossip, but I know where to draw a line. So I went home with her, hung out a little bit, and when she went off to go do whatever it is that . . . *she* does, I came back here."

I wondered if that pause before Sarah said *she* was her stopping herself from saying *fairies*. Jill had confessed to me about being a fairy a couple months ago, after eating one of my scones that I'd accidentally baked some sort of truth-telling spell into. Everyone who had one and was paranormal ended up coming forward to reveal to me what they were. If Sarah knew as much as she claimed she did, then she had to know what her roommate was but didn't want to say it in front of Gram. Although I'd told Gram about the paranor-mals, I had never gone into detail about who was what. Like Sarah had said, that wasn't my right to tell, even to someone who I trusted with all of my secrets, no matter the fact she didn't live here and didn't know everyone I was talking about.

Finally the water boiled, and I cut the heat to the burner before pouring three cups of water into awaiting mugs. I placed two onto the table, allowing Gram and Sarah to take them, then grabbed my mug and sat down at the table between them.

Sarah bobbed her infuser ball up and down in the water. Although it helped with some teas, it seemed like more nervous energy to me.

Guess I'd start. "So what have you been waiting over four and a half years to tell me? And why wait so long?"

"I had to wait for you to accept who and what you are."

"But what does that have to do with how you know what you do?"

"Like I said earlier, you wouldn't have believed me then if I came out and told you that this customer was a fairy or that one was a troll or any of the other beings that we have living here in Heartwood Hollow. You'd have thought I was crazy. Maybe even too crazy to be able to do my job."

I raised an eyebrow at her. "I'd never think you unable to do your job. You're the best shop manager I ever could have asked for." I cracked a smile. "I mean, you can't bake, which might have been helpful at times, but your prep skills have come a long way."

She chuckled at that. "Thanks. Although that wasn't the job I was talking about."

"And are you going to tell me what job you *are* talking about?" I blew across my tea to cool it down.

Sarah took a deep breath, let it all out, then said, "I'm your familiar."

At Sarah's news, Gram, who had been sitting quietly with her hands wrapped around her warm mug, said, "You've got to be kidding. There's no way."

Sarah nodded pointedly. "It's true. I'd never lie about something like that."

"I didn't think people could be familiars," I said. "I

thought it was something only animals were—that Saffy was my familiar."

"Of course that sassy cat is your familiar," Gram replied.

"She's a great cat, no doubt," Sarah began, "but Saffy isn't a familiar."

"But so many of us have had cats," Gram continued, ignoring Sarah. "Me, your mom, both my sisters, and my mother. My father liked cats, but he wasn't a practitioner." I wondered if she was purposefully leaving out my aunt and my cousin. They'd had dogs throughout my childhood.

Sarah sipped her tea with a shrug. She seemed less nervous now, more confident after her reveal. "I don't know what to tell you, but it's the truth."

"But the cat was dropped off on her doorstep in a paper bag with only a note. It was meant to be," Gram argued, shaking her head in such a way that suggested she believed Sarah just didn't get it.

"A coincidence and nothing more."

I'd been questioning the existence of coincidences myself the more they happened to me. Gram, however, hated the idea of them, and her face tensed at the suggestion. "There are no such things."

"And maybe there aren't," Sarah conceded, "but that doesn't change the facts."

This wasn't getting anywhere. I wanted answers, and we still needed to get outside with the crystals. Before Gram could say another word to derail why Sarah had come, I said, "Gram, tea." Hopefully the peppermint would quickly work its magic and infuse some calm energy into her. Could I spell tea the way I could baked goods?

I turned to my assistant and possible familiar, hoping to get back on track. "Do many people have human familiars?"

She stared at me straight-faced. "No."

"That's because it never happens," Gram said.

I nodded toward her mug, and Gram took another sip. "Have you ever heard of it happening?" I asked her. "Ever, even years back."

Gram sighed, a bit of the fight out of her. "It's really rare."

"You have to admit, though, Joanie isn't the typical witch," Sarah said. "She has more powers than any one of you alone, and even more than some of you combined. A matchmaker, someone who can see and talk to ghosts, and a culinary spell weaver? That's rare too."

It wasn't normal to have more than one ability. Miss Susan had told me that much when she delivered a message to me after she died. A *cursed blessing*, she had called it.

"You did tell me that you saw Sarah staying in my life even if she moved on from the bakery," I reminded Gram. "Maybe this is it."

Gram nodded. "I see your point."

"I'm not leaving the bakery," Sarah said. "You're stuck with me. It's best if we work together." Sarah had been a bank teller before working for me. I wondered now what she would have done had I never moved to town. Would she have stayed at the bank or done something else?

Gram sighed. "Oh, Sterling is going to be so disappointed. He's been just as anxious about Saffy starting her real duties as I have. Are you sure she couldn't have two?"

Sarah drank her tea as she pondered her answer a moment. "I guess it could be possible."

"Two familiars? I was just starting to accept having one." I took a small sip of tea to collect my thoughts.

"It's not a given," Gram said. "All it means is I'm still waiting on Saffy."

"Wait. Is that why you always ask about her during our phone calls?"

Gram cracked a smile. "One of the reasons, yes. I also do just like the sassy cat."

At that moment, Saffy let out a long meow that sounded like *now* from by her food bowl. I hadn't even realized she had followed us back in here. She probably came in the moment she heard her name mentioned.

I stood from the table. "Guess we made you wait long enough for a snack, huh?"

She turned in a circle, then sat in front of her dish.

Pulling her treat container from the cupboard, I said, "One more. One. You already had two during the potluck."

No sooner had the treat plopped into her dish than Saffy was chomping away at it, making happy purting noises between bites.

I settled back into my chair.

"See?" Gram insisted. "Sassy cat."

Sarah chuckled. "I can see why you thought she'd be her familiar. She's got such a personality. I wish I could have a cat. Jill's afraid of them. Long story."

That last comment made me wonder if the feline fear was related to Jill being a fairy, but now wasn't the time to ask. "Okay, now that Saffy is settled," I said, "let's talk."

"I'm curious about how you even know you are a familiar," Gram began. "I've never met one. As I said, they're rare."

"Oh, that's easy." Sarah smiled. "I come from a line of familiars. As I'm sure Joanie's powers do, it runs in the family."

Gram's mouth dropped open. "Your whole family?"

Sara held up her index finger, then took a sip of her tea. "Let me backtrack. We're all trained to be familiars. Whether or not we become one is another story. A whole series of circumstances has to be met. One of which obviously is your witch ending up in the same proximity as you. Let's just say, not everyone gets activated."

"So if I hadn't come to Heartwood Hollow . . ."

"I wouldn't have become a familiar. It would have taken some other sort of coinci— *sign* from the universe to get us in the same place at the same time where we could have met and hit it off. A vacation or something." She looked at me pointedly. "And we know how often you take a vacation."

"Wow." I didn't doubt her, but I couldn't believe so much of what I'd chosen to do with my life had such an impact on hers without me knowing. "What would have happened to you?"

"Nothing really. I would have continued doing what I was before you ever came to town. Lived the rest of my life as a normal human enlightened with the knowledge of Heartwood Hollow's paranormal side. But the point is, you did come to Heartwood Hollow, I was activated, and now here we are."

"Okay," Gram said, bringing both my and Sarah's focus to her. "So there's you and how many other familiars in your family?"

"There's me. My uncle, although he doesn't live here anymore. And my grandfather, but he's retired."

I set my cup down on the table. "You can retire from being a familiar?"

Sarah averted her eyes. "Yeah. It's a nicer way of saying his witch died."

"Oh. I'm sorry."

"It's okay. My grandfather keeps himself busy." She chuckled, the air around the table lightening significantly. "He's kind of like one of those nosey neighbors you see on TV now, only he's just genuinely curious about people and what they're up to. He's always liked to be in the know. He made it his job. Both of them."

It sounded like being a gossip came naturally with the territory of being a familiar. But what professional job would have allowed him to be that way too? "Wait . . . your grandfather was the newspaper editor at one point, wasn't he?"

"He was." Her smile grew proud. "We knew you'd figure it out eventually."

"I enjoyed my chat with him, although he is a little cryptic."

"All part of his job. He doesn't believe in handing people the answers. He likes to provide people with enough information for them to form their own opinions and conclusions."

"That fits him perfectly," I said, recalling Vince's and my time together as we chatted about a mis-solved murder last month. He'd believed that the person who was originally tried for the murder wasn't guilty. He'd been right about that, although I should have believed him when he'd said it wasn't who I'd thought it was either. It would have saved me some trouble.

"It was rather infuriating growing up," Sarah continued, "but I appreciate it now. With my uncle out of town with his warlock since before I was born, a lot of my training came from my grandfather."

Like she had earlier when investigating the crystals, Saffy jumped up onto the open chair and placed her front paws on the table.

Sarah stared at her. "You have something to say about all of this too?"

Saffy let out a loud *mrow*.

Gram and I laughed as Sarah sat there blinking in surprise at my cat.

"Maybe I was wrong about her being a familiar," Sarah said. "She's certainly got an opinion on the matter."

Gram seemed to brighten at this possibility. "Well, Joanie is no ordinary witch, like you said."

I went to take another sip of my tea only to discover my cup was empty. Standing, I asked, "Would anyone like a brownie? I'm out of cookies, but brownies have a magic all their own, and that's saying a lot since I didn't make them." Thankfully, Ken had saved some brownies for me before he and Ivy left.

Both Sarah and Gram nodded. Saffy made a noise as well.

"You had plenty of treats today, you silly cat. It's time for people treats now."

She let her front paws slide off the table and plopped back onto her hind legs as if in a huff.

I popped open the lid on the container where the brownies were, then withdrew three. I handed one each to Gram and Sarah. "The question is, why am I a special witch?"

"I'm still trying to figure that out," Sarah answered through a bite of brownie. "I can only go by what I already know about you through either research, what you've told me, observation, or the gossip circles. And let's face it, you've only just started accepting all of this, which has made it harder for me since I couldn't talk to you about it. You've been a mystery through much of this whole thing. It's been fun, you know I love puzzles, but maybe now we can start to put this one together."

"Well, it's one mystery I don't think we're going to solve tonight," Gram said. "We really should get back to those crystals. I take it you're still planning to stay, Sarah?"

She clasped her hands together. "Oh, yes please."

Gram nodded, a warm smile on her face. "See, Joanie? You'll be able to handle charging crystals yourself, but now you have someone to help you do the wards if they ever come undone again."

Sarah grinned excitedly. "Or anything else you might cook up."

I knew she meant that metaphorically, of course. Sarah couldn't bake or cook, but she was the best assistant in the shop I ever could have asked for. Knowing the truth about her now, I shouldn't have been surprised with how well we'd worked together since day one.

"I can't think of anyone better."

CHAPTER 13

After finishing our brownies, the three of us headed outside with all the crystals. Saffy took up her spot on the back of the couch in front of the picture window where she could supervise us.

I put the box, bag, and charging plate on the porch swing. "What do we do first?"

"Give me a minute," Gram said as she leaned over the railing to gaze up at the moon. She pivoted and pointed to the shadows created by the porch railing and posts. "Let's put the ones that will stay steady on the railing and just below. We can bury the others in the garden."

I cocked my head to the side. "But won't those get dirty?" Why had we spent the time to wash some of them only to put them in dirt?

"There is a difference between clean and cleansed," Gram said.

"Some crystals do well in the dirt, I've heard," Sarah said.

Gram nodded. "It's an option for many of them if you ever need to charge them when the moon isn't full. Of course you could always charge them with the sun if that's the case . . . as long as you don't leave certain ones out for too long."

She waved a thought away. Probably a good thing as this was already starting to make my head spin.

Unable to handle the cleansed crystals, Sarah helped hold the box and bag of crystals as I placed as many stones as I could safely on the porch. When that was done, we went into the front yard to the small garden I hadn't done much with since moving here. Daffodils came up on their own in the spring, crocuses and tulips, too, then mums in the fall. Right now, there was some sort of lily. They were orange. Tiger lilies, I think.

"Now, these you'll want to leave in the dirt for about a week," Gram said as I kneeled, "because it's the first time you're cleansing them. After this, you'll be able to shorten it by a day at a time, but always give them at least twenty-four hours to charge. Longer is better."

Sarah kneeled next to me. "Are there some stones that can't go in the ground? Sometimes dirt is damp. Or wet from rain."

I should have thought to ask that. Sarah was already proving her importance in being my familiar.

"You won't want to put iron-rich stones in the ground. The soil could leach it out. So pyrite and hematite especially. Those are up on the porch. I showed them to Joanie earlier, but I'll point them out to you when you're done here."

"I have my own pyrite," Sarah said. "My grandpa's witch gave me some when I was a kid. Called it fool's gold."

"That's it exactly."

"I thought it looked familiar," I commented. "I had some too, didn't I?"

"You had several different small stones as a kid that you

liked to play with. Back then you just thought they were pretty."

"Thea had them too."

"You had the same base kit. Yours lived on your book-shelf. Thea turned hers into jewelry." Gram let out a small cackle at her own joke. "Always knew she'd be into witch crafts."

In the moonlight, I could just make out Sarah's quirked eyebrow.

That sounded rather general to me. "Witchcrafts?"

"No. Actual crafts."

"So you mean, all of those things she sells—the dream catchers, the candles?"

Gram nodded. "Like with your baking, the spell is in the intent of what she makes."

I faced Sarah. "You should see some of her stuff. Has an online store and sells it all. It's beautiful."

Sarah nodded in small, slow motions as she patted the dirt on top of a crystal I'd just placed. She looked up at Gram, her lower lip extended past the top. "Does she have multiple magical abilities too?"

"No. Not at all. She's crafty. That's it." After another moment, Gram added, "Talented, though. Powerful stuff."

"Does *anyone* have multiple abilities in your family?"

"No, just Joanie. What are you thinking?"

"Wonder if it has anything to do with Joanie's father." She tamped down the earth around a tiger's-eye sphere.

"My father? But I don't even know him. He left my mom when he found out she was a witch."

Sarah sighed. "That will complicate some things."

"But why would he have anything to do with this?" I dug into the dirt with my hands, making space for a star sapphire.

"He wouldn't have left Mom for being a witch if he was one too. That doesn't make sense."

"Joanie, that's enough digging," Gram said. "Don't lose your intent."

I blew out a hard breath, then drew in a deep, slow one. "Focus," I mumbled to myself before adding a handful of dirt back into the hole and dropping the sphere inside.

"Sorry. I shouldn't have brought him up right now," Sarah said quietly to me. "I knew he wasn't in the picture, but I didn't realize he'd be a sore subject."

"It's okay. I never talk about him, so how would you know? That's not information you can look up easily." I was quiet for a moment as I placed a smoky quartz sphere I'd cleaned earlier into a new hole. "You've tried, haven't you?"

"Of course I have. It's part of my job." Quieter, she added, "I can stop if you want me to."

Although part of me felt like it was a bit of an invasion of privacy that Sarah had been trying to delve into my past without my knowledge, there was another part of me that knew where she was coming from. I'd been doing the same these last few months as I tried helping the ghosts who were somehow attached to my matched couples. My attempts had gotten me into a bit of trouble, especially when I accused the wrong man of murder, but everything had worked out in the end. Now I knew a little bit about how it felt to be on the other end of that research.

On the other hand, I had to admit that I was curious to know the answers Sarah was looking for too. I put my hand on one of hers, and she looked at me with questioning eyes. "No. Don't stop looking. Please."

Sarah gave me a small smile and a nod before pulling her hand away to push dirt over the smoky quartz.

I returned to the hole I had already made and was about

to place a smooth green stone inside when, from closer than she had been before, Gram said, "Not that one. Too soft. Must have missed it going through them."

"What is it?" I held the stone to the light.

"Malachite. It will help dispel any collected negative energy that's come into the house both of a psychic nature and sometimes of those pesky energy waves that float about from electronics."

Looking at the swirls on the green stone, things started to click. "So like the cell signal and Wi-Fi?"

"Sometimes. Mine do. It all depends on the intent. You know how I feel about those things."

"But you had a cell phone today." That had been one of the biggest changes to Gram since the last time she'd visited. "You used it to check in on your cat. That reminds me, you wanted to make sure he'd eaten."

At this, Sarah turned to look at Gram, but not before a knowing smirk crossed her face. What was I missing? Oh, no matter. I'm sure I'd find out soon enough anyway.

"Only when I travel now. Sterling insisted. He worries." Gram shrugged. "Times change, but that thing goes off and into a drawer as soon as I get home. I can go weeks without using it."

Maybe I could get my malachite to allow a cell signal in the house. Then again, by keeping things as they had been, I'd know when they were broken. Ken's ability to get a text message a few weeks ago, when he'd never been able to before, had been almost as big of a clue to something going on as Miss Susan and Dale showing up in the house.

As if she knew what I was thinking, Gram added, "It's more than just the malachite that will do it. Citrine too, which you have over on the railing."

Having finished burying my last stone, I stood and faced

my grandmother. "How do you keep track of all this? There are so many crystals, and they all do multiple things."

"Simple." She winked. "I'm a crystal witch."

"I knew it!" Sarah said, brushing her hands on her knees as she stood.

I stared at her wide-eyed. "How did you know that?"

She looked like she'd just been given a gold star by the teacher. "All of the bracelets and necklaces were a big clue, but the discipline she's had throughout this whole exercise gave it away."

I hadn't even known it was a possibility. "I just thought there were things like kitchen witches and green witches. Crystals sound specific."

"It can be," Gram agreed. "Miss Susan, like I said earlier, was a green witch, but one of the girls taking over her garden is a tea witch. Miss Susan was great at coming up with a perfect blend of tea, but tea witches can go further and even read the leaves."

"I've always wanted to have that done," Sarah said.

"You should come home with Joanie sometime and meet Tabby. She'd probably jump at the chance to read a familiar."

Sarah spun on her heels to face me, clasping her hands together. "Oh, can we?"

If we left on a Monday after work, we could come back the next day. It could work. "We'll see when we can figure something out." That made me sound like such a party pooper, and she deflated slightly. A smile grew across my face. "I think I'd like to do it too. It does sound fun, doesn't it?"

She brightened again. "It really does. No one around here does that sort of thing."

"I was going to ask you if there were any local covens

Joanie could join," Gram began, "but let's go inside, shall we? We're done out here."

As I followed Gram and Sarah back onto the porch, Sarah quietly told us about the coven her grandfather had been a part of with his witch. I cast a glance back over the yard. It didn't feel any different. Hopefully, now that I was active with the crystals used, the wards we'd create would be stronger than they had been when I had no knowledge they were there. I imagined a barrier going up around the house, ghosts lined up around it unable to get in.

"Coming, Joanie?" Gram asked from just inside the living room. "We have more to do in here."

"Coming," I echoed, then stepped up into the house.

Somewhere nearby, a screen door slapped closed.

Had someone been watching us?

CHAPTER 14

I shook the feeling away as Gram ducked back into the side room. The noise wasn't an uncommon one. It was probably someone letting their dog out one last time. The timing was probably just a coincidence.

I was beginning to dislike that word.

Gram returned a minute later with bundles of dried herbs, flowers, and other greenery as well as short sticks of wood.

"Now this is something I'm familiar with," I said, nodding to the bundle of sage leaves in my grandmother's hand. She and my mom had been using them for years. Now I had my own smudge stick. I'd recently ordered it after repeatedly needing to cleanse my kitchen. The first couple of times, I'd had to use sage leaf spice that I had in my kitchen cupboard. There was a big difference between the two, especially in ease of use.

"Go grab the one you have. Sarah can use the one I brought."

I went to the kitchen to retrieve the smudge stick from the cupboard where I'd been storing my black and white candles, silver candlesticks, and everything else I'd found to be useful during my witchy recipes. It still felt a little odd calling them what they were—spells, séances, or summonings. I also grabbed a box of matches from the utility drawer since I hadn't seen Gram with any. Last I knew, she couldn't command things to light on fire at will.

"Got it." I waved the smudge stick gently in front of me, then held up my other hand. "And matches."

"Wonderful." Gram was holding a rough-cut stick, the other herb bundles she'd had now on my coffee table. Sarah clutched her smudge stick to her chest, looking just like the kids in the bakery after I'd given them the largest cookie or the cupcake with the most sprinkles.

"What do you have?" I asked Gram, approaching her and the stick in her hand for a better look. "I haven't seen you use it before."

"This is *palo santo*, ethically harvested from downed trees in Central and South America. It's holy wood."

I raised an eyebrow at her. "So sacred wood?"

Had Sarah known about this term before? I cast a glance her way, but her widening eyes seemed to say, "Don't look at me." She was right. I wouldn't have expected her to know about this then, back when I thought she knew nothing of the paranormal world.

"You could call it that, yes," Gram answered.

"Why didn't you tell me about this when I asked if you knew what sacred wood was last month?" One of the biggest questions in town had been what sort of wood that was after Lily accused John of having a knife made out of it. Until I could get Lily, who I learned was a dryad, to explain it to me, the meaning behind the term had been a mystery.

"And send you down the wrong path?" Gram put her free hand on her hip, a stance I knew well as both my mom and I stood the same way as we started to take an attitude with one another. In that respect, we were all so alike. "They don't make knives out of this material. It's been used the same way I'm about to for centuries. Besides Heartwood Hollow—the whole Fiddlefern Fjord region and the entirety of New England, really—is far from where this is found. There was no way these were the same thing."

Sighing, I said, "You have a point." Finding out about palo santo a month ago may have only led to my confusion. "So what *do* you use it for?"

"It's another sort of purification method." She pointed to the box of matches, then held out her hand. "I'll follow you both around with this as an added step of our cleansing ritual. We didn't use these until a couple years ago, mostly because I wanted to find a proper source for them. They're used by many, and the tree has been over forested as a result. I was so glad when we found them. I just love the smell."

With that, Gram put the matchbox into her hand holding the stick and struck a match against it. As the end flared to life, she handed me the matchbox. I tucked it into my pocket as she held the match to the palo santo, setting it on fire. She extinguished the match and called Sarah and me over to her, instructing us to light our smudge sticks with the fire from hers. "When you do this yourself, let the stick burn for at least half a minute, but not much longer than that. Then blow it out. The embers will continue to burn"—she blew out the stick as I pulled my sage away—"and the smoke from that will do its thing."

"Oh, that does smell good," I commented, ensuring my smudge stick was properly smoking as Sarah did the same.

Gram smiled. "Told you. And it will always smell a little different. Light, but piney or woodsy, sometimes even lemony almost."

"Really? I get burning sugar, but not in a bad way." I sniffed the smoky air around us once more.

Sarah laughed. "That doesn't surprise me coming from a baker."

Gram took a step backward toward the front door. "Now, as we go along the perimeter of the house, make sure to get all the corners. Energy can get caught in them. Clear your mind and focus on banishing unwanted energies. Sage will cleanse all energies, but the palo santo will take care of the negative ones specifically. For a regular cleansing, you wouldn't need both. You might not even need either. They're not something you use just because."

She inclined her head toward the other smudge sticks on the table. Instead of sage, they contained other herbs. Those, like rosemary and lavender, I easily recognized, but some others I wasn't too sure about.

"We can get into that at another time, however," she continued. "Tonight, the ones we're holding are good."

For several minutes, we blew smoke toward the ceiling where it met the walls as a trio, eventually fanning out to cover more space at the same time once Sarah and I felt comfortable. Gram checked in on us both a couple of times to make sure we weren't forcing the smoke, causing it to dissipate faster than it should—"It's not a candle on a birthday cake, go easy"—or letting too much build in spots because "You don't want the energy and the smoke to linger longer than it should."

"As you pass by the windows, open them to give the energy a place to escape," Gram instructed. "We'll leave the windows open tonight to allow in new positive energies."

I thought back to the time Mom and Gram had cleansed my apartment in the middle of January. It had been cold sleeping that night. Saffy, only a kitten and spending her first night with me, had slept in the crook of my neck to stay warm.

Over the next few hours, Sarah, Gram, and I cleansed both floors of the house as well as the basement. The attic was small and cramped, holding only a few boxes that I still hadn't unpacked from when I moved in, so we didn't bother with it. I'd never heard anything up there, nor had I ever sensed anything, but if we were warding the rest of the house, then at least any existing ghosts would have somewhere to go if they refused to leave my house entirely. I'd met a few wandering spirits over the years, those whose homes or buildings they haunted no longer stood or had become unrecognizable even to them, and I couldn't imagine doing that to a ghost who'd been here longer than I had even if I didn't want them in the main part of my house. The attic was better than nothing.

Without Sarah's help, I had no doubt Gram and I would have been up all night, but shortly after one in the morning, we said goodbye to Sarah. I was grateful she'd been here and was excited by the revelations that she played a bigger part in my being a witch, but as Gram and I got ready for bed, I couldn't help but feel conflicted. Although we weren't the type to hang out together, Sarah was one of my closest friends, so why was I having a problem?

Gram knocked on the open door of my bedroom as I drew the sheet down from my bed, grateful Saffy hadn't left any crumbs from her tuna treats.

"Hey, Gram. You need anything?"

She shook her head. "Only a hug."

I stepped away from the bed and approached her, my arms already open wide. As soon as Gram was within reach, I wrapped my arms around her, and she did the same with me. "I really am glad you're here. And for more than just because you're helping me. It's been fun. And I think everyone liked meeting you at the potluck."

"You have a great group of friends. So many who would support you if you just opened up to them. They might surprise you. Like Sarah. Who would have guessed?"

"Not you, that's for sure," I said teasingly, stepping out of her embrace.

"I truly thought it was that cat of yours." Gram looked at Saffy sitting patiently on the bed. Saffy yawned. "Still might not be entirely wrong. You have multiple powers. Why not multiple familiars? Anyhow, I just wanted to say goodnight. See you in the morning." She gave me another hug and kissed my cheek.

With that, Gram turned around, then shuffled to my guest room. A moment later, her door clicked shut. I closed my door over, unable to shut it completely so Saffy would have access in and out of the room.

"Move over, Saf," I told her as I crawled into bed and lay down.

As I glanced at the clock on my nightstand, the reason for my feelings about Sarah tonight hit me. Gram had been here for a little over twelve hours, and she was leaving later today. I hadn't realized how much I'd missed it being just Gram and me. Then during what I'd been expecting to be a special time for the two of us, I'd had to share Gram and her attention. And there was still so much I needed to know. I'd just have to make today count.

CHAPTER 15

On a normal night, I was asleep in a few minutes, tired from my early mornings at the bakery. Although I'd gotten up just as early today, the day had been vastly different. Cleansing the crystals and smudging the house with Gram and Sarah left me feeling both exhausted and charged. It was late, but I wasn't sure if I'd sleep, even after I lay in bed with Saffy curled up next to me. She must have sensed how unsettled I was and decided against falling asleep between my knees like she usually did.

It was a smart move on her part.

Twenty minutes after flopping into bed, I sat up, then threw the top sheet off me as I swung my legs out of bed, doing my best to not disturb my cat.

Maybe tea would get me to calm down.

I headed into the kitchen and then prepared myself a cup of calming lavender and chamomile tea with a hint of rose petals in it. It was the decaf blend of one of my favorite cozy black teas. Just making the tea was beginning to calm me, and with how long I'd have to wait until it was cool enough for me to drink, I wondered how much I'd manage to drink before sleep took hold.

There were ways to speed the cooling process along, though. Once the tea was done steeping, I popped it into the fridge.

Satisfied enough with its temperature after several minutes, I took the tea into the living room and settled on the couch. I debated grabbing the book I had yet to finish from the coffee table but decided against it. I didn't want to disturb the smudge sticks that were still there, and my desire to always read one more chapter would likely see me finishing the book and not sleeping at all. Instead, I sat peeking out at the crystals on the porch as they bathed in the moonlight, and I reflected on what I'd learned over the last few hours.

Over in my purse hanging from my coat-tree, my cell phone buzzed. The noise puzzled me a moment before I realized what it was. Although Ken's cell signal had recently gone from non-existent to spotty while he was here, I never had service inside. Then again, the wards were completely down now. That must have allowed the message to come through.

But who would be sending me a text at this hour?

I hopped off the couch, then shuffled to the coat-tree. Pulling the phone out of my purse, I clicked on the screen, which had already gone dark, then opened my messages.

Sam: Are you awake?

I'd told him only a few weeks ago that he could call me at any time. Until now, he hadn't, but what would be causing him to reach out now? He'd been fine several hours ago, excited for his friend being offered a chance to work in the bakery and going off to celebrate it with everyone. Had something happened since then?

Me: Yeah. Feel free to call.

I was not a fan of texting. There was too little ability to convey meaning and intent in such short phrases. As a matchmaker, I'd seen people overanalyze texts until it drove them crazy. Even over the simplest things. The word *okay*, for example, and how many ways that word could be inferred when it was a response to something. And don't get me started on if it was followed by a period. That nearly spelled doom for one of my matches in high school. Personally, I needed to hear someone speak to get a full understanding of what they meant.

A moment later, my screen flared back to life with Sam's call. I hoped that with it being on vibrate that it wouldn't wake Gram up. She claimed the cell signal alone messed with her energy, so who knew how she'd react to an actual phone call.

"Hey, Sam. Is everything okay?" I said quietly. Realizing my voice could wake Gram up even if the cell's energy couldn't, I felt it best to go outside. Not wanting to go sit on the porch and possibly draw attention to myself and all the crystals out there, I grabbed my teacup, then crossed into the kitchen and headed out the back door. The hot tub on Nathan and George's deck was no longer occupied, but the light in their dining room was still on.

"Oh, yeah. Everything's fine. I think I had a bit too much chocolate ice cream, and I can't sleep. But you sound tired. I didn't wake you, did I?"

"It's the night of a full moon, and I'm a witch being trained by her grandmother to charge crystals and put wards up in her house. I'm awake." I plopped onto the stairs leading to my backyard.

The line was quiet for several seconds, and I thought I'd somehow lost the signal. It had never been that great in the yard either.

"You're being really open about all that," Sam said after another moment.

I sighed, or was it a yawn? "Yeah, Gram's teaching me to be a little better at that too." I paused. "You don't seem freaked out by my telling you."

"Like I told you before, I wasn't going to believe the rumors, but I'll always believe you if you tell me." I imagined him shrugging. "And I figured as much when you said you thought you accidentally put spells in what we made for the festival."

"Thanks, Sam. I'm really glad you're okay with it all." I hoped everyone else on my team would be too once I told them.

"Look, you didn't bat an eye when I came out to you. This isn't quite the same . . . but then again, it kinda is. It's a part of you that you've been keeping from others, and maybe even from yourself, be it out of denial, fear, or any of the many reasons why people keep these parts of themselves hidden from others. I guess I'll say what you did to me, thank you for trusting me."

"I really am going to miss you when you go off to school, you know. Now, why were you wanting to know if I was awake? What's going on?" I'd been dominating this conversation with witchy things, yet he had been the one to reach out. I sipped on my tea, which was now at the perfect temperature, giving him the time to respond.

"It's weird. I don't know how to describe it, but I figured you'd be the best one to talk to about it because of, well, I guess all the couples you've gotten together."

"What happened?"

"It wasn't that something happened, not exactly. It was more of a feeling."

"Well, what was going on when the feeling started?" My

heartbeat quickened as I listened to him trying to explain what he'd experienced.

"That's the thing. Nothing. I was at the potluck standing in the circle talking with everyone. Brittni had been peeking over her shoulder watching you to see if you'd had the cookie yet. She'd seen you take one, and even though I hadn't told her anything about it being a trial or for a job at the shop, I think she was anxious to have you try it all the same. She's talked about going to culinary school. Todd's not going to go to culinary school, but tonight, he made a comment about the three of us all living together next year. And I don't know. He squeezed my hand and smiled at me. That was it."

I could have kicked myself for giving in to my feelings of being overwhelmed earlier. Could Sam and Todd have been the match I'd run away from and then couldn't feel after eating the brownie sandwich?

"Well, even the tiniest moments can have a great impact. Try to describe the feeling." I'd never had a match express to me the feeling of being matched. Many times, they didn't know it had happened, and sometimes, like with John and Lily, they weren't even in the same room as one another when the match struck.

He took a deep breath. "So we were holding hands, like I said, really a first at something where we weren't just among our friends. When he squeezed it, I looked at him and was flooded with a rush of warmth. It sounds stupid, but it was as if the clouds had parted to reveal the sun shining down on you. Nothing extreme. It wasn't burning. More like a cozy feeling you get putting on a sweater. No, it was like opening the door to the oven and having the heat hit you."

I didn't want to tell him and get his hopes up in case I was wrong, but after hearing that description, I was pretty sure he and Todd had been matched. I vowed to never dull my senses again. Love was on the line, and I had to be able to figure out who was being matched the moment it was happening. I couldn't fail my couples again.

At least with Sam and Todd, I could easily get them together in the same place with me there to confirm they were the newest match in town.

"Joanie? You still there?" Sam asked, a hint of worry in his voice.

"Yeah, I'm still here."

"Have you heard of something like that happening before?"

I'd seen it all. People who were already together like Sam and Todd. Friends who may or may not have secretly thought about what it would be like to date the other person, like Rachael and her husband Mark. Acquaintances, like Ashley and Rich who both wanted the same cookie but then decided to share it. Complete strangers whose pull was so strong I could feel it before they even met, like Lily and her now-boyfriend John. Now that I'd accepted I was a witch, I could see the moment a match was struck for what it was—magic. But because I wasn't sure if magic had struck for Sam and Todd, I deflected a bit.

"There's a first for everything, Sam, but it sounds like love. You were so worried last month about the long-distance relationship, and tonight he was telling you that distance is temporary. He's picturing your future. That's great!"

He let out a long, slow sigh, then quickly followed it with a yawn. "Thanks, Joanie. That makes me feel a lot better."

I responded with a yawn of my own. "I'm really glad I could help."

"I should probably let you go. I know we don't have work tomorrow, but I'm sure you'll be doing stuff with your grandmother that you'll want to be awake for."

"You have a good night, Sam."

"Night, Joanie. Enjoy your day off with your grandma." The line disconnected, so I clicked off the phone screen, yawning once more.

I looked down into my teacup. Somehow, I'd finished it without realizing it until now. It wasn't the first time and wouldn't be the last. It was a little disappointing, though. I would have liked just one more sip before heading inside. Oh well.

Even without that final sip, the tea worked its magic, and my second attempt at falling asleep went more smoothly than the first. The last thing I remembered before sleep overtook me was Saffy crawling between my knees.

CHAPTER 16

I t seemed Gram had the same idea about making the most of our remaining time together count.

Her shaking my legs woke me from not enough sleep.

"Sorry, sassy cat," Gram whispered while my eyes were still closed. "I need my granddaughter."

She hadn't sounded like something was wrong, but I peeked out of one eye at her statement. "Is everything okay?"

Gram was still in her pajamas, a silk button-down shirt, loose silk pants, and her hair in a matching turban. Other than the fact she put my worn-out cartoon pajamas to shame, nothing seemed to be the matter.

"It's time to get up, that's all."

Saffy slowly stood and climbed off my legs as I opened my other eye. Night still clung to the sky. "What time is it?"

"Just before dawn. Come on. Your tea is already steeping."

Lifting the sheet off me, I swung my legs over the edge of the bed and sat up. I wiped the sleep from my eyes, adding in a large yawn for good measure. "I'm up. Let me find my slippers."

"You won't need them."

"I won't?" I wore them whenever I was in the house unless my feet were up on the couch. They were only a few feet away, so I slipped my feet into them. At least they'd be downstairs whenever I did end up needing them.

Gram turned and led the way back down the stairs. Saffy followed me, something unheard of when it was just us in the house. She usually was several feet in front of me in her dash to the kitchen. She had been on her best behavior since Gram got here. If only Gram had seen what had happened between the two of us with the feather duster shortly before she arrived.

I turned into the kitchen, expecting to have to still grab out my honey for my tea, but everything was already set out on one of my tea trays. Two cups with tea steeping, honey, spoons, and two apples.

"How long have you been up?"

"Oh, a little while. These old bones of mine don't like me to sleep in."

"But we only went to bed a few hours ago. This isn't sleeping in."

"My bones know what time it is." Gram grabbed the tray off the counter, then walked back past me. "Come on."

I quickly fed Saffy and then followed Gram outside. She had already set the tea tray down on the little table I had next to the porch swing. Until last night with the crystals, neither had seen much use lately. I loved coming out here to drink tea and read on nice days. But lately I'd been so busy between the ghost stuff and trying to expand the bakery's operations that I rarely had the opportunity to enjoy the space. Instead, I'd been stealing a few minutes of reading time here and there on my couch with Saffy on my feet.

Gram sat on the swing, then patted the cushion next to her, but I remained standing, my head tilted slightly as I looked at the crystals that had been bathing in the moonlight overnight.

"You feel it, don't you?" Gram asked.

"More like I hear it. It's almost like they're humming."

"I call it singing." Gram chuckled softly. "They're getting their energies in tune with one another as well as with you and the house. Go toward them. Allow yourself to feel it."

The difference became noticeable as I stepped a few feet closer to the crystals on the railing. The still morning air felt charged but not in a bad way. It felt like my shop when the lights grew brighter with someone's exceedingly happy mood. The sensation itself wasn't overwhelming, though. Slowly, my mind cleared, and my body unwound from whatever energies I'd been holding on to.

"Now you feel it. Your shoulders just relaxed. Not sure if you realized that."

"I do. It's just, wow," I said, unable to put everything into words. "Is this only because they're so close together or is this how my whole house is going to feel?"

"It's concentrated right now, but as I have you place the crystals in a little while, you'll notice it to some extent throughout the house, more in areas where they're grouped. But we'll get to that." Gram patted the cushion again. "Come sit."

I joined Gram on the porch swing, and she passed me a teacup. As I blew on it softly out of habit before taking a small sip to judge its temperature, Gram lifted her feet into a crisscross position, sending the swing into a gentle rocking.

"This is good," I said of the tea after taking a sip. "One of yours?"

"One of the last bags of Susan's blends. Remind me to give you the bags I brought for you."

"She really was magic with her tea."

"I'm going to miss it." Letting out a long sigh, Gram reached for her tea on the table. "And her."

As she returned to her sitting position, I rested my head on Gram's shoulder, then pulled my feet up under me and to the side, letting my slippers fall off and hit the wood porch with a soft plop. "I know."

We stayed quiet a moment, she and I, letting our thoughts wander. No doubt Gram was thinking about her lost friend. Miss Susan had come to me after she died with a message for me, but she hadn't said much else. It had me wishing I could communicate with spirits who had crossed over and not just ghosts who were still earthbound if for no other reason than to let Gram chat with her friend once more.

Gram sighed once more. "Well, that's not what I've come here for, and that's not what this was supposed to turn into."

Her comment almost seemed like a reply, as if she was talking about not being able to talk to Miss Susan. "What do you mean?"

"We have things to do like bringing in these crystals when the sun comes up, but first I wanted to have a nice morning with my granddaughter. I have a feeling that last night didn't quite go how you expected. That you had been looking forward to it being just you and me."

I sat up and studied my grandma. "Are you sure you don't have multiple powers too? You have this way of knowing what's been in my head."

Gram chuckled, then took a sip of her tea. "No, just the crystals. You can call the other part a grandma's intuition. I've spent the last twenty-seven years developing it and had mother's intuition before that."

Settling my head back onto my grandma's shoulder after drinking some of my tea, I said, "It's not that I was mad Sarah was here, but you're right. I had been expecting it to be the two of us."

"I'll just have to make a point of visiting more often." She wrapped an arm around my shoulders and gave me a squeeze. "You're a powerful witch, Joanie, and just learning about everything. It's an exciting time. That you have multiple abilities and a human familiar only makes it more so."

"I'm glad it's Sarah and not some stranger. I already trust her, and we work well together."

"No reason that shouldn't continue," Gram said, starting to play with my hair. "Despite your feelings last night, you did a good job of sharing me. I can't imagine Sarah's gotten to do a whole lot of this herself. She's learned about it, sure, but she may not have felt comfortable going to a circle without her witch. In a way, she's been holding on to a secret most of her life like you have with your ghosts."

I hadn't thought about it like that. Now I almost felt bad about being jealous last night. "No wonder she'd been so excited when we told her to stay."

"I imagine that was a big part of it." She patted my head. "Come on, finish your tea. There's one more thing I want to do before we get to work."

Too tasty for me to want to chug what was left in my cup, it took me a few minutes to drink the rest. But finally I was done.

Gram stood, and I did the same.

"No slippers," Gram told me as she crossed the porch heading toward the steps. My feet were already halfway in them.

"But we're outside."

She glanced over her shoulder at me and winked. "That's the point." She stepped down from the porch onto the path leading to the driveway and then took two steps into the grassy front yard. "Are you coming or not?"

Knowing not to question her further, I did as she asked and met her barefoot in the grass. It was still cold from the night, the sun's rays only hinting at their arrival.

"All right, now face the sun." Gram oriented herself to look diagonally across the street.

I did the same, memories from childhood overnights at Gram's flashing through my mind. She'd have both Thea and me come outside in the early mornings, sink our toes into the grass, and welcome the sun. I should have known that was what Gram wanted to do when she first said I wouldn't need anything on my feet.

"Ground yourself to the earth. Wiggle your toes and get them into the grass, not just on top of it," Gram instructed, doing it at the same time she was telling me. "Make that connection and feel it. The energy should be similar to what you experienced with the crystals, and that's when you'll know you're doing it right."

Steph and Alex had been telling me to connect to nature, but I hadn't done it more than a couple times. But out here with Gram as we faced the rising sun, this was the first time that I truly felt the connection and grounding that I was supposed to feel. Maybe it was Gram being here. Maybe it was the crystal work and smudging last night. Maybe it was the fact my shoes were off this time. I wasn't sure.

The energy coursed through me, reminding me of the tingling sensation I got when I was around perfect matches. Only this energy was consistent. It flowed evenly through my body. There was no variation accounting for a new match being made, a match going through an exciting time like a marriage or a pregnancy, or one that was on the rocks due to external pressures. This energy also remained circulating, unlike the matchmaking tingle which, under normal conditions, settled in my feet as the match took hold. It wasn't overwhelming either, unlike last night's match energy had been with everyone together and multiple things going on with all of them. No, if this was what I had felt last, I wouldn't have had to retreat into my room to try to calm myself down. This was manageable. Pleasant. I could handle and even enjoy this level of energy throughout my system all the time.

"Did you hear me?" Gram asked, looking back at me with a satisfied smile on her face.

"Hmm?"

"I had asked if you could feel it, but judging by, well, everything, I'd say you can." She turned back around. "Now bring your hands to your navel and place your dominant hand over the other."

I did, then widened my stance a bit as I closed my eyes.

"Empty your mind"—always the hardest part for me—"and your lungs. Hold for one . . . two . . . three . . . four . . . and breathe in deep. One . . . two . . . three . . . four. Hold it. One . . . two . . . three . . . four . . . and breathe out all the way. One . . . two . . . three . . . four."

We repeated the process three more times before Gram told me to open my eyes. It was time to greet the sun.

"Now as you breathe in this time, swing your arms up over your head and bring them palms together." I followed along with her instructions, focusing more on my breathing and the energy than getting the movements correct. My work at the bakery and regular bike riding to make deliveries kept me in shape, but I wasn't flexible.

"Breathe all the way out and arc your arms down as you fold forward," Gram continued. "Let your fingers dance along the grass as you either bring them to touch the ground by your feet or your feet themselves. Hold. Good. Breathe in and lift halfway up so your hands can rest on your knees. And fold forward again just like before as you exhale. Hold. This time as you breathe in, straighten completely and bring your arms back over your head, then your palms together. Now breathe out and bend your knees as if you're halfway to sitting, arms still raised. Hold. Breathe in one more time and stand straight, arms up-up-up. Now this time, exhale and drop your arms, keeping your hands together until they are level with your heart."

Silently she led me through the greeting three more times. As we finished, I kept my hands where they were as the sun continued to rise, and for a moment, I could have sworn I was one with the earth, feeling its energy flow into me as mine cycled back into it. Was this what Steph and Alex had been talking about when they told me to be a part of nature more? Was this what the dryads felt when they merged with their trees?

The energy lessened with each question I asked myself. I was thinking too much. Forcing thought aside, I let my hands fall to my sides, and the feeling returned to how it should have been.

And then Gram spoke once more, breaking the silence of the dawn.

CHAPTER 17

I hadn't been expecting Gram to turn her greeting of the morning sun into a full forty-five-minute yoga session.

Surprisingly, it had been fun, but by the end of it, a couple early risers had already walked past with their dogs or jogged by on their morning runs. A ghost or two had also stopped by to watch the spectacle, although they remained on the sidewalk as they looked at Gram and me. I'd have to reconsider either my cutesy pajama choices or move this into the backyard where fewer people could see me. Or both.

Gram wiped the slight sheen off her forehead. It was going to be a hot, humid day in Heartwood Hollow. "All right, now you can bring your crystals inside."

"What about the ones in the garden?"

"I'll remind you next week to dig them up. Then you can give them a quick rinse with intent or wipe them with a soft cloth to physically clean them. They'll already be *cleansed*. After that, do the same with them that you're doing with these now. Think you can manage that?"

I took a six-inch fluorite tower from its overnight position in one hand and a pyrite cluster in the other. Cracking a smile, I said, "Only if you can get the door."

It took several minutes, but I eventually brought all the porch crystals inside. The entire time, Saffy studied my movements back and forth onto the porch as I placed the crystals on the coffee table for the moment. Her head swiveled this way and that in an almost comical manner, her gaze following me throughout the exercise. Had she been watching me doing yoga in the front yard too? Maybe it was a good thing she couldn't talk. I bet she'd have had an opinion about it.

When I placed the last crystal down, Saffy darted over to the coffee table. She stood up on her hind legs to get a closer look at the stones.

"She feels the strengthened energy of them too, no doubt," Gram started. "You'll want to put your spheres where she can't bat them around or knock them off something in the process. Well, that last part is for all crystals. A lot of them may look hard, but they'll crack or shatter completely if you drop them. Sterling learned that the hard way several years ago."

As if trying to press her luck, Saffy reached for the malachite.

"Saffy, down," I said at the same time Gram chuckled.

"Such a sassy cat."

I put my hands on my hips. "Okay, so where do I put these?" I couldn't imagine having enough room for them all.

"The ones that were over your doors and windows can go back where they were as you think about warding the house, protecting it from those spirits you don't want inside. We can find places to put those that are new to you." As I put back the points that had been resting above my windows and doors for the last few years, Gram instructed me to alternate rose quartz with black tourmaline and to stick extra black tourmaline as close to the corners of the house as possible. Since Gram couldn't touch the crystals, she followed me as she spoke more about the various strengths of the two stones, Saffy trailing close behind.

When I returned to the table, I had several new to me crystals that had never had homes here in my house before as well as the selenite slab that had lived in the storage compartment of my coat-tree. I grabbed the slab and pivoted to head back toward my door.

"You don't need to put it back there, you know," Gram said kindly yet in a way that seemed she felt that it should have been obvious.

"But that's where it's been . . ."

"It's done its job there. But now you know about the crystals and can charge them whenever they need it. It's time for a new home for this one. Let it strengthen some of these." She used her whole hand to point to the coffee table. "It's time for you to make your own altar space."

The idea had been in the back of my mind since Gram mentioned my creating one in the bakery. I'd been a bit dubious about the idea, but after spending more time with her, learning from her, and finding out that Sarah, the person who was with me the most at the bakery was my familiar, an altar there made sense. However, I had yet to figure out where one could go here.

"Where?" I didn't have many options that fit the criteria of being somewhere Saffy couldn't get to easily that was also large enough for what I thought I needed. Now that I knew what it was, I realized that I'd seen Gram's altar. It was huge, encompassing a small table with a beautiful cloth covering it, dozens of towering crystals spread across the fabric or on pedestals or the floor, and beautiful pieces of art on the walls.

"How about where you already have one started?"

I quirked an eyebrow at her. I didn't have an altar. "What do you mean?"

Gram placed both of her hands on my shoulders and turned me around until I was facing the fireplace. "You already have quite the start of one going between your shells, that hairbrush, the hag stone, and all the other bits and bobs you have up there."

I walked toward the mantel to investigate the space more thoroughly. "A hag stone?"

Gram chuckled. "I thought you'd pick up on that. Not the best term to call us witches, but the name for those stones with a natural hole in them has stuck."

A faraway memory of showing Gram the stone I'd picked up after finding it on the Florida beach resurfaced. "You wouldn't touch it back then either."

"No need to add my energy to it when it had called to you."

I picked up the gray stone with shiny flecks. Half the size of my palm, it had a pinky-sized hole through the middle. "But Thea touched it. She didn't want to give it back that day."

Gram waved the statement away. "You were both kids, and she wanted to see through it too. It's fine. It's just your energy now after all these years."

Placing the stone back down, I asked, "Did she ever find one?"

"Plenty. It's like her determination made them come to her. She uses many in her jewelry, some in the other crafts she makes. But her altar space is full of her favorites. I'm sure she'd be happy to make something for yours."

I glanced back at the mantel, still wondering where I'd fit everything. "But it isn't going to look like yours."

"That's the point. It's not supposed to. Sure, it will have some of the same elements when it's finished"—she came up to stand next to me and wrapped an arm around my back to give me a squeeze—"but it will be all your own, as it should. An altar is, after all, a place you get your strength from, from those things that have called to you over the years. You may add more over time, or things will lose their meaning and you'll remove them. As you learn more about your path, you'll find that it may change with the seasons or certain elements will only be needed when you're working toward something particular. It's where you'll cast spells . . . well, those that aren't in your baked goods, anyway, contemplate your intentions—whatever you choose to do that you are comfortable with."

She let me go and walked back toward the coffee table. As I turned to follow her, she glanced over her shoulder at me. "You only half dusted that, by the way." She winked. "Don't think I missed that sassy cat with the feather duster when I got here."

Through laughter, I confessed the story of my attempt to clean before she got here. My laughter disturbed Saffy, who had gone up to her spot on the couch to sleep in the morning sun once she realized she wasn't allowed to touch the crystals. Yawning, she stood and stretched before circling her spot three times and lying back down.

As I talked, I moved several of the crystals over to the mantel, arranging them just so and moving some of the things I already had up there to encompass the new additions. After some time, the altar seemed to hum harmoniously, and I stopped to take it all in. Although there were still crystals left on the coffee table, I wanted to keep some space available for anything that was in my garden that I might want to put up there. But for now, I was done. What I had left could go in the bakery.

Except for the fluorite. I took the short purple and green tower and brought it into the kitchen, then placed it on the windowsill where the afternoon sunlight would hit it just right and make it seem like it was glowing.

Gram followed me like she had been doing all along.

"Tea?" I asked, already reaching for the kettle so I could fill it.

"Please." She took a seat at the table.

After the kettle was full, I placed it back on the stove, then turned on the burner.

"I don't remember it being like that when I was younger," I finally confessed after a few moments as I watched the flame under the teapot. "The whole yoga and greeting the sun thing."

"It was when you were little. Both you and your cousin could feel it. But after a while, you lost it. You still came out and did this with me, but I think you humored me more than anything for a few years."

"I take it Thea could always feel it?"

"Correct. Occasionally she'll still come over and meet me in the mornings to do it."

Pulling open the tea cupboard, I sighed wistfully. "The benefit of living in the neighboring town."

"Now, now. You know I'd love you closer, but you're meant to be here. I saw all your friends last night. It's like you've always belonged."

I paused what I was doing, my hand holding two infusers swinging gently in mid-air. "Huh."

"What?" Gram came up behind me to choose her tea, taking one of the infusers and setting me back in motion.

"Ken said the same thing not too long ago."

"I like him." I could hear the smile in her voice. "And he doesn't mind all of this?"

I shook my head, ducking under Gram's arm as she sorted through the teas so I could turn the burner off on the stove. "Not anymore. We had that misunderstanding a while back, but he sees how important it is to me. He gets it now."

"Good. You know, for a while, I thought you'd end up with your neighbor. George's son." She pulled out a bag of blueberry green tea.

"Nathan?"

"Mm-hmm." She put her tea into the infuser, then backed out of the way so I could do the same with my black tea with pecans. "I met him that time we moved you in here, and he was such a nice boy to help even though he was just here for the day. Then when he moved in to take care of George and was thus around all the time . . ."

I giggled. Actually giggled. Partly because I was discussing my dating life with Gram, which felt surreal in itself, and partly because, Nathan? No. "You're right, he is nice, but I've never felt anything but neighborly toward him. Well, that and overwhelming gratitude for the one time he helped me out with Ivy, but that's it."

"I can see that now, but you should try to find him someone." I started to turn toward her, but before I could say anything, she held up a hand to stop me and added, "Now, I know your abilities don't work like that. It was more of an 'I hope that if you are there when a match happens, you'll help them.'"

As I poured the steaming water into our teacups from earlier, I said, "I'd love to see him be matched. He deserves to find someone perfect for him. And of course I'd help it stick."

Gram took her cup, and she dropped her infuser into it, bobbing it up and down in the water. I'd contemplated making her a proper breakfast, but as I took stock of the kitchen and how much I had in the sink from last night, I decided to take her out for breakfast instead. If I timed it right, we could get to Donna's at Olde Templeton as Walter and Paul were leaving to take their spots at the counter.

We had just enough time for tea.

CHAPTER 18

Although it was a perfect day, Gram and I drove toward Main Street. I felt a bit silly for not walking, but we planned to be down here until after she got her tattoo, and I didn't know how she'd feel afterward. No way was I going to make her walk back to the house or even to get food if she didn't have to. Gram didn't seem to mind driving. I think she liked the idea of having her car parked on the street where everyone could see the vintage beauty and admire it.

Right now, however, the car was drawing plenty of attention with its noise as we went down Main Street. Gram smiled and waved as I pretended to ignore the heads turning our way. No doubt several customers would come into the bakery tomorrow to let me know Gram's car needed work of some kind. I passed several open spots, including a surprising one right in front of Olde Templeton, favoring a spot closer to the tattoo parlor. It was only a short walk to Donna's diner from there.

Fortunately, we'd timed our arrival as perfectly as I'd hoped. Walter and Paul were just leaving as we walked in, and after a quick hello, we took their stools at the counter while Donna was back in the kitchen, likely having taken the men's dirty dishes to the sink. She hated to leave spots dirty for even a moment on busy mornings.

"Now isn't this a pleasant surprise," Donna said as reentered the dining area. She set down a white ceramic diner mug in front of each of us, then reached behind her for the coffee. "Joanie, it's good to see you on your day off. I'm sorry I couldn't make it to your shindig last night. Who is this you've brought with you?"

"Donna, you remember my grandmother, Carol."

"Sure I do. It's been a few years, but no way is this your grandma. She hasn't aged a day! And look at me"—she mock-primped her bun with her free hand—"I'm more gray than anything now."

I studied Gram. She'd always looked beautiful to me. But she really stood out when compared to my friends' grandmothers because of her age. She was a younger grandma, only sixty-five. Now I couldn't help but wonder if there was a little something magical behind it as well.

Gram pulled the braid she'd done up after we finished our tea so that her hair wouldn't be in the way while she got her tattoo, and brought it over her shoulder. "I wouldn't exactly call this not aging."

Donna sighed. "I always wanted white hair. Instead, I'll settle for this."

"Isn't that the look now?" I offered. "People are dying their hair gray."

She considered this a moment, her lower lip stuck out and to the side a bit as she looked to the ceiling. "Guess that's true, but what I'd do is go crazy with some wild color if I had the guts to."

Gram perked up at this. "I think you'd rock it." She winked.

"You think so?" Donna's initial warm smile faded. "Ah, but what would people think of me if I did that?"

This was the first time I'd ever heard Donna worry about the town's rumor mill focusing on her. I'd always thought she was one of its leaders, same with Sarah, although Sarah's surprise revelation had turned her part in the mill on its head. Did Donna gossip so as not to be talked about for similar reasons?

I quickly chided myself. Not everyone could have paranormal motives in this town. "Who cares what people might think or say," I finally said. "What matters is how you feel about it once it's done."

"You know? You're right. I might just have to do it." Donna took our order then, and by the time she'd finished ringing the bell to let the kitchen know another order had come in, two of the tables in the tiny diner had cleared. She darted off to clean them and put out new place settings.

"Gram's getting a tattoo today," I announced when Donna came back around the counter a few moments later to continue our conversation.

Her eyes widened. "Now that is something I'd never be able to do. Don't like needles. Do you have others?"

Behind us, the door chimed with more customers coming in.

"First one," Gram answered as Donna reached back for the pot of regular.

Donna sped away with the coffee but came right back after making her rounds filling and refilling mugs. She checked our cups before setting the pot down in its spot. Gram hadn't had anything. She didn't care for coffee, but she was too polite to say no, much like I was.

"What are you getting?"

"There are a few things I'm still going between. Can't

quite make up my mind. Guess if I like this one, I can always get more." She shrugged, seemingly downplaying the whole idea of the tattoo to make it seem as if it were no big deal. But if Gram was getting something on her body, it was a huge deal.

"Well, more power to you," Donna said.

"That's the goal," Gram replied, a wry smile forming on her face, and she turned her head to give me a wink. I chuckled at her veiled witchy reference.

Donna nodded at Gram's answer, but before she could reply, her nephew Elliot, who worked in the kitchen, rang the bell in the window.

He placed two dishes on the sill, then smiled at me. "Enjoy your breakfast."

I gave him a small wave, and he quickly ducked back into the kitchen as his aunt turned around to grab our plates.

"Here you go," Donna said, setting our breakfasts in front of us. "Can I get you anything else?"

Neither of us needed anything, so Donna took off once again to check on her other customers, who kept her busy for a while, preventing her from doing much more than making sure our breakfasts were good. Working at the bakery six days a week, I rarely got the chance to have breakfast here, but Donna had some of the best home fries around. Small, seasoned, and with just the right amount of crispiness to them that allowed you to sink a fork through them without them breaking apart. I had to pace myself so I wouldn't run out before I was done with my ham and cheese omelet. Gram munched on her chocolate chip pancakes almost absent-mindedly, not saying a word. It wasn't until she took a sip of her coffee that she snapped out of it, making a face.

I giggled, then swapped my empty mug for her nearly full one. "We can go get some tea after this."

"Something to relax me," she said. "If I'm being honest, I am nervous about getting a tattoo."

"Gary has a great green rooibos tea with rose hips and buckthorn berry that will be great for you." I reached over and patted her hand. "And I'll be there the whole time to hold your hand if you need me."

She flipped her hand over so it was palm-side up and grabbed mine to squeeze it.

At that moment, Donna walked over with her coffee pot and tried to pour Gram some more.

"Oh, no thank you." Gram placed her hand over the mug's opening. "Don't want to get too jittery for my tattoo."

"No, I can't imagine that would be good." Donna drew her hand away, then set the pot back on the warming plate behind her. She turned back around and faced Gram. "Now I don't think I've ever asked, but are you Joanie's grandmother on her mom's side or her dad's?"

Gram nearly choked on her pancake, and she grabbed her mug back from me to wash the bite down.

"Mom's mom," I said as Gram recovered. "Truth is, I don't know anyone on my dad's side, including my dad."

Donna's face fell. "Oh, I'm so sorry. I shouldn't have even brought it up."

"It's all right," Gram said after another sip of coffee. "You didn't know, and you only find out by asking."

I considered Gram's comment. She had a point. I'd never really been interested in my father after finding out he'd walked out on my mom, but now, I had tons of questions. Maybe now was the time to ask.

Well, not right now. I'd wait until it was just Gram and me, but the time for me to get some answers was coming.

CHAPTER 19

I had my opportunity to talk to Gram alone as we walked up Main Street with our teas from Leafs and Grounds.

"What do you know about my dad? You had a big reaction when Donna asked whose mom you were."

She sighed. "I knew this was coming eventually. Sarah put questions in your head mentioning him last night too, didn't she?"

I nodded, blowing through the little hole on the lid of my tea to cool it down as I collected my thoughts. "Mom told me he left one day soon after she found out she was pregnant, and that was it."

"I'm going to stop you right there." Gram stopped walking and turned to face me. She put a hand on my shoulder and, looking me straight in the eye, she continued, "He did not leave because of you. I don't want you to even think it. Your father didn't know about you when he left. Your mom didn't know she was pregnant until shortly after. She suspected it, but there was no confirmation of it until after he left. He never knew."

That hadn't actually been one of my questions, but that saying about answers leading to more questions rang true. "Do you think he would have stayed had he known?"

She turned away and resumed walking. "You know as well as I do that's not a good reason to stay."

I did. My aunt and uncle had tried to make it work on account of my cousin, but he left all the same. Thea and I were both little at the time, but I had vague memories of him.

"Did you know my father well?"

She shook her head. "This is probably a conversation you should have with your mother. Your mom was off . . . doing her own thing for a while, shall we say. That's when she met your father. Truthfully, I never met him."

My mouth dropped. I'd had no idea. Sounded like I was going to have to talk to Mom again soon about visiting. This was a conversation to have in person.

Knowing I'd get no further about my father, I asked, "So mom wasn't always this by the book witch that she is now?"

Gram laughed. "No, but she was always a witch, even when she thought she'd run away from the lifestyle, just like you've always been a witch despite being oblivious to that fact for most of your life. You can stop practicing witchcraft, but that doesn't stop you from being a witch. Now, I'm not talking about those who practice Wicca. Someone can choose to stop practicing that like any other belief system, and before you ask, yes, witches can also be Wiccan. I am and many I know are. But I'm referring to witches in the strict paranormal sense here. Your magic doesn't go away simply because you say you're not a witch."

That led me back to all the *why me* and *why am I different* questions, but that wasn't what I wanted to talk about right now. We'd figured out as much as we could these last couple of days about me and my abilities, getting some answers but a ton more questions. We could talk in circles at this point about those and never get anywhere.

Besides, right now, the image of my mom as some sort of witchy rebel seemed fascinating. "So what happened? Why did mom leave and stop practicing?"

"That's probably something else you should talk to her about too," Gram said to my momentary disappointment, "but in my opinion, it was all part of her growing up and finding herself. We all have our own paths to how we got to where we are now. For your mom, her way was to leave Sunny Valley and come back. Yours was coming to Heartwood Hollow and finding out about everything here. As much as I would have loved for you to stay in Sunny Valley, that wasn't the way for you."

"What about you, Gram?" I took a small sip of my tea to check the temperature, then a larger sip when I determined it was fine.

"Sunny Valley has been home to the Sunevalls for generations. I may only be one through marriage, but I've lived there my whole life. Been a part of the coven there my whole life. I'll live there for the rest of my life. I have no desire to leave"—she bumped her side into mine—"unless I'm visiting you or your cousin, of course."

We turned off Main Street and down Cooper Court. The tattoo parlor was just up ahead, down a tiny alley. It had likely been an outbuilding for one of the larger homes that fronted River Street but whose property lines backed up onto the alley.

Through the window of the parlor, I could see David sitting behind the counter, a pencil in hand, furiously at work, scribbling away. He looked up as I pulled open the door, allowing Gram to go in before me.

"Hello, ladies," he said with a smile. "Good to see you today. You ready to get your tattoo?"

There was a nervous edge to Gram's voice as she said, "As ready as I can be." It reminded me of my answer to her before we started cleansing the crystals.

There wasn't anything out here for them to do the tattooing, so I assumed they did it somewhere in the back. I tried peeking behind the curtain separating the two parts of the building.

"Dylan's just finishing up with his client, and then after he cleans up, we'll head in there. Tim's in the other room adding color to a sleeve. They'll be in there awhile."

"Is there any way I'll be able to go back and sit with you both, or do I have to wait out here?"

"There's a chair for you in there if you want. Not the comfiest of things, but it will do." David looked at me and chuckled. "That's as long as you can stay out of trouble while you're in there."

Had it been almost anyone else, I'd have commented about how I never got into trouble. However, he'd been witness to some of my latest paranormal-related antics as I solved the case related to his now-wife Chelsea's haunted tiara.

"I'll be on my best behavior," I promised instead, "and thanks. I kind of already told Gram I'd be there to hold her hand if she needed it."

He smiled at my answer but said, "And no ghosts. There isn't enough room for one of them to pop up unexpectedly in there." He'd seen that happen, too, meeting Chelsea's great-aunt Sandra face to face despite her having been killed fifty years prior.

"Ghost-free today." I hoped it would stay that way. I'd had

a quiet few weeks since uncovering Sandra's murderer, and I didn't want anything to prevent me from having a nice day with Gram before she had to go.

"Well, then there will be plenty of room for the three of us." He tapped the counter and waved Gram over. "We were talking about doing a small sigil yesterday. Have you settled on a design? I can get it transferred over to the paper I use to put an outline on you while we wait."

Gram removed a piece of paper from her pants pocket. "I want something like this."

I'd been looking at a wall of finished tattoos, photos that were taken moments after completing a piece of body art, but as Gram unfolded the white paper, I crossed the tiny shop to see the drawing. Although I'd heard parts of her conversation with David yesterday, with everything we had to do, she and I hadn't talked about the specific symbol she was going to get.

I came up next to her as she showed David the line drawing on familiar paper.

"Hope you don't mind I used one of your recipe cards," Gram said, "but it was what I could find."

"Not at all. I wonder if it will make whatever recipe I end up putting on it taste different." When she returned a side-eye, I gave her one of her signature winks. "I'm kidding. But if I could keep it when we're done, I would appreciate it. I'd like to learn. What does it mean?"

The line drawing vaguely looked a little like a cat with a circle for a head, its nose at the center with two whiskers on one side but with arrows on it, one pointing to the center and the other pointing out. On the other side was a semi-circle, the line thicker at the middle, reminding me of a sliver of the moon. Extending up from the center was a pointy heart, the upper parts forming the triangular ears of the cat.

"This is a sigil of protection," Gram started, pointing at the center. "This dot here inside the circle is me. The circle encompasses everyone I hold dear." She traced the top whisker. "This line is that which seeks to do me and my circle harm, and here it is being cast away, hence the arrow pointing out." She let her finger follow the lower line away from the middle of the circle.

As Gram explained, David sketched the design on a fresh sheet of paper.

Gram moved her finger to the top of the design. "This here is the truth. It radiates from me and my circle. And this is the moon. It's waxing, still reaching its full potential. We go forward while that which seeks to do us harm is forced backward, so we reach our destination without negative influences."

"That sounds very powerful," David replied, not batting an eye at all the witchiness that had just come out of Gram's mouth. I wondered if he had done these sorts of tattoos before. After all, he had known what they were called. Maybe he could point me to other witches in town.

"It is," Gram said confidently. "I wouldn't put it on my body if I didn't believe it was."

"Did you design it yourself, Gram, or did you see it somewhere?"

"The circle created it after what happened to Susan, but I'm the first I know of to get it as a tattoo."

At that moment, the hum that had been background noise to our conversation stopped, leaving a weird silence in the air.

"That must mean Dylan is finishing up."

Farther away, a hum resumed.

"And that must be Tim getting back to it after a break. Sleeves take a bit of work. He's been at it since we opened today."

A hand poked through the curtain between the front of the parlor and the back, then the curtain shifted, revealing Dylan holding it open for his customer.

"I find the lighting so much better in here for photos," Dylan was saying, looking over his shoulder at his client with bubblegum-pink hair. On her calf was a large pink and yellow flower, the area around it slightly swollen and red. Dylan faced forward, noticing us at the counter. "Oh, hello. Give me like five minutes and the room will be ready."

"Perfect, I'm just cleaning up the sketch," David answered.

Dylan nodded at me as he passed. We had never really talked much beyond his coming into the shop for baked goods. But then last month at the police station while we were there for separate but related matters, a few kind words to one another made all the difference. Turned out he was there to provide information about the actions being taken against the merrows in town. His doing so became a catalyst in healing a decades-old rift between the merrows and selkies.

Pulling his cell phone out of his pocket, Dylan followed his client closer to the window, "All right, let's get a picture of this." He squatted and extended his arms forward to snap a few pictures of the young woman's leg.

Once that was done, David passed Dylan some sort of

ointment, plastic wrap, and gauze, and Dylan covered the flower tattoo. The two walked over to the counter, where Dylan rang up her body art.

"It's a beautiful piece," I told the girl. I didn't recognize her, so I doubted she was from town.

She gave me a warm smile. "Thanks. Are you getting something done?"

My eyes widened. "Me? Oh, no."

"I am," Gram said, turning toward her.

She looked surprised for a split second before turning seemingly impressed. "Rock on." It was then I noticed the girl had several other tattoos, many referring to video games, including one behind her ear of a circular yellow face in profile, its mouth pointing toward a path of dots.

After paying Dylan, the girl headed for the door, telling Gram "Good luck" over her shoulder as she left.

Dylan headed back past the curtain, leaving David, Gram, and me alone.

David spun the sigil he'd redrawn toward Gram. "Just give this a quick look for me and let me know if it's okay."

Gram studied the piece for a moment before nodding. "Looks fine to me. Good size too."

"That was going to be my next question." David tapped on the counter. "Great, let me get this printed on the transfer paper, and we'll be ready to go."

Behind David was a small machine that reminded me of a desktop printer. He spun to face it and then placed the drawing he'd done of Gram's sigil between other papers. He fed the bundle into the printer, then pressed a large green button, causing the machine to beep to life. A moment later, David removed the stack from the printer. He separated the papers, then turned toward Gram, placing his original drawing on the counter and holding up the new one. The design was in a light-purple ink.

"One more time to okay it as is," he said. "Next time will be after we place it to make sure you like it there."

Gram nodded. "Let's do it."

"Okay, I'm just going to see if Dylan needs any help—"

"No help needed. All set," Dylan said, walking back into the room. He and David swapped places, and then Dylan pulled out a sketch pad from somewhere under the counter.

"Right this way, ladies," David said, sweeping one arm in front of him as he held back the curtain with the other.

Gram and I headed around the counter and into the back area.

"To your left," David instructed as he let go of the curtain to follow us. "Carol, take a seat on the big chair. Joanie, you'll see the chair to the side of the room."

We entered the small room, and Gram plopped herself into the padded seat as I took the spot in the chair by the door. It moved slightly, and when I glanced down, I realized it was on wheels.

"You can move it closer to your grandmother if you'd like," David said as he came in. "Just stick to the opposite side of where I'm working."

"You got it." As David prepped inks and the needle, opening the hygienically sealed bags where we could see and transferring everything to a tray with wheeled legs, I scooted my chair to Gram's side. "Do you need me to hold your hand?"

"I'm okay right now. He hasn't even started." She gave me a loving grin. "But I'm glad you're here just in case."

David approached Gram's other side, then washed her arm with a paper towel and a special soap. After he was done, he returned with the purple drawing that he'd cut out of the larger piece of paper. He pressed the paper up to Gram's arm. "This where you want it?"

After a slight adjustment to the drawing's orientation, Gram nodded hard once.

David pressed the drawing over her arm, explaining how the purple dye would transfer to Gram's skin and show him where to put his needle.

With one final look in the mirror once the design was on her upper arm, Gram said, "Good to go." She settled back into her chair as David pulled up the tray as well as a stool.

David warned her that the outline would be the worst part of the tattoo, and I wondered if that was the right thing to say, more a force of habit than anything. Wasn't the sigil pretty much all outline?

Gram reached for my hand. I gave it to her, and we shared a small squeeze as I smiled reassuringly at her. I'd never seen Gram nervous before. She'd always been calm and composed even when she didn't quite know what she was doing, including the time she helped me with the bad ghosts.

A few minutes into the outlining, Gram eased up on my hand. "That isn't so bad."

"It's not a bad spot for your first tattoo," David replied. "Right on the bone hurts more."

"First tattoo?" I asked. Gram had mentioned the possibility of getting more if this one went well, but she was still in the chair, and here he was already bringing up getting another. "Isn't it a bit soon to talk about more?"

David chuckled. "It can get pretty addicting." Soon he announced he was ready to start filling in the design. Guess there was more than outlining after all. Gram adjusted her hold on my hand but said nothing to me. Instead, she made small talk with David, asking him how long he'd been tattooing, how many he had, and more. Somewhere in the middle of their conversation, I zoned out with the hum of the needle.

Gram hadn't given me many details about her solving Miss Susan's murder. The killer had been arrested and was awaiting trial. What had transpired that her entire coven still thought it necessary to create a symbol of protection? I didn't want to press her, but I hoped she'd tell me in time. Did I have reason to worry about her?

I found out about Miss Susan's death before Gram even had the chance to call me about it. I'd heard the news from Miss Susan herself when she visited me to pass along a message. I was the convergence of two cursed blessings. I hadn't known what she meant at the time, neither did she, but I believed I was beginning to understand. Matchmaking and seeing ghosts had both led to quite the experiences lately, everything from rescuing ghosts who were trapped in objects, reuniting lost loves, repairing relationships, shedding light on town mysteries, to confronting serial killers. It hadn't been easy, and at times it was potentially even dangerous. I believed that to be the curse of it all. But I was blessed too. It wasn't easy to do what I did, but it was rewarding to see couples matched and to help ghosts cross over. So that was my blessing. I hadn't realized how much so until my bakery was forced to shut down. I'd been afraid of losing it, knowing that the bakery helped me do everything else I did.

Of course, there was a chance I'd misinterpreted the message, but like with so many of my questions, I'd find out eventually.

The humming stopped as Gram released my hand, drawing me from my thoughts.

David put the tattoo gun onto the tray. "And you are all set." He wiped Gram's tattoo with a paper towel.

She turned her head to peer over her shoulder at her new ink. "I love it. You did very well."

"Would you mind if I take a photo of it for my portfolio? Understanding its importance to you, I promise to never reuse the design, but I want to be able to show people what I can do."

"Well, I could see one person you might reuse the design on." Gram cast me a look.

"Maybe a temporary one," I said with a laugh. Tattoos were pretty, but this experience hadn't changed my opinion about needles.

"You could always do henna," David suggested.

"Might be worth trying," Gram agreed before turning back to David, "but yes, that would be fine."

Unlike Dylan, who'd led his client back to the front room for photos, David took his cell phone out from his pants pocket, then snapped a few pictures right there. He proceeded to apply the same ointment I'd seen Dylan use, followed by the gauze and plastic wrap, the whole time explaining to Gram how to take care of her new body art.

After Gram paid, we strolled back up Main Street. We'd done Olde Templeton for breakfast, Leafs and Grounds for tea —plus a marshmallow rice treat for me—and now it was time for lunch at Founder's Fresco. It was the perfect day to sit outside on their patio to eat.

I didn't get a chance to talk to Gram about anything witchy while we ate. Summer tourist season had been in full swing in Heartwood Hollow for several weeks now, and even though it was a Tuesday, the restaurant was packed. Instead, we sat on the top patio, dining on strawberry grilled chicken salads and sipping on mango lemonades. Conversation revolved around my recent business expansions into making candy to sell at the bakery and edible raw cookie dough for the ice cream parlor. That then turned into a promise to grab an ice cream cone so Gram could try it before she left.

All in all, it felt like one of our regular Saturday phone calls, only in person.

And it was wonderful.

CHAPTER 20

The bell above the door chimed, signaling Gram's and my entrance into With a Cherry on Top Ice Cream Shop. Lucy greeted us with a smile, and I introduced her to Gram. At that moment, Todd walked out from the back, and I hoped that meant Sam would show up while we were here. Then I could find out if he and Todd were officially my mystery match from the potluck. Since our talk about making his remaining time here count when it came to his love life, Sam had been spending as much time with Todd as he could, including having ice cream for lunch every day Todd had a shift. Of course, I only knew that because I had been having ice cream just as often . . . for flavor research. A perk of my job.

"Hey, Joanie," Todd said, a bright smile on his face. I took him in for a moment. He'd come a long way from the polite but reserved waiter I'd had on my first date with Ken. But he seemed even happier today, and hopefully it was because my theory was right.

"Hey. Sam been around yet today?"

He glanced at the ice-cream-themed clock. "He should be

here soon. Went school shopping with his mom and grandma." Even the mention of Sam getting ready to go off to college couldn't shake Todd's chipper demeanor. "Are you looking for him?"

I shook my head. "Just forgot to tell him something last night, that's all, but I'll see him tomorrow."

"All right, then. What can I get you?"

I looked at Gram, who pointed at Lucy already scooping something for her. I placed my order, and as I waited, the familiar tingle started in my toes.

"Sam will be here soon," I announced, barely able to contain my excitement. The tingling grew stronger with each passing second as Sam drew closer to the shop.

When the door opened, the bell chiming overhead once again, the last sliver of doubt left my mind with Todd's "Hey, Sam."

Even as I stood there waiting for Todd to get my s'mores ice cream, the tingling from his match with Sam flooded my system. It was the only match in the nearby area, however, so the sensation was more manageable than it had been last night when it joined all the others, causing me to flee.

Now, rather than making me want to run, the new match made me want to cheer. Sam was special. He'd come to me on his own wanting to intern in my bakery even though it meant crazy hours for him to balance the internship and high school, and now he was leaving in a few weeks to go to the same culinary school I had attended. He'd gotten me started in the candy business, introducing me to his grandmother, who had been the candy maker in town years ago and ended up giving me all her recipes. He effortlessly accepted my ability to put spells into what I baked, refusing to believe the rumors in town about me and letting me tell him under my own terms, then trusting me enough to tell me his truth about who he was before he came out publicly. I was an only child, and Sam had stepped in to fill a little brother role for me. I was going to miss him, and I needed to do something to mark his leaving. A small bakery family party perhaps.

After Sam said hello to everyone, he turned to me. "I would have thought you'd been having leftovers after last night. There was so much food."

I chuckled. "I made sure a lot of it went elsewhere after you two left. Still have plenty, but I couldn't pass up an opportunity to have some ice cream. Gram's not had it from here."

Todd handed me my single scoop of s'mores ice cream. "Thank you."

A moment later, Lucy said, "Here you go" to Gram, handing her a two-scoop cone with what looked like the peanut butter cookie and brownie pretzel. The bakery had supplied Lucy with the dough for both flavors on Friday.

Gram eyed the waffle cone, either in wonder or in disbelief of what she had just gotten herself into. Lucy's scoops weren't small. "Oh, wow. I'm glad I only had a salad for lunch."

And the salads hadn't been small either.

No matter my experience in the kitchen, there would always be a part of me that anxiously waited to see someone's reaction as they tried something I'd had a hand in making. I watched as Gram licked her cone, first up, then around both flavors.

She closed her eyes and visibly relaxed, her shoulders drooping. "Mmm . . . this is good." She looked first at Lucy, then at me. "Well done, the both of you."

"Thanks, Gram. I'm really glad Lucy came to me with the idea. It's only been a few weeks, and we've already had to increase the frequency of my making dough for the ice cream."

"They've been some of our most popular flavors. We have people come in just to try them whenever I announce we have a new flavor on our social media pages," Lucy added.

That was something I'd never considered doing before, social media for the bakery. I barely touched my personal accounts, and by that, I meant I'd probably last updated them when I bought my house here in town.

I probably should have had Sarah create and manage something for the bakery all these years. As a major participant in the town's gossip circle, social media was probably something she enjoyed. But with the revelations about her being my familiar, I didn't want to add to her responsibilities. Now Sam was leaving for school, and Lily was with me on borrowed time. Bryan mentioned there being a baker group chat a few weeks ago. Perhaps he'd like to do it. Or Gina. Or even Lauren once she picked up shifts in the shop for the summer. It was something one could do between customers, right?

At least I had a basic website. That was a start.

"Careful, Joanie. Yours is dripping on that side." Sam pointed toward my fingertips.

"Whoops! Good catch." I quickly licked that spot, then cleaned up all the soon-to-be drips around my cone.

"Well, shall we get going?" Gram asked.

I glanced at the clock. If Gram was going to get home without hitting traffic, she'd have to leave soon. Unable to prevent my disappointed sigh, I let it out, then replied, "Okay."

We said our goodbyes and then shuffled out the door, back onto Main Street, and toward Gram's car.

Our time together was growing short. I still had so much to learn. What more could I find out from her before she left?

CHAPTER 21

I had to prioritize what I wanted to know with how much time we had left, but when I opened my mouth, a question failed to come out. "I wish you didn't have to go already," I confessed to Gram as we crossed the street.

"I know you don't, and I'm reluctant to go as well. This has been fun. But Sterling only has enough food to last him through dinner. You know how he is with strangers."

"No better with them in his old age? He must be getting up there. You've had him for ages."

Gram laughed. "He's only thirteen, maybe fourteen. He's got plenty of time left."

"But he wasn't a kitten when you got him," I protested.

"Well, he wasn't old either." She licked her ice cream. "Besides, Silver lived until twenty-two. I still potentially have many years left with my handsome fella."

Sterling loved to be called *handsome* and would tolerate wearing anything as long as he was told so—bow ties, hats, sweaters. Even as a young teen, it was fun to dress him up when my cousin and I stayed overnight at Gram's house.

After catching another drip of ice cream, I asked, "He's your familiar, isn't he?"

Gram nodded. "I said as much yesterday when I said he was going to be disappointed that Saffy wasn't yours."

"Now when you say disappointed . . ."

"I mean it. I wouldn't make something like that up."

"He told you?"

"Well, no, but only because I haven't broken the news to him yet. We'd been thinking Saffy was your familiar ever since she showed up on your doorstep. Now I'm going to have to tell him that after six years of waiting for Saffy to do something, he remains the only cat familiar in the family. How could he not be disappointed? You know how much he got along with your mom's cat Paige."

I took a bite of my waffle cone and thought of my mom's seal point Siamese. Gram walked Sterling every day—telling him he was handsome as soon as she put the harness on him, of course—and Mom's house was a regular destination along their route. The two cats got along fabulously, perching in the same sunny window or chasing each other through the house as Gram stayed for tea. Sadly, Paige had passed shortly before I first visited Heartwood Hollow. It had been her death that prompted that initial trip to the town I now called home.

"So Paige was Mom's familiar?"

Gram nodded, her mouth too full of ice cream cone to verbally answer. Somehow, she'd gotten through more of her gigantic cone than I had of my smaller one.

"And she's not gotten another one?"

"Well, she has Lio, but he's a regular cat. You don't just get familiars at the store, or animal rescue in this case. I mean, you could, but it's all a matter of timing. There's no guarantee yours will be there when you go. If it's supposed to happen, it will happen when the time is right."

"What about Aunt Pat?"

Gram chuckled. "Remember Randall?"

"That drooly thing was her familiar?" The big, old St. Bernard was such a mush, but he dripped drool everywhere. You could never escape the slobber. "And what about Thea?"

"Oh, you can ask her all you want about hers. I'm sure she's bursting to talk to you about all of this now that you've accepted you're a witch."

My cousin and I had been close as kids but grew apart once I got into high school. She was two years younger than I was, but three grades in school because of how our birthdays fell, so we only spent a year in school together after elementary school, my senior year, which was her freshman year. Then I left for college, but she remained at home. "I should reach out to her. I enjoyed seeing her at your commendation."

"I bet she'd like that. She's missed you." She popped the bottom of her cone into her mouth and opened the door to her car, the driver's side this time. I did the same on the passenger side, and we both sat in the seat. Gram had swallowed her bite by then, and as she adjusted her seat and mirror back to how she needed it, she continued, "We all have missed you, but I think things will be different now."

I agreed. Weekly phone calls with Gram had been great, but there was no way I was going to go as long as I had without seeing everyone in person again.

We walked up the driveway and on the slate-stone path to the house. Saffy waited for us in the window.

As we stepped inside, Gram said, "Now, how about you follow me as I pack up my things. You can ask me as much as you can with what time we have before I go. But first, go make some tea. I'll put it in my travel mug to have on the road."

Gram dropped her purse on the couch, and Saffy immediately went over to investigate. She always liked people's bags, including mine, but this one had the extra enticement of smelling like Sterling. Gram didn't seem to mind, however, and she headed upstairs to grab her things.

I scooted into the kitchen, where I filled up the kettle, then set it on the stove to boil.

That's all it took for Saffy to come running, so I gave her a treat to keep her happy before heading upstairs to help Gram with her bags.

She was placing a small pale-blue crystal cluster back into a velvet drawstring bag. "Some come with me no matter where I go," she said, never turning around. She must have heard me coming. "These ones here help me sleep."

"There's still so many I don't know about."

"Downstairs in the suitcase in the side room, there are reference books on all sorts of things. Gifts from the ladies in my circle. You'll know which ones came from me." She glanced over her shoulder with a wink as she cinched the velvet bag closed.

A wave of warmth—love, peace, and acceptance—washed over me as the realization that there were so many looking out for me settled into my mind. Despite my hesitations and my many questions, I'd come out of this self-discovery okay. I was a witch. There was nothing wrong with that. In fact, many would tell me to celebrate it. After this weekend, it seemed I was well on my way to doing just that.

"Talk to me about witch types. You are a crystal witch and I'm a kitchen witch. You've mentioned several others. What's Aunt Pat?"

"She's a textile witch. Makes all of our robes."

"Huh." I liked how her and my cousin's powers were related. "And your sister Barbara?"

"She was a matchmaker like you and your mom." I didn't

need to ask about Gram's sister Pegee. She saw ghosts like I did, not that anyone had seen or heard from her in years to know how she was dealing with that.

"What's mom?" I'd almost not asked her, expecting her to tell me to ask Mom directly, but since Gram had brought her up, I figured, why not?

"She's a literary witch."

"I thought literary witches were just that, witches that are in books."

"Well, they can be that too, but literary witches are also those who look at witchcraft from the more scholarly aspect of things."

"That kind of fits mom perfectly."

Gram wordlessly mumbled an agreement as she placed another crystal into her velvet bag.

"And there's no extra magic to that the way there is with my spells in food?" Could they have been overlooking the possibility of her having multiple abilities?

Gram shook her head. "Not for your mom. Her magic is in matchmaking, but she also knows a great deal about general witch history, writes spells, and has an extensive grimoire. She could teach you a lot, you know."

"I'll be talking to her again soon. You can be sure of that." Beyond being able to teach me more about witchcraft, she had to have answers for me about my father. At least I hoped. She'd quickly shut me down the only time I'd ever asked about him before. But maybe now things would be different. I was older and a witch too. "I promised I'd give her an update on how I handled the rest of the potluck. Guess I have a lot more to say now, especially with Sarah being my familiar and all."

Gram placed the velvet pouch next to another in the small pocket of her suitcase.

I picked up Gram's pajamas and slippers, then placed both in her suitcase, her slippers upside-down to keep the soles off her clothes. "Did you know she was—"

"Your familiar? No, as I said, I thought it was Saffy."

"I was going to say *special*."

Zipping the small pouch, Gram nodded. "After all you've told me about her making comments to you about your being witchy, I thought I'd test her. She was so excited when I gave even the slightest hint of my being a witch. And then she was ready to burst when I mentioned the ladies in my circle. I had to suppress a laugh when Lauren asked if it was a knitting circle."

"I can't see you knitting . . . ever."

"Nope." She shook her head slowly. "That is a type of magic completely lost on me. Although I do benefit from your aunt's ability to do it so well."

"I'm glad that's not my magical skill. It took me six years to knit a scarf," I said with a chuckle. "I did make those paisley pillows on my couch pretty quickly, though."

Gram flopped the top of her suitcase back over, then zipped it up. "Here, help an old lady with her bags." As I picked it up, she grabbed her smaller toiletries bag, then followed me down the stairs back into the living room just as the kettle for the tea water whistled.

We placed Gram's bags by the couch, then headed into the kitchen.

"Even Nathan picked up on the way things always seem to be perfectly timed here in the kitchen," I said, turning the knob for the burner off, "and he's rarely here when I cook."

Gram opened my tea cupboard. "I've always said there were no coincidences. It's all a part of your magic." She pulled out my jar of lemon raspberry green tea and an empty drawstring tea bag. I rarely used bags, preferring my infuser balls or baskets, but I always kept several fillable tea bags on hand in case they were needed. Gram reached into the drawer under the counter beneath the tea cupboard. She grabbed my teaspoon and used it to scoop out a generous amount of tea that she then dropped into the bag. She handed it to me, and as I cinched it closed and dropped it into her travel mug, she put away the tea and cleaned my spoon.

Gram nodded to the sink as she turned off the faucet. "Do you want me to stay to help you clean up all of this?"

The sink was still full of dishes left behind at the potluck last night. I wasn't looking forward to washing it all since I had to do it all by hand—someday I'd get a dishwasher—but Gram had to get on the road.

Pouring water into Gram's travel mug, I shook my head. "Gives me something to do while I wait for you to call to say you're home."

She took the mug from me and then capped it. "I'll call you as soon as I walk in the door."

After I made my tea and set it to steep while we said our goodbyes, Gram led me out of the kitchen and into the living room. She grabbed her toiletries bag and started for the front door. I followed behind with her larger suitcase, grateful I didn't have to also grab the other one she'd brought with her. I couldn't wait to dive into all the books she'd brought for me to study.

We returned to the house after putting the bags in her trunk, and Gram grabbed her purse, disrupting Saffy who had decided to use it to prop herself up as she leaned on her side. "Sorry, you sassy cat. I have to take this back now, but I'll be sure to tell Sterling you say hello once he smells you all over this."

Saffy dramatically flopped to her side before picking

herself back up. Then she jumped to her spot on the back of the couch as if nothing had happened.

Gram chuckled but sobered as she looked around. "All right, I think I have everything. Any last questions before I go?"

"I'm sure I will as time goes on, but— Oh! Your apples!" I dashed into the side room where we'd put them yesterday when we got back from the cider mill, then returned holding the bag out for Gram.

"Thank you. I would have been disappointed to go without these."

"That's not all," I said before rushing into the kitchen. Returning a moment later, I stopped at Gram's side, holding the pastry boxes and fudge I'd grabbed from the fridge.

She was pulling something from the cider mill bag, which she had put on the floor. She straightened, several papers in her hand, and smiled upon seeing the boxes from the bakery. "Of all the things to almost forget. The ladies never would have let me live it down."

"What's in your hand?"

"Looks like coupons and whatnot. I'm not going to be here for any of it, but you could always use them. I know how much you like it there." She passed them over to me as she took the boxes from my hands.

I flipped through the papers as I righted them all. Then I went back to the second one in the stack, certain I hadn't seen the announcement correctly.

But there it was in bold green letters.

Fifth Annual Memorial Road Race and Apple Float

Beneath that was a picture of Cindy Bug, the woman who

regularly helped me at the cider mill as she chatted away about her favorite new products.

I said nothing, just kept staring at the picture of the helpful old lady who was always so happy to see me. I remembered the first day I went to the cider mill when Mom and I first visited the area. It was a weekday but still so busy. Cindy was there, standing at the door like she usually did, and had said hello. I'd said hello back. In a cider mill uniform like everyone else who worked there, I had no reason to suspect she was anything but alive. But there was no denying that she had already died.

Somehow I had missed finding out about the other events in her honor.

"Joanie, what's wrong? You look like you've seen a ghost."

I didn't think she'd realized what she said, but she wasn't far off.

"She's dead," I whispered, still not believing it. She'd been dead the whole time.

"Who's dead?"

"The woman from the cider mill."

"Just now? Is she here?" Gram looked around, a puzzled look on her face. "The wards should have worked."

I held the flyer out to her, shaking my head. "No. She's been dead."

She glanced at it and said, "Oh. Is this who you were talking to yesterday?"

I raised an eyebrow at her. "You knew I was talking to a ghost and didn't say anything?"

"Well, yeah. I thought you knew, though. You didn't introduce me and went on your merry way trying samples. I had no idea that you thought she was alive. You'd never done that before in front of me, so I figured she was like your trench-coated friend in the park that you've told me about. The one with the dog. It was fascinating to see you in action. Just like my sister when we were kids. I'm sorry. I would have said something otherwise."

"It's okay. You didn't know." I sighed long and hard. "I just can't believe she's dead. All this time . . . I never even suspected."

Gram placed the pastry boxes on the coffee table, then took the flyer from me. She pulled me in for a hug, and I rested my head on her shoulder. "I really am sorry, Joanie. Are you going to be okay? I can call your mom to check in on Sterling and give him some more food if you need me to stay tonight."

"No, it's all right. Sterling misses you, and you're right, he does get a bit ornery when his routine is disturbed. Having you stay longer will only make it more so. Besides, you're already all packed, and you're meeting with the ladies tonight. I'll be fine. Just a little shocked more than anything. It's been a while since I've been taken by surprise like this. Especially after this much time and interaction."

Gram put a bit more squeeze into her hug before letting me go. "As long as you say so."

I stepped back, then stooped to get the cider mill bag at Gram's feet.

Gram picked the pastry boxes back off the coffee table. She followed me to the door, which I now held open, and she cast one last look over her shoulder before stepping outside. "Goodbye, you sassy cat." I didn't hear a reaction from Saffy, but as we crossed the porch, movement in the window caught my eye. Saffy stood pressed up against the glass, watching us.

We placed the bag and boxes into the trunk with Gram's other things, only after I made sure the suitcases wouldn't crush anything. Gram didn't want them in the car with her.

"Can't have a box of pastries go flying away because the top's down."

She had a point.

I wiped my hands, making a clapping sound as my hands came together. "Well, I guess that's it. Thank you so much for coming to visit. I don't know what I would have done without you. The crystals, the wards, the smudging, all of it."

"I'm so glad I was finally able to come. Let's not make it so long next time, and maybe you can take a day off and come home for a real visit sometime."

"I'd like that."

Gram pulled me in for a hug, squeezing me tightly as she rocked from side to side in short motions, humming as she did.

"Love you, Gram."

"Love you too, Joanie."

As we stood there in a hug I doubted either one of us wanted to break, I could hear the hum of the earth like I had when Sarah and I buried the crystals and again this morning when Gram and I greeted the sun. I wondered if this would be how it always felt now, at least if I paid enough attention.

Finally, but much too soon at the same time, Gram released me and then reached behind her to open the car door. She took two steps backward before sliding into the seat of her car.

When she was properly situated, I closed the door for her. "You call me as soon as you get home, okay?"

She promised she would as she turned the key in the ignition. Her car roared to life, sending a nearby squirrel running for a tree. "You do me a favor," she said in a way that made it a statement, not a request. "Believe in yourself and your magic. It will go a lot further if you do. I know you can feel it now, so don't deny it."

I nodded as she released the brake on her car and put it into reverse, letting it roll back down the driveway. She stopped the car before it could go into the road, looked both ways, then backed into the street. Before pulling away, Gram gave me a large wave using her entire arm.

I followed her car to the edge of my yard, then went back to my porch to sit on my swing until I could no longer hear her car's engine. In quiet Heartwood Hollow, that was longer than it would have been elsewhere. I stood, turning back toward the door. Saffy was sitting in the window, alert, likely still able to hear Gram's car at least a little bit.

My tea had steeped more than needed, but the honeybush tea with apple and mango was exactly what I needed to settle down for the rest of the day. First, I had a mountain of dishes to do, but after that, I'd be grabbing one of the books Gram had left me.

I was ready to dive right in.

CHAPTER 22

The mountain of dishes morphed from one chore to another as I dried everything and put away what was mine. That still left me with several dishes on my counter. Then I remembered a few more dishes in the refrigerator that still had food in them weren't mine either. There was still so much food and no way was I going to eat it all, but I knew someone who would be happy to share with me. So I cleaned out the fridge and split the remaining leftovers into two sets of containers.

I placed one set in a bag, then carried it to the living room. After slipping on my shoes, I opened the front door. There on my porch railing was a small purple box like one would get jewelry in. It certainly wasn't mine. Or at least, it hadn't been.

How had I missed someone dropping it off? My house wasn't that big, and I'd been home for hours. Whoever it was must have come while I was doing the dishes and talking to Mom on the phone. Although she was still busy at her library and couldn't talk longer than it took for me to tell her Gram had left, it would have been just long enough for me to miss the noise of someone on my porch.

As I stepped outside, I glanced back into my house through the picture window. Saffy was asleep on the couch just a few feet away from where the box had been placed. She'd followed me into the kitchen earlier hoping for a snack, but I refused to give her another one. She'd had plenty when Gram and I first got back. So she'd returned to her spot and had been there ever since.

She still wasn't fond of unknown people coming over, and she hadn't made a noticeable fuss of someone coming onto the porch. So did that mean she knew who it was? If only she actually could talk. Then she could tell me who she saw.

There was no note with the jewelry box, although I didn't look as hard for one as I had yesterday. I only peered over the railing to see if it could have fallen. Nothing. And there was no breeze to have blown one somewhere had it existed.

I took the small velvet box in my hand and opened it. Inside was a pendant on a chain featuring a newly familiar symbol. The Triple Moon Goddess. A full moon flanked by waxing and waning moons. Solid and sturdy, it wasn't a cheap piece. I didn't wear jewelry because part of me worried about something falling into cake batter or frosting or that I'd lose a ring taking it off to wash my hands yet again, but I could see putting this on for special occasions once I figured out who had given it to me. It would be too weird to wear it without knowing that.

At that moment, Matt stepped out of his house, closing the door behind him.

I shut the jewelry box and slipped it into my pocket before calling out to him, "You heading out somewhere?"

He waved. "Only for a walk. How are you doing?"

"Good. I was about to bring you some leftovers. I have way too many for just me to have, and my freezer is full. But you have plenty of room since you only took cake last night."

I couldn't hear it from here, but I saw him chuckle. "And that's already gone. Had it for breakfast."

"Well, I have everything gathered in a bag already, so stay right there. I'm coming."

"All right." He pushed his front door back open.

I ducked back inside to grab the bag, then crossed the street toward Matt's house. His house was similar to mine in size and style, but our front yards were completely different. Where mine was all grass minus the small gardens around the bushes by my porch, Matt's had only a hint of grass toward the sidewalk. The rest of his yard consisted of ornamental bushes and trees. Occasionally I'd see him out doing things with them, but he had a landscaper come by to maintain the shape of anything that needed help.

Matt's yard was always a favorite of hummingbirds and butterflies. I couldn't remember seeing either of those in my yard, only those black birds with iridescent wings. Their name escaped me. I'd always found birds interesting, but beyond the names of a few common ones—cardinals, crows, blue jays, and robins—that was all I knew. Saffy, understandably, loved to watch the birds from the window. She probably could have told me their names with how much time she spent chattering at them. I momentarily wondered if there were such things as bird witches and if they'd be able to tell me the names of the various birds.

Despite our similar porches, I tripped up Matt's top step, too wrapped up in thoughts of birds to see where I was going.

"Careful there. Can't have you dropping my dinner." Matt chuckled again as he reached out to help steady me. "But seriously, are you okay?"

"Oh, I'm fine, just a bit of a porch klutz today, I guess." I handed him the bag.

His eyes widened as his hand dipped from the bag's weight. "Wow. Wasn't expecting this much. Thank you."

"It's a little bit of everything. And I do mean everything," I said as he peered in the bag, a smile growing on his face. "You should be well stocked for a while."

"I do believe this is going to delay my walk a bit as I put it all away," he commented.

I rubbed the back of my neck. "Sorry about that."

"Aw, that's all right. Happier to have all this, and as long as I get a walk in, everything's fine. Have you recovered from your late night?"

"Late night?" A nervous pit formed in my stomach. What had Matt seen?

"I heard you come outside last night talking to someone on the phone. I was just leaving George's. After the hot tub, we went in and played cards. I hadn't done that in ages. Not used to staying up quite that late anymore, but it was fun. Took it a bit slow this morning as a result. It's why I haven't had my walk yet."

I let out a mental sigh of relief. He may have heard me come outside and talking in general, but there was no way he had heard what I was saying or to whom. I'd been quiet. "I'm not used to such hours either with having to get up early for the bakery, but one of my friends was having an issue and texted me. It was easier to talk, so I came outside to not wake my gram up."

"Everything okay?" He seemed genuinely concerned.

I nodded, smiling at the thought of Sam and Todd's match. "It will be."

"Good. Glad to hear it. Did you have a good time with your grandmother?"

"I did. Wish she could have stayed longer."

"You'll have to take more time off next time she visits. I

don't think I've ever seen you not head into work except when you're closed on Tuesdays."

That made me laugh. "You're not the first to say that. Everyone tells me that I should take a vacation. Someday I might just do that."

"You're always on the move. I think you've earned it." He reached back for the screen door.

"Say, Matt, you didn't happen to see anyone come up on my porch earlier, did you?"

He dropped his hand from the doorknob, then scratched his head. "Can't say that I did. But I was busy in my backyard before I came out here for my walk. Why? You get something else without a note?"

I'd already asked him if he'd seen someone leave the altar cloth yesterday, and I didn't want to worry him again by admitting I'd had another mysterious delivery. Nor did I want to say what I'd been given this time either. "Saffy went a little crazy as if someone was coming on our porch, but no one was there. Must have been a bird on the railing or something."

"Cats are funny critters, aren't they? My Petunia and Cosmos were a riot when they were younger."

"You have cats?" I had no idea.

His usual smile faded. "Not anymore. Lost 'em both a few years ago shortly after Henny died. Petunia had mostly been hers, but Cosmos preferred me. You know how cats are with picking their favorite person. They were from the same litter, and at nineteen, I think Cosmos was ready once Toony went."

"I'm sorry to hear that." Matt had been coming for dinner all this time, and we'd talk throughout our meal, yet I'd never known about his pets. I vowed to be a better neighbor. "Think you'll get another?"

He shook his head. "I'd never say never, but it would take a cat getting dropped off on my doorstep." He chuckled.

"Funny you should mention that. That's how I ended up with Saffy."

"Well, now, isn't that something?"

I nodded. "Best mystery present I've ever been given." It hadn't dawned on me until then that Saffy's origin was similar to how I was getting things now. Hopefully whoever it was knew not to give me a cat. "All right, I should let you go. I've taken up enough of your time, and here you are still holding that bag of food."

"It's not too heavy. Was just surprised by it all at first." He reached for the door behind him once more. "You have a good rest of your day and thank you for all of this food."

"Oh, you're welcome. You know that I'll always share if I have it." I turned and started my descent from his porch.

"Careful on the steps."

Once I was safely on the walkway, I called over my shoulder, "See you Monday!"

Now I was ready to dive into everything Gram had left me.

Once I made more tea, of course.

CHAPTER 23

The next morning, Walter and Paul arrived at the diner as Donna wrote the muffin flavors on the specials board. They plopped onto their stools at the counter and then turned to face me, spinning in their seats as they did.

"Are you feeling okay?" Walter asked me.

Immediately my thoughts went to the potluck and all the food. Had he or Martie gotten sick from something they'd eaten? He looked fine, and he'd left his wife to come here, so that meant she was fine too. It couldn't be anything too serious, right?

Before I could answer, Paul added, "Because you look fine, and you seemed fine Monday at your potluck."

"Didn't seem the time to ask you all this the other night," Walter said, "but we had to after yesterday."

Yesterday? Okay, so it wasn't related to the food. I had no idea what they were talking about. "I'm perfectly fine, gentlemen. What's going on?"

Paul and Walter exchanged a glance with one another as Donna set coffee mugs in front of them.

Walter turned back to me. "Something was off with your muffins."

"Yeah," Paul continued, reaching for the sugar as Donna poured them coffee. "They had no pep. Yesterday or the day before."

"They were like regular muffins. You didn't make them ahead of time, did you?" Walter raised a brow at me. "Not trying to pass off Sunday leftovers as fresh muffins or anything like that?"

Ah. Now I understood, but I also felt a little offended. "No, I can assure you they were made on Monday. And I would hope you both know that I'd never make false claims as to the freshness of my baked goods. I have a day-old shelf in the store for what little we have left each day. Besides, I know how much everyone likes the Monday muffins. I'd never risk doing something different to them."

"Then what happened?" Paul said before I could continue.

"I wasn't there on Monday. I was preparing for my gram's visit."

"Ah. Nice woman," Walter said. "Martie and I enjoyed meeting her at your potluck."

Paul set his coffee mug down after taking a sip. "Same. But you not being there to make them certainly explains why your Monday muffins were, well, regular muffins."

"We were dragging all day," Walter explained, stressing the word all, before pausing to have his first sip of morning joe. "And as you know, we have them on Tuesdays too, so that was two days without your magic muffins."

I struggled to keep a straight face, wondering if they realized just how close they were to the truth about my magical influence over what we made at the bakery. I was surprised by how evident the difference apparently was, though. "Was it that noticeable? The lack of, what did you call it, pep?"

Both men looked me square in the eye, their lips drawn together, and nodded slowly.

"It's true," Donna said, putting the lid on the top of the stand where she kept the muffins. "No one complained that they were bad or anything—I don't think you could make something bad—but no one marveled at how good they were like they usually do either. You know we have people come here just for the muffins on Mondays."

"They're the best," Paul confirmed.

"And you not being there on Monday explains all of it. People are already talking, I'm sure," Walter said. He sat up straighter as Donna set his breakfast down on the counter.

And they would know if people were talking. The two older men and Donna were three of the biggest gossips in town, perhaps only rivaled by Sarah. I'd have to ask her if she'd heard anything once she got to the bakery.

Donna set Paul's plate in front of him. "It's just like your good luck cookies, and let's not forget your curing Rachael's morning sickness not too long ago. You know this is only going to strengthen what everyone says about you, has been saying for years."

This was the first time Donna had ever mentioned the rumors about me outright. "Oh? And what is it that they say?"

"You know . . ." She reached back for the coffee pot on the counter behind her, then topped off Paul's mug. "That you're a witch."

I knew it was coming, but even still, I nearly choked on my saliva. "A witch, huh?"

"Isn't it ridiculous?" She let out a hearty chuckle. "I've been telling people that since I first heard it. No way are you a witch. All that nonsense is just people thinking your treats make whatever was already going to happen actually happen. Just a big coincidence. A placebo effect. You know how people talk here in town."

This was as good an opening as any to test what would happen if people beyond the paranormal support group and a few select others knew about me. "What if I was a witch?"

Donna's face went blank, and both men's forks stopped midway to their mouths.

All right, then. Maybe now wasn't the time to reveal my secrets. They could live with the rumors for now. I blew out a quick puff of air before cracking a cheesy grin.

Donna pursed her lips and shook her finger at me. "Oh, you had me there for a second. I didn't realize you were such a kidder."

I shrugged, and my smile returned to its normal appearance. "Nothing I haven't heard before. Gotta have some fun with it every now and then."

Donna nodded in understanding. Beside me, Paul and Walter resumed eating, but Paul muttered, "Four years of a placebo effect?"

Next to him, Walter mumbled, "No such thing as coincidences."

That was Gram's belief too, and after this week especially, I was thinking the same. I wondered how much the two men believed in the rumors—or cared about the truth to them—as long as their Monday muffins did their job.

"Well, it was good to see you all this morning." I slid off my stool. It was time to head back to the shop. "Next week's Monday muffins will be back to their usual standards."

As I turned to head around the building to collect my bike, I caught sight of Donna out of the corner of my eye, leaning close to the men, propping herself up with one hand placed square on the counter, already engaged in conversation. No doubt they were already crafting something to add to the rumor mill.

I directed my bike back onto the sidewalk. At the last minute, I turned right on Main Street instead of left, setting me on course for a longer trek back to the bakery. In reality, going the back way along River Street, which gracefully curved back up toward my end of Main Street, only added another two minutes to my ride. But I needed the extra time to process what the three at the diner had revealed.

I hadn't wanted to let on my true reaction to hearing about the Monday muffins being different. I was fully aware of their power. They even had an effect on me.

It had nothing to do with the physical ingredients. That recipe didn't vary no matter who made them. Despite what some may have thought, there wasn't caffeine in the muffin except for the negligible amount in a few chocolate chips I'd sometimes add depending on the flavor.

I understood why some thought there was caffeine in them. It was almost like a tiny jolt of energy came with each bite. By the time the muffin was gone, it was like having had an extra-large coffee—only there was no afternoon crash or withdrawal later on. So if someone hadn't felt as if they'd woken up from a Monday muffin, then it made sense to me that they'd describe it as a vague *off*. They didn't understand why it was different while the taste was the same.

My only experiences with eating spelled foods—that I knew of—were the Monday muffins and the brownie apple sandwich from the potluck. Both had immediate effects. I didn't know if that was the case for everything I made, however. One wouldn't necessarily feel that they were eating a lucky cookie or a pastry instilled with a boost of confidence. There wasn't a way to know if something had worked until they went and did whatever they felt they'd needed the treat for. That's probably where Donna's comment about the placebo effect came into play.

This was all still new to me, but I should have known better with how popular Monday muffins were. Why hadn't I considered that when I took Monday off?

One thing was certain, though, as I pulled into the back lot behind the bakery. I wouldn't be taking another day off for a while.

CHAPTER 24

Everyone was busy with their baking tasks when I returned, and I hopped onto my station to split the Danish pastry dough I had been letting rise while I made my morning deliveries into thirty-six smaller balls. The strawberry jelly that I'd use as filling for what would eventually be *piroshki* was already chilling in the fridge. I quickly got lost in rolling each ball out into a flat oval. Next came dropping a bit of the jelly onto the middle of the ovals, then folding one short edge over the jelly to create a pocket. After scoring the opposite edge, making tiny slices through the dough, I folded it over the pocket. With that done, I had to let them rise a bit more before baking. Once out of the oven, each hand pie would be a puffy dough log with a fruity center running through it. It was one of the more time-consuming things we made, which is why I did them in small batches and only as one of my rotating monthly specials.

"Those are my favorite," Gina said from her station behind me. "It's a real shame we're limited to only sweet fillings. We could do so much if we were allowed to use more savory ingredients."

With my tray in hand, I passed Gina's station and told her I agreed. Although sweets were my first love, baking with savory things was a lot of fun too. However, using ingredients like meat or cheese or even onion would step on Zeke's toes. Then again, after having to work with him out of his shop while mine was closed, he'd agreed to let me use candied bacon.

Maybe it wouldn't hurt to ask him if it would be okay if we limited it to this one item for now. I could envision it. Ground beef and onions, sausage and peppers, and curried chicken. And many of those could be made ahead to let the meats soak in the flavor of whatever spices we used.

I shook the thought away as I placed my tray on a baking rack to let the dough finish rising. We could consider asking Zeke about that in a few weeks, but for now, we had more candy recipes to learn and hopefully, after today's meeting, a new baker to train. I glanced at the clock. Sarah would be here soon to help me open the shop, and Brittni could arrive anytime after that. I should have given her a time. That would have been the professional thing to do, although my offering her the job hadn't happened in a traditional manner either.

"Hey, Sam," I said on my way back to my workstation with a rack of cooled cookies to decorate, "do you know when Brittni is planning to come by?"

"I told her that we typically wrap up enough around ten and that you make your next round of deliveries by eleven thirty, so sometime between then. I know Wednesday afternoons are slow, but I figured you'd want us here to officially meet her as you showed her around."

I turned back to smile at him. "Smart move."

He shrugged before cutting a scone round into wedges. "That and it means she and I can go grab ice cream for lunch afterward to celebrate."

"Didn't you celebrate on Monday?" Bryan asked with a laugh, taking Sam's tray from his workstation to put it into the oven. "You left before the rest of us, saying you were all going to get ice cream."

"That was to celebrate the offer. Today's celebration will be for making it official." Sam walked over to the refrigerator.

"You can celebrate just about anything with ice cream," Gina said, glancing over her shoulder at Bryan, who was back at his station prepping more muffin batter.

Sam opened the door to the fridge, then pulled some cream cheese frosting that had been chilling before returning to his station. "Besides, I'm loading up on all the ice cream I can get before I have to leave." He looked over at me. "Are there good places for ice cream near campus?"

"Well, they have a soft-serve machine in the cafeteria, but depending on the units you're doing, you'll be fully loaded on desserts, some of which involve ice cream."

"Fully loaded? I don't think so." He laughed. "There's always room for ice cream. You've said it yourself."

"That I have," I admitted, turning back to finish the last few cookies on my tray. "I can give you a list of my favorite places that were nearby. You might need to take the campus shuttle to get to some, but I think you'll be satisfied with what's available." That was the nice thing about living in a city. Lots of variety, even of the same types of foods.

We all fell into conversation with Sam about school. He'd been quiet about it for most of the summer, but recently, he'd started talking about the prospect of leaving and expanding his culinary skills. Part of me believed it had something to do with our conversation a few weeks back. I'd told him to let his relationship with Todd take its course and not end it just because they could break up in the future. It was as if that had given him permission to be excited. But now they were a match. Sam had felt the shift himself. As a result, I only expected his eagerness to grow.

Through the window in the door separating the kitchen from the bakery, I saw the lights turn on, signaling Sarah's arrival. I grabbed my completed tray of decorated cookies, then headed into the shop.

"Good morning. How was your day off?" I placed the tray on the counter.

"Spent it doing some research for . . . everything." She followed me as I reentered the kitchen to grab another tray. She put her purse in the closet, then took a tray of her own to bring back into the shop.

I slid open the case closest to the window. "Anything interesting?"

"Lots." She handed me one of the trays. "You have anything planned tonight? I could come over so we can talk about it."

I slid the tray into place. That sounded great. I had plenty to talk to her about too. "Pizza okay for you?"

"As long as there aren't mushrooms." She made a face, then passed me the second tray.

"Deal." I took the third tray from her hands, then went back to grab more from the kitchen.

By the time we were done loading the first case, Gina and Lily were ready to help get the rest loaded. Soon they were joined by Sam and Bryan, and the six of us quickly loaded the remaining two cases and restocked the fudge shelf.

Before we got back to work prepping my midday deliveries, and while we were all together, I asked, "Who made the muffins on Monday?"

They all glanced at one another, unsure of how to respond.

Finally, Sam spoke up. "You know we all kinda do a bit of

everything back here. Monday was no different. Maybe even a little more so with you gone. Why?"

"Umm . . ." I sighed heavily. There was no time like right now to address the rumors head-on. In this small town, my team would eventually hear them anyway, and since three of them already knew, it was only fair the other two did as well. "People noticed they were different."

"Different, how?" Bryan asked.

Lily tilted her head back in understanding. "They lacked that bit of something extra that makes the Monday muffins so popular."

Bryan shook his head. "But we made them the same way we make all the other muffins on any other Monday, or any day for that matter. These shouldn't have been any different."

"That's the thing," Gina said, likely starting to realize what I was getting at. "They weren't any different from the muffins we make the rest of the week. That's it, right?"

I nodded.

"But what do you do to them?" Bryan asked. "I've had them. I know they're different somehow. Where did we go wrong?"

"You didn't. You did everything right." I glanced at Sarah for some reassurance. She nodded. "It's magic. I didn't know it until recently, but I'm a witch."

Bryan cocked his head to the side. "Like hocus-pocus witches? With pointy hats and brooms? For real?"

"Well, I don't have a hat or ride a broom, and it's not like I'm baking things in a cauldron or anything like that. I just kind of think about something while baking and it happens. The Monday muffins have been different all along because I go about making them with different thoughts."

"So when you make the muffins on Mondays, you think about everyone being awake?"

206

"Pretty much. Awake, alert, enthusiastic, and ready to start the week on a good note. You've said it yourself that you know they're different. So what do you think?"

"I've noticed how they wake me up. Is that why you started keeping a few for us in the kitchen?"

I nodded.

"All right, then. I mean, it's weird, but"—he shrugged—"I believe you."

"I didn't believe it myself until Walter and Paul convinced me to try one a couple months back."

Gina squinted her eyes, studying me. "It's not just the muffins, though, is it?"

I shook my head. "If you've heard about something happening, like good luck cookies or getting rid of morning sickness, then it's probably right."

"What about the caramel a few weeks back? I know part of it was sabotage," Bryan started, "but it was still really popular."

"No, that had nothing to do with me. Just a coincidence." It wasn't really, but I was not going to go into an explanation of how the whole town was full of paranormal beings. Some of them already knew, but not everyone. Maybe they'd find out someday.

"Well, I think it's wonderful that you're embracing who you are," Sam said. "You let me be me, so all I can do is let you do the same."

His reply warmed my heart, and the lights in the shop brightened.

Bryan looked up. "Do you do that too?"

"Honestly? I'm not sure." I looked around at my team. Lily and Sam were smiling proudly. Sarah looked excited. Gina and Bryan still seemed to be processing everything, but if I'd needed as long as I did to accept it, I couldn't expect them to do it in only a few minutes. I realized then that I'd have to tell Lauren, and eventually Brittni if she became a true part of the team. It wasn't something I'd spring on her right away, certainly not today.

"So are we all set out here? I need to flip the sign in a few minutes." Sarah walked to the windows and lifted the shades.

Bryan shrugged. "Guess so."

Gina looked at Lily and Sam. "We're good."

"I'll be back out in a minute or two," I told Sarah, then led my team back into the kitchen. They all got back to work with whatever they'd been working on before the tray load-in started.

With everyone settled, I returned to the shop. Sarah took one look at me and her mouth dropped a little. "I cannot believe you just told everyone like that. Who are you, and what have you done with my boss of almost five years?"

I quirked my lips and lifted a shoulder. "I had a good opportunity with the muffins. And I had to bring those up. They were the first thing Walter and Paul mentioned when they saw me this morning. They thought something was wrong with me." That earned a chuckle from Sarah. "Besides, it was time. Lily already knows after I helped her and John, and Sam has kinda known since I accidentally spelled the scones for the Love a Tree Day Festival, but I told him outright Monday night after you went home."

"I'm just surprised, that's all. But in a good way. Accepting your witchiness has been good for you." She walked over to me, then gave me a quick hug before spinning on her heels to head to the front door. She flipped the sign from *closed* to *open*.

"Gram also may have had a hand in it. She made a comment about how I've been trusting the PSG, but if I couldn't trust my team here, then why were they working for me?"

Sarah returned to her spot behind the counter, ready to start the day. "Your gram's a smart lady."

"That she is," I said over my shoulder, my hand on the door to the kitchen. "Oh, she also suggested we make an altar in the basement here. Focus on the business side of things with our intentions. I'm hoping to get a cupboard with doors or something for it."

"Are you thinking of getting John and Lily to make something?"

"I hadn't even thought of that. I was thinking of something that spoke to me when I came across it."

Her eyes lit up. "Oh, I love antiquing."

"We just need to make sure there are no ghosts attached to whatever we get because I am not introducing one into the bakery. The ones that end up visiting wreak enough havoc sometimes, and I don't want to waste any more flour." I threw my head back and laughed, and before Sarah could respond, I pushed open the door to the kitchen, calling, "Let me know when Brittni gets here."

CHAPTER 25

The bakery brightened so much that it was noticeable to me through the kitchen window. I wiped my hands on my apron, no longer needing Sarah to come tell me when Brittni had arrived. She was here. There was no way that much energy to cause such a reaction with the lights could have come from anyone but my excited new baker ready to talk more about the job.

I darted into the bathroom to clean up and was just coming out when Sarah popped her head into the kitchen.

"Brittni's—"

"Here. Yes, I thought so." I pointed to the lights, and Sarah nodded in understanding.

"Do you need me to finish anything back here or can I grab you tea or something?" Sarah asked as I scooted past her and into the shop.

"How about you stay a few minutes, and then when I start showing her around the kitchen, you can grab something for all of us?" I pointed up, circling my finger around. "I'd like to have you here to talk schedules and specifics if you don't mind."

"Sure!" The smile on her face was evident in her tone as well.

I pivoted to face Brittni, who was standing in the center of the room, her hands folded in front of her and clasping a piece of black fabric, an apron, I assumed. She appeared ready for an interview. Her hair was in a ponytail like it had been on Monday, minus the sticks, but unlike her casual style from the other night, today she was wearing khaki pants, and only the top button of her solid light-blue button-up was undone.

"It's good to see you, Brittni. Thanks for coming in. How are you today?" I approached her with one arm outstretched, my hand open.

She took mine in hers, and we shook. Her grip was firm and strong. Good for working with dough.

"I'm good. Nervous, but good," she replied, letting go of my hand.

"Nothing to be nervous about. Job's already yours if you want it."

Her eyes widened and her eyebrows raised. "Oh, I do."

"Wonderful." I motioned to the tables to the side of the shop. "How about we all sit and talk a bit. Did you get a chance to meet Sarah the other night?"

Brittni and Sarah shook hands. "No, but I've obviously seen you around town. You were talking with Gary from Leafs at the potluck, right?"

Sarah nodded as the three of us sat down, and was she blushing? I'd have to ask her about it later.

"Sarah is my shop manager and all-around assistant. She doesn't bake, but she's the person you go to if I'm not here and you're having problems for whatever reason."

"As long as it isn't a problem with figuring out why something isn't rising or browning or solidifying or . . . I think you get the idea." She laughed.

For several minutes, we talked about the bakery dynamic, my expectations, the daily schedule, and what Brittni's goals were while working in the bakery. I was excited to hear her confirm what Sam had said about wanting to go to culinary school and that my alma mater was at the top of her list.

"There's also the option of picking up shifts in the shop once you get used to everything so that you can be as well-rounded as you can be going into college. That's what Sam has been doing some days."

"I'd like that."

"Good, I'm glad you do. Now, how about we go in the back and I can properly introduce you to the rest of the team."

The three of us stood, and we took Brittni into the kitchen.

Sam rushed over to us but stopped about a foot away as if realizing he should be professional. "Good to see you, Brittni. I'm excited to get the chance to work with you for a few weeks."

Brittni beamed. "I am too."

I quickly estimated the open space I had right here in the doorway and stepped out of the way. "Okay . . . go ahead and do the bouncing thing you two do. But just this one time. We can't make a daily habit out of it."

Brittni squealed as she and Sam grabbed each other's fore-arms. They jumped several times, laughter bubbling out of them, as I shook my head, a big grin on my face.

"Okay, you two. Out of your system?"

They each took a calming breath, then stepped away from one another.

"Yes," Brittni said.

"Thanks, Joanie," Sam added as he moved to Brittni's side.

I nodded. "Okay, everybody, this is Brittni. I know you met her at the potluck and that I offered her a job, but consider this her official interview and hiring process. We haven't scared her off yet with our early morning schedule, so things are already looking good."

Bryan laughed. "She'll be fine. Just give her a Monday muffin for a few days."

"That's probably not a bad idea." Guess that meant he was okay with what I'd confessed earlier.

"I like your muffins," Brittni said. "Mr. Johnson gives them to us before tests."

"Oh, you have, Ri—Mr. Johnson as a teacher?"

"Last semester, I did. I will again in the fall."

"He's one of my best customers."

She laughed. "With as many tests as he gives, I'm not surprised."

Gina snorted as Bryan barked out a laugh.

Brittni shrugged. "He's tough, but he's fair."

"He also gets stuff for the cross-country team."

"Oh, that's right. I forget that he does that too. I . . . don't do sports."

"Don't worry, it's not required, although you're going to get pretty good at lifting bags of flour and sugar working here."

Sam flexed his arms. "See? I didn't have these before I started. I gotta say, I shaped up nicely."

What we did every day was a good workout. I'd met a guy in culinary school who lost a hundred pounds while working at a patisserie. The idea of a pudgy baker wasn't always a true stereotype.

"All right, everyone, back to work. I'm going to be bringing Brittni around to all of your stations, so be prepared to talk about what it is you're doing." As everyone returned to their tables, I showed Brittni around the kitchen equipment, then gave her an overview of what we made on an average day, how we handled deliveries, and how we decided who took what task when a special order came in. After that, I led her to everyone's spots to see them in action. As I did, Sarah took drink orders from us all, then excused herself to Leafs and Grounds.

"Once Sam leaves, that will be your station," I told her, moving from his table toward mine, "but until then, you and I will be sharing as we get you up to speed. I'm off making deliveries twice a day, so sometimes you'll have the table to yourself. I have plans to put a candy station behind me, but that is still to come. We're selling fudge now, as I'm sure you're aware, but we have a lot more we want to do. You're coming at an exciting time."

"Thank you so much for the opportunity."

"You're welcome. You earned it after those cookies. If the other things you make are even half as good, you have a great foundation for working here. And I absolutely want that recipe."

"That I can do." Brittni reached into her pocket and then pulled out an index card. She handed it to me. "Here."

"Wow. You came prepared. Thank you." I glanced down at the card and scanned the recipe. I couldn't wait to make these cookies. "So I have been doing a lot of the talking. Do you have any questions for me?"

She smiled. "When do I start?"

I tucked the recipe into my apron pocket. "I'm more than willing to have you start tomorrow, but if you need time to adjust your sleep schedule, Monday is fine."

"Oh, my mom doesn't let me sleep late. That's for when I stay at my dad's on the weekend. Well, it was. I'll probably be a little tired tomorrow, but that's better than starting Monday."

"Then, great! I'm sure we can whip you up something in the morning that will wake you up if you need it."

Behind me, Bryan coughed over a laugh. I hoped I wouldn't have to worry about him. He still seemed okay, but with these sorts of reactions would he be able to keep my secret?

"I'm really looking forward to it," Brittni said.

"And I'm really glad to have you as a part of our team. Let's make it official, shall we?" I put my hand out, and she did the same. We shook once more, sealing the deal. "I have a few papers I'm going to need you to fill out, so how about we go back into the shop and you can do that at one of the tables. I have it under good authority that someone wants to grab ice cream for lunch with you once you're done."

She cast a look over to Sam, a big smile on her face. "Mmm . . . ice cream sounds good to me."

Yep, she was going to fit in here perfectly.

After getting Brittni situated with the forms, I sat across from her and we continued chatting, although not about anything too distracting so that she could focus on the paperwork. As she flipped to the next page, I caught sight of a necklace she was wearing. It must have slipped out from under her shirt when she was jumping up and down with Sam. But now, it drew my attention because of the pendant hanging from the chain.

"That's a pretty necklace."

She paused mid-writing and grasped at the pendant with her free hand, letting out a small gasp. "Thank you," she said quietly and went to tuck it back under her shirt.

"That's the Triple Moon Goddess symbol, isn't it?"

She nodded but wouldn't meet my gaze.

"I have a similar one." Had she been the one to give it to me?

"Wait, you're actually a witch?"

"I take it you've heard the rumors about me." Unsurprising, but so much for not telling her about me on her first day.

"Well, yeah. But I thought that's what they were. Rumors."

I shrugged. "I'm still learning it all myself."

"Emily gave it to me. Please don't tell my parents. I don't think either of them would be cool with this." So did this mean Emily was my mystery gift giver? I'd suspected she was a witch, but this confirmed it. If not, it had to be someone she knew.

"I'm not going to tell anyone, but you don't have to hide it with me. I have no right asking as your boss and especially not in the job hiring process"—I nodded to her paperwork— "but it doesn't matter to me what you practice. We're accepting here, no matter who you are. There's no tolerance for any sort of discrimination."

"Thanks, Joanie. Sam said you were cool with stuff, but I didn't realize that would extend to this."

I smiled warmly. "Thanks. I'm glad I'm cool. Can't say I heard that a lot in school." Losing my best friend after telling her I saw ghosts had put a kink in my social circles. Ginny kept most of our friends, and although I made more, I made sure to protect my feelings as well as my secret. It wasn't until recently here in Heartwood Hollow that I'd begun to trust others with what I could do.

At that moment, Sarah returned with drinks for everyone. She poked her head into the kitchen to tell everyone she was back, and over the next couple of minutes, the team filed out as they finished their cleaning tasks. Sam plopped down next to Brittni and sipped away on his frozen coffee drink as he waited for her to complete her forms. I stood and headed for the counter. The lid on my chai tea had already been popped off to let it cool.

"Thanks, Sarah."

"Wasn't sure how long you'd be sitting there, so I figured I'd take care of it." She sucked down some of her iced mocha. "So shop manager, huh?"

"I'd wondered if you picked up on that. It was time. You've already been working full-time for me, and let's just say your 'other duties as assigned' will only continue to grow."

She let out a small chuckle.

"Comes with a pay raise too."

"Really?"

"Least I could do."

"Thanks, Joanie."

I cleared my throat, and the conversation in the room died down. "I wanted to let you all know that in addition to Brittni joining our team, Sarah has been made our official shop manager." Everyone clapped, so I waited a moment to continue. "As we add more offerings within the shop, this title acknowledges that more responsibilities will be put on her shoulders. We are still working out what those will be. So, Brittni, welcome to the team. Sarah, congratulations. And everyone else, whenever you're ready to go, you're done for the day." I glanced at the clock. "I have some deliveries to go make, so I'll see you all tomorrow if not before."

I walked back into the kitchen and then out the door to the back parking lot, having grabbed two packed pastry boxes off my workstation as I passed it. Crossing the parking lot to provide the yogis with cookies for their cheat day, I was feeling good about the latest staffing changes at the bakery and hoped it was a sign of things to come.

CHAPTER 26

Sam bounded into the kitchen, slight concern on his face. "What did you need me for?" I'd asked him to come back after lunch, not telling him why.

I held the book of candy recipes out toward him. "Pick your favorite, Sam, and let's do this." Although he was leaving for college in a few weeks, it didn't feel right to start my new Wednesday afternoon routine of practicing his grandmother's recipes without him here.

It would also give me the chance to talk to him about my latest match.

Sam's eyes lit up with excitement, and he began flipping through Trudy's *grimoire*, as she'd called it. After a few minutes, he loudly tapped at one of the pages. "This one."

I came up next to him and peered at the recipe. "The base recipe we can do. I have some leftover pretzels from the brownie batter we made for Lucy if we want to try mixing those in. We don't need to worry about all the varieties until we've perfected the basics."

We prepped some muffin trays with paper cups, then Sam set to work melting semi-sweet and milk chocolates in a double boiler on the stovetop as I mixed confectioner's sugar and peanut butter together in a bowl. When it seemed to be incorporated, I tried it. It needed a bit more . . . something. A note written next to the original recipe in a second handwriting said to add butter and a bit of brown sugar to taste.

"So much of this is 'to taste,'" I began, stirring in a teaspoon of softened butter, "but everyone's tastes are different."

"That's why you have taste testers, silly. Go with the consensus. Even in Grama's last few years at her shop, she would have us try her new candy creations until they were just right. And she'd been doing it for decades by then."

I grabbed a new spoon and dipped it in my mixture so I could try it once more. "Better."

"I think this has melted down enough," Sam said, giving the chocolate another stir.

"Set it to low, and let's crush up some of these pretzels."

We put some pretzels in a bag, and Sam took a rolling pin to them, creating way more crumbs than I believed either of us expected.

As I added half of them into the peanut butter mix, Sam grabbed the melted chocolate. He poured it into the bottoms of the muffin cups, and once I'd mixed the pretzel crumbs in, I followed with dollops of peanut butter. Sam came back around to top all the cups with chocolate, and then we popped the trays into the fridge to let them set.

We set to work cleaning, and after about an hour, we pulled the cups out.

"I think we need to work on the chocolate's tempering to get the shine one would expect from finished candy, but let's give them a try." I poked my head into the shop. "Hey, come taste these." Wednesday afternoons were our slowest of the week. The shop would be fine for a few minutes.

Sarah scooted into the kitchen, and she, Sam, and I each tried a peanut butter cup.

I studied their faces, trying to gauge their reactions. "What do you think?"

"Not bad for our first attempt," Sam said.

"Agreed. We're not quite there."

"What about a little salt on top?" Sarah asked.

I nodded. "That could work. Almost balance the sweetness of the peanut butter mix back out, and for this variety, at least, it would go with the pretzels."

Sam pointed to the bag of pretzel crumbs on his workstation. "Or even just more of those."

"All things to try next time. But for now"—I popped the remaining cups out of the muffin tins—"these are good enough for us to snack on back here."

"Sounds good to me." Sam grabbed another before I could get them all into a storage bag. He took a bite, then quickly followed it with a second.

"Probably not so good for my waistline," Sarah said, a hint of laughter in her voice. "Can you spell them to not have calories?"

"Not sure it works like that," I confessed, "although I could probably make something that would prevent you from worrying about how many calories were in it."

She shrugged before popping the last of her cup into her mouth. "I had to try. Okay, I'll be back in the shop if you need me." She headed into the kitchen, leaving Sam and me alone.

"Thanks for this," he said.

"You're welcome. I thought it could be fun, just you and me making something. And I wanted to talk to you about our phone discussion the other night."

He drew his lips to the side. "Sorry for calling you that late."

I waved him off. "That's really okay. I said to call anytime, and I meant it. No, I wanted to talk to you about what you said you felt. I know why. You and Todd are a match."

"Wait, what?" His eyes widened and took on a sparkle I only saw when I talked to people about their matches.

A smile grew across my face. "You heard me."

"I don't understand."

"I do more than just spell baked goods." He'd mentioned my matchmaking before, but I confirmed it, confessing it all to him. What I could do, that it was magic, what it felt like, and what had happened at the potluck. "I had to be sure before I got your hopes up. I confirmed it when we got ice cream. I'm sorry I didn't know it was you two as soon as it happened."

"Hey, it's okay. There were a lot of us around."

"You're taking this really well."

He shrugged. "I'm just excited that he and I are meant to be. Thanks for not letting me break up with him last month." Worried about leaving Todd to go to school out of state and a few hours away, Sam had asked me if it would be better to end their relationship despite his feelings. He'd been fretting over the possibility of a future long-distance breakup, despite how he felt for his boyfriend.

"You're welcome. Match or no match, you two are great together." I was glad he'd decided to let things progress how they should. Maybe this was why the magic had finally struck. Maybe it always would have. I didn't understand the hows and whens and whys of my matchmaking. But I doubted the magic would have had the chance to take hold had Sam made a hasty decision.

"Would you mind if I go see him? I won't tell him. I don't know if he'd believe me anyway."

"Go on. Go see your match."

"Thanks, Joanie." He wrapped me in a big quick hug before tossing his apron into the bin. "I'll see you tomorrow!"

After Sam left, I headed into the bakeshop with the broom and dustpan in one hand and the glass cleaner and a rag in the other. I passed Sarah the broom. It was time to get ready for closing, but our day was far from done.

CHAPTER 27

Less than an hour after Sarah and I closed the shop for the day, she was knocking on my door.

"Come on in." I walked into the living room from the kitchen, a menu to Mama à la Pizza in my hand. "Have you tried them yet?"

She laughed as she pulled the door open and came inside, a canvas tote bag slung over her shoulder. "Oh, I've done more than try them. Jill and I get them at least once a week."

"Great. Know what you want?"

"Hungry?"

"No. Anxious to get started is more like it." Not wanting to lose time figuring out food, I'd decided on what I wanted as soon as I got home.

After setting her bag down, Sarah wrote her order down, and then we called for delivery.

"What's in your bag?" It wasn't something she usually carried with her, and I was curious to see what she'd brought.

"Books mostly. I know how you tear through them, so I figured I'd bring you my small collection to get you started." She retrieved her bag from the floor next to the couch, then transferred the books onto the coffee table. "I've had a general upbringing with this sort of knowledge. My grandfather said it didn't make much sense to go deeper until I knew what type of a witch I had if I ever got so lucky. I don't think any of us expected that you'd be all sorts of things."

"Awesome. We can add those to what I have." I hurried into the side room, where I grabbed the suitcase Gram left.

Sarah raised an eyebrow as I reemerged pulling the suitcase. "What is all that?"

"This is what Gram brought." I set the bag down on its back, then unzipped the entire thing. Pulling the top open, I stopped when Sarah gasped.

"Your gram gave *that* to you?" She pointed to the altar cloth I had put in here for lack of somewhere else for it to go. I'd forgotten all about it as I set up my mantel. "How did she get it?"

"She didn't. I put this in here. Why, do you recognize it?"

She sat on the couch and reached out for it, so I handed it to her. "It's covered in symbols for the Moonshadow Coven."

"Moonshadow Coven?"

"That's the coven located here in Heartwood Hollow. The one I told you and your grandmother about. See? These are the phases of the moon. The larger design has all of them casting light on a tree at various angles, creating the moonshadow. But if your gram didn't give it to you, how did you get it?"

The celestial design took on a whole new meaning for me. "It was given to me. I think."

"You think?" She crossed her arms.

I explained to her how Gram and I found it when we came back from the cider mill.

"It was just there? No note or anything?"

"I looked. Even under the bushes."

She let out a small snort of amusement. "Can't say you're not thorough."

"What do you think it means?"

"I don't know," she admitted, examining the cloth more closely. "It's old. See? There's a patch here mending the fabric."

I leaned forward and lifted the corner of the cloth to inspect the plain dark-purple patch near the edging. "Almost like where you'd put a name. Too bad there's nothing here."

"That would be too easy."

"Maybe I could ask my aunt. Gram said she's a textile witch."

"Your family has the coolest powers." She let out a wistful sigh.

I drew my lips to the side. "I wouldn't know."

"I mean it. Joanie, do you realize how big of a deal your family is in the witching world? Even among those who aren't paranormally magical."

Standing, I let the corner of the fabric fall from my hand and back onto Sarah's lap. "It is?"

"You have a whole town named after your family," she said, nodding her head emphatically. "That's huge. Everyone here knows the Suncraft Coven, and I'm sure many of the witches here have visited Sunny Valley a time or two."

I paced the floor. The idea seemed so foreign to me. I knew Sunny Valley was popular among tourists, but I'd never have suspected that so many could have been witches. How had I been so unaware of where I'd come from?

"I have to admit something." Sarah averted her gaze.

I turned back to her. "You aren't going to tell me you're not actually my familiar, are you? I'd be a little disappointed at this point."

"No, no, nothing like that. Just . . . I was really excited

when you turned out to be my witch. I was much older than either my uncle or my grandfather when they found their witches. So when I found you, and you were a Sunevall with ties to the Suncraft Coven, well, that made me feel a lot better about coming into this so late. It was big news when you moved here and called your shop what you did. A lot of people took an interest in you."

"Well, I'm only a Sunevall because I don't know who my father is."

"I doubt that matters. A lot of witching families follow a matrilineal line anyway." She folded the altar cloth. "I wonder if you're being courted by the coven."

"Excuse me?"

"Has anyone else in your paranormal support group said they are a witch?"

I shook my head.

"But if someone was there and went and told the coven—"

"They're not supposed to take anything out of the group."

She shrugged. "It's just a theory. Or maybe someone saw your grandmother, and knowing who she is, decided to act now before she got you to join the Suncraft Coven. You did say you got this after she got here, right?"

"Yeah," I said as the doorbell rang. "And you know what Gram says about coincidences."

I opened the door, and there stood Larry with our food. "I didn't realize you delivered for Mama's too." I'd last seen him delivering Chinese food for me and Ken a while back.

"I deliver everything," he said quietly, handing me the slip. "The tips are good, and I like being outside." Like me, he made a lot of his deliveries on a bike.

"Hi, Larry," Sarah called from the couch.

I signed the slip, giving him a hearty tip like always.

Anyone who brought me food deserved one. We traded the slip for two small pizza boxes and a full plastic bag of food. "Thanks. You have a good night."

"You too." He turned and left as I closed the door.

"Food's here. Let's head into the kitchen."

As we ate our fill of pizza, garlic knots, and fries, we talked about Sarah's growing up in Heartwood Hollow and her training as a familiar. She could write a book about it. Afterward, we headed back into the living room, where the suitcase was as we had left it.

I put the altar cloth on the open flap of the suitcase. "The cloth isn't the only witchy thing I've received lately."

"What else did you get?"

I pulled the pendant out of a side pocket and handed it to her. "Just this."

"These I've seen around. I wouldn't be surprised if all the witches in the coven have one. Yeah. You're definitely being courted by them. When did this one come?"

"Yesterday afternoon."

"It has to have been because of your gram. But on a related note, I talked to my grandfather, and he said the next coven meeting isn't until the full moon. They meet less in the summer. I guess even witches need to go on vacation." She eyed me.

"Why does everyone want me to go on a vacation? I'm not taking any more time off until we figure out how I can pre-spell the Monday muffins. Have you heard anything more about that?"

She passed the pendant back to me. "No. Well, nothing more than what you heard from Walter and Paul. I don't think it will blow up or anything like that. Full moons always bring a rush of rumors to town, and your muffins not being as magical as they normally are is not the weirdest thing being said."

I started stacking the books from Gram's suitcase onto the coffee table. "What on earth is weirder than that?" Then I thought about it for a second. "I don't know if I want to know right now. It's probably more than I want to deal with."

Pausing her scanning of the book titles, Sarah laughed. "Probably for the best. It's very north woodsy if you get my drift."

"That could mean anything!" When I looked into what had happened in the north woods before learning about the dryads, I'd been told stories involving everything from killer trees to wolves to other sorts of monsters. Although the killer trees weren't real, I wasn't ready for more that could be.

Time to change the subject and get back to work. I plopped the final book on the table. "That's the last one."

She picked up a book and opened the front cover. "What else do you have in there?"

"Well, you already saw all the crystals . . ."

"I did. I like what you did with your altar space, by the way."

"Thanks." I glanced at the mantel before returning my gaze to the suitcase. "And I already took out the tea, but there's still a lot of stuff in here. I don't know what to do with half of it. There are metal bowls, candles, I think these are tuning forks"—I picked one up—"but they're in all sorts of colors."

"Wow," Sarah closed the book and placed it next to her on the couch. "That is a great start to a witch's kit, especially for a beginner."

"Gram said all of her ladies contributed to it. I bet my

mom is responsible for most of the books. She's a literary witch."

"Fitting since she works in a library. So you said you don't know what everything is?" I shook my head. "Well, why don't we start there tonight? You were right. Those are tuning forks," she said pointing to them. "The colors are to help you differentiate between the frequencies that each fork vibrates with. Each one is attuned to a different chakra."

"Chakra?" I'd heard the term before but didn't know what it was.

Sarah dove into an explanation, pulling out one of the books from the stack to show me. From there we moved on to the singing bowls, then the bag of runes. The suitcase was so full we wouldn't have time for all of it tonight, so we made plans to meet after work tomorrow . . . and probably again next week too. Even then, these few nights would only introduce me to everything I got, nevermind go in depth with how to use it all.

I foresaw a lot of hanging out together in our future, no skills in fortune-telling needed.

CHAPTER 28

Somehow, I lucked out. Someone was just leaving the front parking lot at the cider mill as I approached the entrance. That never happened. Had I not stayed talking with Rachael's mom after the baby shower brunch—it was a boy—then the timing wouldn't have been right and I'd likely have ended up in the far lot. She'd wanted to tell me the brownies I made for the shower were delicious. I didn't have the heart to tell her I'd made those for more than one reason. The second reason was why I was here right now.

Knowing that I was possibly going to pick up a peck of apples, at least a gallon of cider, and whatever else struck me while I was here, I took the parking spot like it was a gift . . . a sign that what I was about to do was meant to happen.

Cindy wasn't at the entrance like she usually was when I came, but then again, I wasn't regularly here at this time. Some ghosts stuck to routines, and if Saturdays at the cider mill weren't a part of Cindy's, then she wouldn't be here. I'd hoped to talk to her, but right now it looked like I was going to have to come back another day for that. Talking to her wasn't the main reason I'd come, however.

It felt strange not taking a cart when I walked in, but despite my plans to grab stuff while I was here, my goal wasn't to shop either. I glanced around, trying to locate the office.

"Can I help you?" a cashier asked from behind the fudge stand.

I gave him my politest smile. "I'm looking for Zach. I'm meeting with him to discuss the memorial event coming up." And to find out more about his mom, but no one needed to know that but me.

"Office is right behind the checkout area," the cashier said, pointing to the next room over. "Nora's running the room and can put you in touch with him. She's got a walkie in case he's out feeding the chickens."

"Thank you." I headed left past the cheeses and into the checkout area where they had single-serve cider jugs, candies, and nuts in front of three checkout counters.

The woman with the walkie-talkie was easy to spot. Her shirt featured the same design as the rest of the staff shirts but was red instead of green. The giant walkie-talkie was also a big clue.

"Excuse me," I said, stopping in front of her with a small wave, "I was told you could help me find Zach."

Her smile widened. "Sure can. Who can I say is looking for him?"

I stuck my hand out. "Joanie Sunevall, owner of Suncraft Bakery in Heartwood Hollow."

"I like you already. You had me at *bakery*. I've had some of your stuff over the years at various events." She thrust her hand toward mine and grabbed it. "Nora. Zach's wife. Nice to meet you."

"Likewise."

"You're here to talk about my mother-in-law's memorial

event." It wasn't a question.

"I am. I didn't move to town until after she passed, so I didn't have the pleasure of meeting her, but I love this place and wanted to see if there was any way I could take part."

"Cindy was a lovely woman. Really the heart of this place. Zach's the sixth generation to run the mill. Come on, I'll take you to him." She let the girl at checkout know she'd be gone a bit and brought me through the office and outside. Cindy had been sitting at the office desk as we passed, bent over some papers studying them. Guess that was her routine on Saturdays. She hadn't seen me, and for obvious reasons, I couldn't say anything to alert her to my presence.

The door to the office closed behind us as Nora led me across the back lot.

"How did she die? Your mother-in-law."

"Peacefully in her sleep. Just went to bed one night and didn't show up for work the next morning."

Not alive anyway. Hearing that she'd died overnight, I believed that she woke up the next morning and went to work, never realizing she was dead.

"Zach went over to check on her and found her." Nora sighed. "Guess it was just her time to go."

We walked up a wood ramp toward several picnic tables overlooking a pond where dozens of geese and other waterfowl swam or basked in the sun along the shore. I'd been here dozens of times before. This was one of my favorite spots to enjoy a frozen treat from the cider mill's food stand.

"He's probably in the feed shed. Let me call him." Nora tugged the walkie off her belt, then brought it to her mouth. "Joanie from the bakery in Heartwood Hollow is here to meet with you."

A moment later, the walkie crackled. "Be right there. Thank you, dear."

Nora smiled at me. "Take a seat. Can I get you anything? Probably should have grabbed you a cider on our way through. How rude of me."

"Oh, don't worry about it. I'll be okay. Thank you for helping me."

"Stop back in with me before you go. I'll make sure you go home with one."

"I will, thank you."

She gave a quick wave to someone over my shoulder. I turned and saw who I assumed was her husband stepping out of a small shed on the opposite side of the pond, which bordered one of the apple orchards.

"Well, fancy meeting you out here," a voice said from behind me. When I turned, Nora had already started back to the mill building, but Cindy stood before me, smiling as she always did when we said hello.

"It's good to see you. How are you doing?"

"Just checking the numbers. Thought I saw you walk through the office. You didn't say anything. Figured you didn't want to bother me."

"Cindy, why don't you sit down. I've recently learned something that I wanted to talk to you about." Now was as good a time as any.

One of her eyebrows furrowed as the other lifted in curiosity, but she sat down. "What is it, Joanie?"

Breaking the news to someone about a death was never easy. There was a whole new layer of complexity added to it when the person I was telling was also the person who had died. "There's no good way to ask you this but, are you aware that you're dead?"

She sputtered a breath of air at me with a *pfft*. "Me, dead? Well, that's certainly a new one. I didn't take you for a joker. What are you getting on about? I'm right here."

I gave her a consoling grin. "I'm sorry, but it's true. Almost five years. The event they're having here in a few weeks is the fifth memorial road race and apple float in your honor."

"I do love that event. Seeing all those red rubber apples floating down the mill creek is so much fun."

I pulled a piece of paper out of my pocket, then unfolded it to show Cindy the flyer about the event. Featuring in the center was a photograph of her. "See? It's right here."

She took the paper from my hands. I'd never get over how well some ghosts could manipulate objects while right in front of me. Usually, it was a door or a chair. Something that would have impeded their path. Many rarely walked through things. A few months ago, I'd watched as a hairbrush stroked my cat Saffy. The ghost was in the brush then. But the scene for me then was likely how someone else would be seeing the paper now. Hovering in mid-air. No one holding it. They'd likely think I was doing some sort of magic trick. It wouldn't do well for the things that were said about me, although I doubted most here would ever connect me to rumors from the neighboring town. They likely wouldn't have even heard of me or my witchy ways. Thank goodness for tourist spots.

"But I'm right here," Cindy said again.

"I know it's a lot to take in—"

She scoffed. "This has to be some elaborate prank that they roped you into."

"This is no joke," I said, shaking my head in short, slow strokes. "That would be cruel."

She pursed her lips to the side. "And they aren't that."

"No," I agreed. "Have you not noticed anything different?"

"No, I mean, I wake up every day, get ready for work, go to work, and go home. Repeat. That's been my life for years."

"Five years, perhaps? How do you get to work?"

"I drive, of course."

"Do you? If we went to check right now, would we see your car?"

"Well, not today. Have you seen how busy it is? I can't stop everything for this silly errand."

"Then how did you get here today?"

"Like I do every day. It's routine. I barely even notice the short drive anymore after all this time."

"Cindy"—I placed my hand on her arm, pulling it down and thus lowering the paper she was holding too—"you barely notice it because one minute, you're home, and the other, poof! You're just here. Same thing at the end of the day. What do you do when you go home?"

"I'm always so tired . . ."

She was out of spiritual energy at the end of a long day interacting with so many people and objects. I'd never seen a ghost last that long. Her strength amazed me. "You don't think you do anything. But in reality, you disappear and recharge however it is that ghosts do that wherever it is they do it. Then the next day is the same."

"But I come to work every day. I talk to customers, my coworkers."

"Do you?"

She tilted her head down and looked up at me. Mumbling, she answered, "I'm talking to you right now."

"I've been able to see ghosts since childhood. I don't count."

She handed me back the flyer as footfalls sounded against the wooden steps on the opposite side of the deck from the ramp.

"Hello, there, Ms. Sunevall. Sorry I took a few minutes longer than expected. Name's Zach. Nice to meet you." He stuck his hand out, and we shook.

"Nice to meet you as well. No worries about the time. It's a nice day, and I just love it here, which is really what brings me here to talk to you."

Behind me, Cindy said, "He didn't even acknowledge his own mother . . ." Maybe before she would have written the slight off. Now she had to be seeing it with new understanding.

"Yes, you said you wanted to take part in the memorial event for my mother if you could. You're a baker, right?"

"Sure am. I own Suncraft Bakery in Heartwood Hollow."

"Ah, yes." He lifted his head slowly before bringing it back down. "Heard good things. Tried a few good things, too, at your tree festival. We had a cider stand."

"I remember." I'd stopped by to get a cup. "It's my favorite cider. Always so fresh. But I must admit, the floats are my favorite." Cider, ginger ale, and soft-serve vanilla ice cream. The combination was perfect.

"We'll have to make sure you get one before you leave."

I smiled. "Your wife said the same."

Zach laughed, but behind me, Cindy wasn't laughing. "You should tell her how it was my idea for the floats."

With her statement, Zach sobered. "My mom created the drink. Figured she could make something better than the root beer floats we kids could get from the corner store. They had a soda counter along the back."

Huh. Cindy had spoken, but I was sure her son hadn't heard her. Not out loud anyway.

"Well, she had fabulous taste."

Cindy chuckled. "Thank you."

Zach smiled fondly. "It was an instant hit at the snack bar."

"She sounds like a smart woman," I continued, hoping if I kept him talking, it would get through to Cindy that she was truly dead. His seemingly responding to her comment could have cast doubt in her mind about her death.

"She was. The best mom too. I always planned to take over the cider mill, but I never expected to be doing it so soon and without her here."

"I'm sorry for your loss. Your wife said she passed in her sleep. Was she ill?"

"Nope. Perfect health. Freak aneurysm."

That could certainly attribute to her waking up dead the next morning not knowing she wasn't alive. Sick people knew they were sick, so it wasn't a shock to them when they passed from their condition. But in healthy people, if they didn't cross over right away or realize what had happened, the fact of their death took a bit more convincing. Like now.

"Oh, that's terrible."

He nodded.

"But I'm right here," Cindy said.

Zach sighed. "Sometimes I feel like she's right here with me."

Again he was responding to something she'd said without hearing it. Her energy must have been powerful. No wonder she hadn't noticed being ignored while she was at work. She could speak something and the idea for it would come to whoever she was talking to. Wicked impressive.

"It's nice that you do this event in her memory. It sounds like a lot of fun. Well, most of it. I'm not much of a runner. The floating apples are more my speed."

That brought a smile to Zach's face. "It's fun for the whole family. Now, what brings you here today? You know we have our own stand that sells sweets, so I don't know quite where you'd fit in."

Chuckling, I said, "I am very familiar with your sweets. But you concentrate so much on the cider with your cider donuts or your apples in their entirety with the apple crisp, apple turnovers, pies, and let's not forget your apple fries. But I'm thinking something more like this. I pulled out a container I'd been carrying in my bag.

Zach looked with interest as I popped the top, revealing a sampling of my apple treats.

"This here is my apple brownie, made with your Cortland apples." And this time, they lacked oils from the pierogi lasagna, a vast improvement over my impromptu sandwich. They'd been a hit at the shower.

Zach broke off a piece then popped it into his mouth. He chewed slowly, letting it sit. After a moment, he closed his eyes. "Mmm . . . That's delicious."

"Thank you, I'm glad you think so." I handed him a cookie. "This is an iced-oatmeal cookie. Each batch uses a half cup of applesauce. I used your Fuji apples this time, but I bet they'd be great with your Paula Reds."

As he took this one, I told him I could also do an apple-sauce cookie variety with chocolate chips, and plain sugar cookies with apple-themed designs.

His mom studied me. "She's got good ideas, Zach. Shame to just use her at only one event."

I wanted to smile at Cindy's comment, but I didn't want to seem too eager in her son's eyes. Not everyone wanted to be watched while they ate.

Zach swallowed. "You know? I think I'd like to do one better. You can absolutely have a table at the memorial event for my mom, but how about you start baking some of these things for our snack bar all season long? We'll put a little standing card up next to the treats to say they were from you, and your business cards can go in our partner tourist area for anyone to grab."

I hadn't been expecting this. My baking had been an

excuse to come and get more information about Cindy's death. But expansions and partnerships seemed to be the third theme of my summer . . . behind helping my couples with ghosts interfering with their relationships and accepting my witchy identity. Why did big things always come in threes?

I'd been studying with Sarah and knew a little bit about the significance of the number, mostly about maiden, mother, crone. I thought back to the last time I was at the cider mill, when Gram gave me a numerology lesson. Gram had taught me more about the few numbers we'd covered then than the books had so far. No doubt she would have more to say about this too.

"So, what do you say?" Zach prompted. "We'd love to have you as a community partner, and it would bring in some extra revenue for you, of course. We'd never expect this to be one-sided."

One-sided . . . That got me thinking. I broke out into a smile. "Rather than money, how about we trade?"

He quirked his head to the side. "I'm listening."

I explained to him my sitting area at the bakery and my desire to provide customers with things to drink, then further expressed how I was limited so as not to compete with other businesses, ruling out most coffees and teas. "What if I sold your cider? Like you for me, I'd put a little card on the cooler window and provide business cards."

"I like your thinking, Joanie. That sounds like a great idea. A wonderful start to a new partnership. How about we go grab some floats and draw up some paperwork in my office?" He stuck out his hand. I took it and we shook, sealing the deal.

"Sounds good to me."

We stood, and as we walked back to his office, Zach

radioed the snack bar for two floats. By the time we were sitting down in the chairs, one of the servers from the stand had arrived with our drinks and a side of apple fries for each of us. Cindy had followed us in, and she hung out behind her son, looking mildly put off that he had taken the cushy desk chair.

We sipped and looked over the terms of Bug Creek Cider Mill's typical partnership agreement, modifying it where needed to reflect our trade of goods rather than compensation for my baking. As Zach typed up a contract tailored to us, he told me more about the history of the cider mill and his family. It was a long story tied to that of Heartwood Hollow and the Dunmores. The Dunmores got to the area first, setting up their mill on the larger and more powerful Mill River. Zach's family, the Bugs, had been among some of the original Dunmore lumber mill workers, and when the Dunmores began leasing tracts of land so others could set up mills of their own, the family jumped at the chance. The cider mill was founded on a smaller creek of one of Mill River's larger tributaries to feed the loggers. Soon their families joined them, and a little hamlet grew between the wood mill and the cider mill. As loggers cleared the land of the forest, others replaced the pines and oaks with the apple orchard. The cider mill continued to grow, even after the lumber and textile mills in the area closed. Today the cider mill and its store was one of the biggest employers of people living in the hamlet, followed by the hospital in Heartwood Hollow.

Zach's printer flared to life, causing Cindy to jump. A moment later, it spit out a piece of paper with such force the paper overshot the cradle and fluttered to the floor.

"Always hated that thing," Cindy commented as her son reached over to pick it up from the floor saying, "Mom always hated that thing."

I took the paper from Zach's outstretched hand. "It gets quite the distance."

He laughed. "It's a pain sometimes if you forget what it can do and it's printing out multiple pages. Gotta number your pages or else good luck to you. But it's nice and fast and still works, so there's no reason to replace it."

"I can appreciate that. Shows good business sense."

"I never like to waste something if it can still be useful. Some places would have replaced their cider presses in their entirety by now, but we still have parts on ours that are original to the mill. It's one of the draws for tourists who are excited to see the cider being made right in front of them."

"I taught him well," Cindy quipped, a satisfied and loving smile on her face.

"I'd like to think I'm making my mom proud."

Looking at Zach, I replied, "I'm sure she is."

He pointed to the paper in my hand. "I'll let you look that over at your leisure, but it includes everything we talked about here. If you have any questions, drop me a line, and if not, you can come back anytime so we can ink this deal. I'm looking forward to what I hope will be a beneficial partnership to us both. Kicking it off at my mom's memorial seems like the right move to make. Bring you right on into the Bug family."

"Thank you so much for meeting me today. This is more than I had hoped for, and I am so excited for it."

We stood and shook hands once more.

"Can I see you out?" Zach asked.

"Oh, that won't be necessary. I still have some shopping to do. I can't go home empty-handed."

He nodded. "All right, then. You have a good day now, Joanie. It was nice meeting you."

"You too." I folded the copy of the contract, then placed it into my bag before opening the office door to a swell of noise.

CHAPTER 29

The cider mill store was much busier now. The checkout area was crowded with people. It made no sense for me to try to weave my way in the opposite direction of everyone. So instead, after giving a quick wave to Nora, I exited the store, then went around the front so I could get back in using the main entrance.

Cindy was waiting for me in her usual spot. "I used to think you were my favorite customer. Then you told me I was dead, so that might kick you down a few notches." She cracked a small smile.

"How are you doing with everything? Are you starting to believe me?"

"Well, considering I was just in the office with my son, and now I'm talking to you with no memory of how I got here or how I beat you to this spot despite all the customers . . ." She sighed. "I'm starting to."

"I'm sorry. I've seen this a time or two before. It's usually the result of an unexpected death, which yours was, but I've never seen someone quite like you." I motioned to a bench sitting in front of the mill store away from the entrance. "Why don't we go sit and talk? That way people won't think I'm talking to myself, or worse, the wall."

She nodded, and the two of us headed toward the bench made out of an old wooden barrel cut in half. The two halves were placed side by side, the widest portion down, and three wood planks on top of that formed the bench seating.

"I meant what I said," I began once we were settled. "You're not like other ghosts."

"Why, because I can talk to you?"

I stifled a chuckle. "No. That's been happening to me a lot lately. I mean someone as powerful as you. You're not quite bound to a place, nor are you bound to a particular person, nor are you here for a reason beyond just not realizing you were dead. I've seen two out of the three together, but you are something else. Not to mention you fooled me for nearly five years. I'm not perfect with my abilities, but for someone who's been doing this for most of her life and knows the signs, you surprised me."

She seemed pleased by this.

But I wasn't done. "Then there's the whole you can talk to other people thing. It's not just me you've been communicating with all this time."

"I don't know what you saw, but I can't talk to anyone."

I quirked an eyebrow at that statement. "Until you learned you were dead, you thought you could."

She opened her mouth as if to speak but closed it again.

"You saw how your son was repeating what you said. That's what has been going on all along, hasn't it?"

"I always thought they were just repeating me to confirm they'd heard me right. Sometimes they'd come back with something else as if countering what I'd said." She turned to watch a family walk by on the way to see some of the antique farming equipment at the far end of the parking lot. I wondered if she'd done it so that I wouldn't be speaking as they passed and thus wouldn't look like I was talking to myself. I appreciated the consideration.

When they were likely out of earshot, her gaze returned to me. "Does that sound possible?"

"For the last five years, you've been asserting your influence on anyone you thought you were talking to. You'd suggest something, and if they liked it, they repeated it as if they were agreeing with you. If they didn't like it, they'd come back with something else. Do it enough times and it almost feels like a conversation. It's like you've been planting ideas in their heads. Ideas that, to them, feel like they've popped up out of nowhere, but it's been you all along."

"I think I understand."

"Take today for example. You put the idea of partnering with me into your son's head. He seemed on board for my coming to your memorial with my brownies and cookies, but who knows if he would have partnered with me beyond that if not for your suggestion."

She smiled that proud smile I'd seen earlier. "Oh, he's a bright boy, I'm sure he would have."

"Eventually, sure, but maybe not after the first bite. He doesn't know me. You, however, have been talking with me for the last four-plus years, suggesting this and that to try, and I've told you plenty of things about my bakery and what I've made with the foods you sell in the store. You were on board right away and made that known to your son without him realizing."

"And all ghosts can't do that?"

I shook my head.

She sat quietly for a moment, staring off at somewhere I didn't see, her expression wistful. I couldn't imagine how she felt. Learning she was not only dead but that she was uniquely dead all in one day. It had to be a lot to take in, especially after five years.

"I just thought the new employees were less talkative. My son more busy as he took on additional responsibilities. I never imagined it would be that they didn't talk to me because they couldn't see or hear me. Or that the added responsibilities my son had were because I wasn't around to do them anymore. We'd always said he'd run the place one day, and it had been our plan for him to do more and more so that I could take it easy and do what I liked best, talking with customers." She sighed once more. "So I'm really dead, huh?"

"Afraid so," I replied, nodding.

"But why am I here? I don't have unfinished business or any of that nonsense you see in movies about why ghosts are around."

I reached for her hand, and she let me take it. "Sometimes it just happens. Now that you know, nothing is keeping you here. I can help you cross over if you want. You don't have to stay. I'm sure you have others waiting for you."

Her mouth tightened into a straight line as she shook her head. "While I would like to see them again, I just learned after five years that I'm dead. I don't know if I'm ready yet."

I squeezed her hand. "I understand. It's a lot to take in. You've had five years of existence like this, and no one can expect you to let it go all in one day. If you ever do decide it's time, it's looking like I'll be around even more than before. I can help you if that's what you'd like."

A slight smile formed on her face. "Thank you." Her gaze fell to our hands. "Now, how is this possible? I always thought—"

"That ghosts weren't solid?"

"Yeah, that's what all the movies have always shown.

They can walk right through anything, even people. So how . . . just, how?"

I shrugged. "You can do all sorts of things like that if you want, but it's not your natural state." I told her about how John's grandfather, Dale, had paced between my shop and the kitchen by going through the door rather than opening it, preventing anyone from seeing the door move seemingly on its own.

Another family passed by us, this one with two toddlers. They waved at us when we smiled at them.

As they walked away, Cindy frowned.

"Those waves were for you too, you know."

She shook her head.

"I'm serious. Little kids can see ghosts. It's just something they can do until they grow out of it."

"Or not, in your case."

"True. I never grew out of it. But that doesn't change the fact those kids could see you. Had I not been here, they still would have waved at you. Their parents would likely have chalked it up to excitement or an imaginary friend or something."

She brightened. "I've always loved the kids who came here. It makes me happy to know that they can still see me. Oh, how I'd so been looking forward to grandkids. Thank you for telling me."

"You're absolutely welcome. I'm glad I could bring a smile back to your face."

"You know what will keep it there for a while?" She stood, then extended her hand to me. "Let's go shopping."

"Now that sounds like a good idea to me."

We went back into the cider mill store, and together we loaded up my cart as we'd been doing since I first started coming here. I didn't know if Cindy would ever want to make her final transition to whatever came after death, but I'd not make her leave. Sometimes my ability wasn't about helping a ghost cross over, sometimes it was about giving them a bit of normalcy. And for the hour we shopped, that's what I did for Cindy, and for now, that was what mattered.

CHAPTER 30

I stood at my mirror holding up two dresses. "Which one, Saffy?"

I watched her reflection as she stood up and stretched. When she settled back down, her gaze was on the cyan-colored dress. It had been a while since it had last come out of my closet. I was sure I'd worn it at a shower a couple summers back, but I couldn't remember if it had been baby or bridal. Didn't matter. I loved this one because of how it played up my eyes.

"Good choice, thanks."

She plopped her head back down, letting it and both front paws hang over the edge of the bed.

"Looks like you have your night planned out, huh?"

She let out an audible yawn but didn't move otherwise.

Me, I didn't know what the plan was for tonight. I'd been told to dress comfortably, and when I pressed Ken further, asking if this were a shorts and sneakers date or a dress and heels date, he said a summer dress would be fine but that I'd want to skip the heels. Considering my penchant for klutzi-ness, I didn't know why I had even offered to wear them.

Probably because they were still at the top of my closet after Chelsea and David's wedding.

I quickly got dressed, then applied minimal makeup. As I headed downstairs, Saffy charged in front of me, and she beat me to the kitchen by several feet. So much for that catnap.

The late afternoon sun was streaming through the window as I entered the room, the fluorite in the window boldly showing its bands of color thanks to the backlighting. Out of all the crystals, this one was my favorite. Gram had said it was for neutralizing negative energy and stress, as well as a few other things, and in the research I'd been doing with Sarah, I'd learned that fluorite was also used to help improve balance and coordination, both things that sometimes eluded me. I'd thought about buying a piece of fluorite jewelry so I'd always have it on me as a safeguard but hadn't gotten around to it yet.

Saffy tapped her bowl, adding a quick meow for emphasis. I grabbed her crunchies out of the cupboard, then poured some into her empty bowl.

"There you go," I said, resealing the bag. A few minutes later, I added a spoon of wet food on top.

As I was putting the remainder of her wet cat food can in the fridge, the doorbell rang.

"You have a good rest of your dinner. I'll see you later tonight."

Ken's smiling face greeted me as I pulled the door open, his hands behind his back. "It is so good to see you."

It felt like I hadn't seen him in ages, even though it had only been since the potluck. Though, since we'd gotten back together, the few days was one of the longest stretches of time we'd gone without seeing one another. I pushed the screen door open for him since he hadn't grabbed it himself. "How are you doing?"

He stepped into the living room. "Better now that I'm here. It's been an afternoon."

"Is everything okay?"

"Yeah. Nothing to worry about. I'll tell you over dinner. But first—" He leaned toward me and gave me a kiss, sending heat into my face. I'd missed this. But something was off. He wasn't touching me. Usually he'd at least wrap an arm around me or touch my cheek.

"What's behind your back?" I asked as the kiss ended, quirking an eyebrow at him.

His smile lit up. "This." He brought his hands in front of him, revealing a great big bouquet of flowers. But they were unlike any bouquet I'd gotten before. "They're paper. Specially made for you out of pages from various cookbooks."

"It's amazing!" And hopefully something that Saffy won't eat. I took the bouquet from him and studied the paper flowers. Pages had been cut to form petal shapes that were then gathered and curled to form roses. Others were folded to be angular daisy-like flowers or frayed and piled into bulbous puffs. Accenting them all were sprigs of buttons and pearls. The whole bouquet was wrapped with a piece of pretty yellow cotton fabric.

"I was going for something a bit more cat proof, knowing how she likes to get a hold of them."

"Where did you get these?"

As I ducked back into the kitchen for a vase, Ken explained, "I found a girl online who makes all sorts of crafts. I was searching for flower alternatives, and when I saw this, I knew it was perfect. I even got to specify the type of books I wanted the flowers made from. Ended up having to get Ivy a few single flowers. Since Matt gave her carnations the other day, she keeps talking about getting more."

"Well, I love them. And I bet my cousin would too. She's a

craft witch and can put spells in the things she makes." I'd walked all around the living room and had yet to find a suitable spot. The bouquet was a little too wide for my mantel or else I would have put it as part of my altar space. Instead, I pulled out one of the roses from what I deemed to be the back of the bouquet and set it there instead. "I'll be right back. I think I have a good spot in my room."

I returned a moment later after placing the vase on my nightstand behind my alarm clock. Now it would be one of the first things I saw every morning.

Walking back to Ken, I said, "Thank you so much for the lovely surprise." Once I reached him, I wrapped my arms over his shoulders and stood on my toes to give him a quick kiss.

This time, no longer trying to hide a surprise behind his back, he pulled me toward him. "I kept her business card so that you could have it. Maybe you can pass it along to your cousin," he said once he let me go as he steadied me on my feet. "Are you ready to leave?"

"Just need to throw my shoes on." I opened my closet door, then pulled out my yellow thin-canvas sneakers. They seemed to be a happy medium for whatever we were going to be doing. Not heels or even ballet flats, so I could still get around comfortably and do something active, but not so casual that they didn't go with my dress or would stand out somewhere on the nicer side. I slipped my feet into them, then bent to tie the laces. Straightening, I looked into his warm green eyes and said, "Ready."

As Ken approached the parking lot a mile past the town golf course along the river and turned into it, I grew more and more excited. The Last Hole was a restaurant situated in the middle of a private golf course . . . a miniature golf course. The restaurant was, fittingly, part of the last hole. Its floor consisted of a thick layer of plexiglass, and underneath it, one could see the elaborate system golfers had to blindly shoot their balls into. Slanted so all balls came out, the giant pegboard was dizzying to watch as balls bounced back and forth between the pins that would determine where a player's ball would roll out on the green. If you got a hole in one, you got free dessert.

Usually family-friendly given the location, one Saturday night a month, the restaurant went upscale to cater to a different clientele. Adults only. This extended through the whole complex, including the putt-putt. Any adult group could access the miniature golf course during the evening, but the restaurant was by reservation only. From what I heard, it booked out quickly each summer. There were only so many Saturday nights during the season. I'd been mini-golfing several times over the years here with friends, but I'd never been to the restaurant on one of these famed Saturday nights.

"I can't believe we're here!" I nearly squealed with excitement as we got out of the car. "How on earth did you get a reservation?"

Ken smiled at me. "I may have booked us a table back in May after seeing it advertised when I brought Ivy and a couple of her friends. I know you're not the most athletically inclined, but I took a chance hoping you'd like it. Based on your reaction, I guessed well?"

"Really well. Miniature golf might be the one sport I'm good at."

Ken took my hand, and we crossed the parking lot, and after checking in at the entrance where we'd typically get our golf ball and club, we walked along the path that wove through the putt-putt course. It was already fairly crowded with couples on their date nights, and laughter mixed with the sounds of putters tapping golf balls and the occasional plunk into the water hazard.

"Our dinner reservation was on the earlier side, so I figured we could eat first, then golf, and then grab dessert."

"Just in case we hit a hole in one?" It wasn't easy. In addition to the free dessert, those who did it earned near-perpetual bragging rights.

He chuckled. "You never know."

We were seated at a table overlooking the back side of the course, and beyond that was the river. It was probably one of the best views in the restaurant. The two of us chatted as the waiter took our order for drinks and an appetizer, me filling Ken in on how things had been going since Gram left. I was telling him about hiring Brittni when the waiter returned for our dinner order. By the time dinner arrived, I was giving him the exciting news about the bakery's newest partnership with the cider mill.

"That's all great," Ken said as his steak dinner was set in front of him. "The partnership sounds like a terrific opportunity."

"I think it will be. And the idea all started thanks in part to one of Ivy's brownies."

Ken's smile didn't reach his eyes. "She'll be happy to hear that." He poked at an asparagus spear as the waiter walked away.

I reached across the table and grabbed Ken's hand. "Is everything okay? You said you were going to tell me what was bugging you at dinner. Now, here we are. Is it Ivy? Your demeanor changed as soon as her name came up. Is she okay? Is it something to do with your custody?" There hadn't been an update on that in a while. Had Ivy's mother done something?

He shook his head. "It's nothing. I'm making it out to be more than it is. It's just that it happened right before picking you up, so I haven't figured out what to do yet." He smiled, some of the warmth and charm returning.

"Well, whatever it is, I'm here for you."

Ken squeezed my hand. "Thanks. Know any good daytime babysitters? I know Lichelle's out with her shifts at Double Aitch."

"What happened to Heather?" She'd been sitting for Ken during the day throughout the summer.

"Nothing." He released my hand. "But with school starting up again soon, so are sports. And varsity soccer has practice Wednesday afternoons, leaving me short a few hours. I've already moved my schedule around to accommodate the summer fundraising events as well as making sure I'm there for as many of Ivy's larger activities as possible. Her games and such. I don't know if they'll like me shifting more."

I gave him a hopeful smile. "Doesn't hurt to ask. And even if they say no, something will turn up. It's only one afternoon."

"Thanks." Ken cut into his steak. "Sorry for bringing down the mood."

"Don't worry about it." I popped a roasted brussels sprout into my mouth. "If something's ever bothering you, I want to know about it. We'll think of something."

He cheered up after that, seemingly relieved that it was off his chest. We finished our delicious dinner, then after Ken paid, our waiter handed us each a golf ball and putter.

"Good luck," he said as I looked at the purple ball in my hand before pivoting on his heels to check on one of his other tables.

Ken stuck his elbow out. "Shall we?"

I looped my arm through his, and we strolled out to the miniature golf course.

My lack of practice was evident as we progressed from hole to hole, but Ken wasn't much better, and I didn't think he was holding back. But it was the perfect activity, full of laughter, some of it so hard we had to lean into one another to hold ourselves up. I hadn't laughed like that in ages, but when my ball skipped up and over an obstacle, then landed on the fairway of the next hole, everyone laughed, even the people around us.

"I swear I used to be better at this," I said as Ken teed off, still chuckling.

We watched the ball as it rolled down the slight incline, bouncing between the brick borders to the tiny path that funneled the balls over the small water hazard that most balls had no problem traversing unless they hit that one spot in just the right way . . .

Plop!

"I used to think I was pretty good at this too," Ken replied as he went to fetch his ball from the water. "Where do you want me to place this?"

"After the bridge. I won't make you try to do that again."

He nodded, then stepped over the water hazard to the other side of the course.

"It was Wednesdays, you said, right? That Ivy needed to be watched."

Ken squatted, placing the ball a putter's length away from the brick wall. "Yeah."

"Why don't you have Heather drop Ivy off at the bakery?

She can hang out there until you're done for the day, or I can bring her home with me if you won't get out in time."

He leaned on his putter. "I couldn't impose on you like that."

I sized up my shot and took a swing. The ball took a similar course as Ken's but fortunately didn't end up in the water, instead coming out the other side a few feet from the hole. I passed him on my way to the ball. "You didn't. I offered."

"Are you sure? This is Ivy we're talking about."

"Wednesdays are the slowest days in the shop. We can handle it. I'll just load her up on sugar for you, that's all." I tapped my ball, sending it only a few inches away from the hole. The next shot sunk it.

Ken pulled the scorecard and a pencil out of his pocket. "Four."

"I'm not saying you have to take me up on my offer, but it is an option. We could always try it for a week while you find other alternatives. Or better yet, why don't you ask Ivy?"

Ken hit his ball, getting it in the hole. Somehow, even with hitting the water hazard, his score tied mine. "Okay. Let's try it. She's enjoying all her baking lately. She might just love this."

"I think she's going to surprise you."

"*You* surprise me." He reached into the hole, then stood, holding my ball out to me. "You're something else, you know that? I don't know how many people would date a single dad going through custody stuff, let alone offer to watch said dad's kid at their place of work. How'd I get so lucky?"

Taking the ball from him, I giggled. Heat had already rushed to my face. "I'm the lucky one. Who else would have given a girl a shot when their first interaction involved her being covered in salad?"

He belted out a laugh before pulling me toward him and kissing me on the forehead. "I'm really glad you're a klutz sometimes."

We moved on to the next hole, and as if fate wanted to prove a point, I tripped on the brick wall dividing the green from the path. We dissolved into another fit of laughter that more than made up for the fact neither of us won a free dessert at the last hole. Instead, we bought our dessert and took it to the benches they had along the river. The berry mascarpone napoleon looked too good to pass up.

Ken walked me back to my door and said goodnight on my porch, never noticing the one thing that was amiss. But I saw it right away. A tiny black cauldron sat on the table next to the swing.

As soon as Ken drove away, I darted back outside to pick up the cauldron. If Ken had noticed it, he probably thought it was mine. It was actually kind of cute. Plain for the most part, but one side had the phases of the moon stamped into it. The empty little cauldron was the third gift I'd gotten from someone I didn't know who knew I was a witch. If Sarah was right, it was from someone in the Moonshadow Coven here in Heartwood Hollow, the one I'd likely be joining soon if I found it to be the right fit. I hoped Sarah was right. It limited who could be giving these to me, but this was a strange way to be acknowledged by anyone.

I carried the cauldron inside, and Saffy immediately came up to investigate it. "Sometimes I wish you really could talk, then you could tell me who dropped this off while I was gone." I set the cauldron down on the couch so she could continue sniffing it, then headed upstairs to change.

Although it was late enough for me to go to bed, I was too happily wired from the date and felt I should study a little bit.

Tea was required for both calming down and reading, so once I was in pajamas, I went back downstairs. Saffy had returned to her spot, leaving the cauldron where I'd placed it only tipped on its side. She must have deemed it safe and hopefully ghost-free.

After making my tea, and giving Saffy a snack after she charged into the kitchen demanding one, I returned to the living room. But before I could get comfortable, I had to do something with the mini cauldron. Whereas my paper flower bouquet wouldn't fit on the mantel, I spotted a suitable spot for the cauldron. Behind my chunk of amethyst and next to my rose quartz sphere. Then I put the smudge stick made out of colorful flower petals that Gram had left inside it. Doing so freed up more room. Maybe I'd find a home for all of the crystals still in the dirt after all.

As I stood back from the mantel to take in my altar, I thought of my mystery presents. In a way, the things I'd been given over the last few days reminded me of the suitcase Gram had left me. Although the witch's kit contained a wealth of objects, strangely, there had been no pendants, altar cloths, or mini cauldrons. There were no such things as coincidences.

Like the gifts from the ladies in Gram's circle, the gifts that had appeared at my doorstep seemed harmless, even useful. It all begged the question why was all the mystery surrounding who had given them to me and why necessary?

CHAPTER 31

A whole week had passed since Gram's visit, and now it was time to uncover the crystals in my garden. It was not as bright this evening as it had been under the full moon, but the air was just as warm.

Although Sarah couldn't touch the crystals, she'd come over to help me dig them up. At the very least, she could hold the bowl I'd be using to carry them inside. After taking Saturday night off so I could have my date with Ken, Sarah and I had spent our evenings hanging out and getting to know one another more, both as witch and familiar, and as friends. I'd always considered her to be one of my friends, but whereas Steph and Courtney and I had fallen into the routine of girls' nights and lunches, Sarah and I hadn't ever done that.

"I was already pushing you about the witchy stuff at work," Sarah said when I asked her the second night she came over, "and I didn't want to push you too far too fast by inserting myself elsewhere in your life. Did I expect you to take over four years to get to this point, no, but I had to strike a balance. But I'm glad we can start hanging out now."

At least for now, hanging out meant going through all the books Gram had left me plus those that Sarah had brought. We'd have dinner delivered to give us as much time as possible to study, but tonight was Monday, and Matt was coming over.

Matt was used to me having other people here for our Monday dinners. Ken and Ivy were our usual companions, and they were again tonight, but Matt didn't bat an eye when I'd told him Sarah was joining us.

"You're going to need a bigger table soon if you keep adding folks," he said with a chuckle as he followed me into the kitchen and spotted the special arrangement to fit everyone. I'd had to pull my desk chair out from the side room to use at the table. It was only large enough to fit four comfortably, so we had to squeeze in a bit, but I had a feeling Ivy wouldn't mind sitting next to her favorite person.

"Don't worry," I replied, opening my cupboard doors so he could grab out the plates. Setting the table was his job on Mondays. "There will still be plenty of leftovers for you to take home."

He let out an exaggerated relieved sigh before smiling at me, his hazel eyes twinkling and the crow's feet settling deeply at the corners. But then he grew serious. "You know I don't come only for the food, right?"

"Of course I do, but that doesn't mean I'm going to stop giving you food just because there are more of us sharing a meal." I spun around to face him and put a hand on my hip. "How long did the potluck leftovers last you?"

"Got some of them frozen. I like my food, but even I couldn't eat that much. I'm not a strapping lad anymore like your man friend is." He pulled down a stack of plates and placed them on the counter, then eyed the slow cooker a few feet away. "It smells good in here. What are we having tonight?"

"Pulled barbeque chicken sandwiches." I opened a cupboard above me, then reached into it before pulling out a bag of rolls I had picked up from the Corner Bakery yesterday in preparation for tonight. Zeke still hadn't found anyone to work for him in the shop and had to scale back some of his bread offerings again. He'd seemed tired when I talked to him, but he remained hopeful that it was only a temporary setback. He said he had a bit of a way to go to recover from his gruff attitude these past few years that spooked anyone from working with him. I hoped he'd find someone soon. Rested Zeke and tired Zeke were very different people.

"Oh, doesn't that sound good."

"Ken and Ivy are bringing some pasta salad, and Sarah is bringing potato salad." When I hired her, Sarah claimed she couldn't bake or cook. So when she offered to bring something tonight, I had assumed she meant store-bought but was pleasantly surprised when she said homemade. "I don't know about Ken and Ivy's, but Sarah's making hers."

"If it's her grandmother's recipe, then it's a good one." He opened a lower cupboard where I kept my napkins. We'd need extra of those tonight.

"You knew Sarah's grandparents?"

"Well, I still know Vince, her dad's dad, and Evelyn, her mom's mom. Did you forget how small Heartwood Hollow is? We all grew up together."

"Huh," I replied, reaching into my utensil drawer to grab out my meat hooks and some tongs. "Guess I did."

"Anyone who's been here long enough pretty much knows everyone. Especially when you're my age, even if it's just as so and so's grandchild. You'll have the whole town figured out eventually. That's just the way small towns work."

He chuckled. "Henny said that's what made the gossip so good."

Seemed gossip circles in Heartwood Hollow hadn't changed much over the years. I'd tried to avoid it, but I'd come to accept it as part of my life in recent months. It certainly made finding some things out easy, like where someone was if I was looking for them. But gossip sometimes complicated matters too. Like when everyone had a theory as to what had happened years ago in the north woods. Or who mysterious strangers in the neighborhood were twenty-five years ago. Then there were the rumors about me that had swirled for years . . . although those turned out to be true.

"There does seem to be a lot of that here," I finally agreed, wondering if he was right in his statement that I'd have Heartwood Hollow figured out someday. I could only hope so. The town that had once seemed so normal—ghosts aside, but that was *my* normal—kept revealing new secrets and mysteries, regularly surprising me. Dryads, merpeople, fairies, trolls, witches, and now familiars. Of course, I seemed to be the biggest mystery of them all, but hopefully everything Sarah and I had been studying over the last week would start to help me in that regard.

The front screen door opened slowly. Without seeing who had entered, I knew it was Sarah. Beyond the fact I'd grown accustomed to how she opened the door, which vastly differed from Ivy's rushed opening, the energy making its way inside now was eager but much calmer than that of a seven-year-old. Ivy's excitement over seeing Matt at Monday night dinners was palpable. It coursed through the house as soon as she entered.

I'd always been able to figure out who had come into the bakery, too, once I got to know them for the same reason. Was that another power or just part of one? Or perhaps it was from being a kitchen witch, a skill I had strengthened over the years to make the bakery feel warm and welcoming to everyone.

"Hello!" Sarah called from the living room.

"We're in here," I called back, lifting the lid off the slow cooker, the steam from the chicken rising in a large puff.

Sarah stepped into the room, holding a large white plastic bowl with a blue lid. "Is there anywhere special you want me to put this?"

"How about right here on the counter." I pointed to an empty spot next to the plates Matt had set out. "Ken and Ivy should be here shortly."

She set the container down, then gave Matt a quick hug. "Good to see you again."

"Likewise. I rarely see you kids now that you're all grown up and not coming to your grandparents' house to swim in the pool."

"Oh, that was so much fun. They threw the best parties." She cast me a look and a mischievous grin. "Maybe Joanie should get a pool. That potluck reminded me so much of back then."

Laughter bubbled out of me. First Ken had said it wouldn't be a bad idea if I got a fire pit, which I was actually considering, and now I was supposed to get a pool? In addition to the garden I wanted to put in, where would I put everything? Fortunately, I knew the pool comment was only a joke. Mostly. "If you want to bring one of those inflatable kiddie pools over sometime, feel free. But I'm not blowing it up."

"Oh, I'm sure I can find someone who will," Sarah replied at the same time the screen door swung open once more. At my look of panic that Ivy would hear something about the possibility of a pool, Sarah added, "I'm kidding!"

Footsteps that could only be from Ivy thundered onto the hardwood floor and across the living room. Moments later, she popped into the doorway, a full grin spread across her face. What was it they said? Small size, big personality? That was all Ivy.

She launched her tiny body across the short distance and flung her arms around Matt, who had already braced himself in anticipation of her ginormous hug. "Matty! I missed you!"

"It's good to see you too, Miss Ivy. How was your week?"

As she dove into recounting everything that she'd done over the last several days, Ken walked into the house.

"She was so excited to get here today, she ran up ahead," he said, explaining why she had come in by herself. Not that I minded. She was welcome here anytime. Saffy still wasn't too sure of her, especially on days like this when she charged into the house, but somehow Saffy always managed to find herself upstairs before Ivy came. On Mondays, she took her cue to leave when Matt arrived after a quick hello to him.

I rose on my toes slightly to kiss him hello, then took the pasta salad from his hands. "That's all right. We knew you were on your way, and you knew where she was going."

"Besides, if you try to keep up all the time with this one, you'll be run ragged by the end of each day," Matt added before looking at the little girl who had released him from her hug but was still wrapped around him, leaning into his side. "Isn't that right?"

Ivy looked up at Matt, beaming. "Yup!"

"Well, now that you're all here," I started, setting the pasta salad next to the potato salad, "I say let's eat."

We spent the next few minutes serving ourselves, then shared our meal, falling into easy conversation and lots of laughter. My later activities with Sarah weighed gently on my mind, but that was nothing new. There was always a corner of my thoughts occupied by witchy things now.

An hour passed with seconds—and for some of us thirds, Ivy loved the chicken—as we talked and ate. But eventually the meal was over, and it was time to clean up.

As Sarah and Ken helped clear the table and bring the dishes to the sink, I packed take-home containers for everyone while Matt and Ivy continued to chatter away. She'd moved her chair even closer to him and had turned to face him, bringing her feet up under her. Looking at the two of them, I thought back to Matt's comment about knowing Sarah's grandparents and how everyone in Heartwood Hollow at least knew of everyone else in town at his age. That meant he'd known Ken's father, Danny, who had grown up here, as well as his parents, Kate and Edward. I wondered if Matt was telling Ivy stories of her family, of people she never got the chance to know but who would have loved her immensely. Anyone who met Ivy did.

Then somehow their conversation evolved into one about ice cream.

"Daddy, I want ice cream." Ivy turned toward Ken. "Can we go get some?"

Ken and I had already talked about making this an early night so I could do what I needed to with Sarah. This seemed like a good opportunity for them to leave without much fuss, although I wanted ice cream too. We'd made a new batch of birthday cake dough for Lucy over the weekend, which was delicious, but I didn't know what she'd made for her second special flavor of the week. Naturally, I wanted to try it no matter what it was.

"Sure, kiddo. But then it's bath and bed when we get home, okay?"

"Okay." She looked up at Matt before returning her blue-eyed gaze to her father. "Can Matty come too?"

Ken's eyes widened, and his shoulders went up in a small shrug. "I don't see why not, but have you asked him?"

"Matty, will you come get ice cream with us? Please say yes."

"Well, who can refuse a request like that? I'd love to. Unless, of course, you've made something for dessert, Joanie."

"Nothing planned for tonight. Seems like a great excuse for ice cream."

Ivy gazed up at me with a hopeful expression. "Are you coming?"

Even though I had a good reason, it was tempting to give in. "Oh, not tonight."

Before I could say more, Sarah cut in. "She's helping me with something."

I smiled. "But you have a great time and get something good." I hoped that my excitement for her sounded convincing enough, but I was a bit jealous.

Ivy frowned momentarily until the realization that she was still getting ice cream likely kicked in. "Oh, I will." Then she hopped off her chair, turning into quite the little helper in an effort to get out the door and to ice cream even faster.

A little while later, we said our goodnights as I tried to hide my disappointment over not going to get ice cream. But I had important things to do. I closed the door, then turned back to Sarah.

She must have known. After all, half the time, when I went to get a cone for lunch, I was bringing one back for her. "You know, if we're only concentrating on digging up the crystals tonight, we can go join them. The crystals won't take too long, and I know you'd prefer fewer people around to see you doing it. That's only going to happen if it's later."

"Really? You wouldn't mind? I've been taking up so much of your time lately."

Sarah placed a hand on her hip. "As your familiar, I'm here to tell you that's not going to change. If you want ice cream, let's go get ice cream."

She didn't have to tell me again.

CHAPTER 32

W e'd managed to catch Ken, Ivy, and Matt before they were able to leave for the ice cream shop. Matt had delayed them by running his leftovers into his house. So the five of us headed down in my station wagon to Main Street. There, we all topped off our already full stomachs with delicious ice cream. That was the nice thing about ice cream. Its melted goodness filled in all the cracks. There was always room for it.

By the time we got back to my house, night had fully fallen in Heartwood Hollow. Windows in neighboring houses were still illuminated, but porch lights had mostly been turned off. Sarah and I said goodnight to Ken, Ivy, and Matt once more before heading toward the house to get ready for the crystal retrieval.

There in the corner of the screen where the storm door held it in was an envelope. Under the porch light, the golden lettering on it seemed to glow.

I grabbed the envelope as I opened the door. "This is addressed to both of us."

Sarah and I rushed inside, and she spun to face me. "Who's it from?"

"There's no return address." I flipped the envelope over. A golden wax seal held the envelope closed, and pressed into the wax was a familiar symbol of a moon and a tree in shadow. "It's from the Moonshadow Coven."

She peered over my shoulder as I opened the envelope. "That's way fancier than anything I've ever seen from them."

I pulled out a piece of handmade paper. Natural fibers, including some flower petal fragments, were easily visible. I unfolded it. The handwriting inside was written with the same gold ink as the envelope, and it had the same glowy appearance even inside the living room. The message was short.

"Dear Mses. Sunevall and McAlister," I began. "You and your familiar are cordially invited to attend the gathering of the Moonshadow Coven at the next full moon, followed by the inner circle meeting."

I folded the paper. "That's it. It's not signed aside from the coven symbol again."

"That was a lot of buildup for an invitation." Sarah put her hands on her hips.

Slipping the paper back into the envelope, I asked, "What's the inner circle?"

"My grandfather's never said anything about it. But he has to be a part of it. Or at least he was."

"Maybe he's not allowed to. Kinda like a secret society or something." At least in my mind, it would explain the strange way I'd been getting presents from them.

She shrugged. "Do you mind if I bring this to him?"

"Go right ahead." I passed her the envelope, and she slid it into her bag.

"Well, there's nothing we can do about the coven tonight, so shall we head outside?"

I nodded, then peered out the window. Although I was fine with those in the paranormal support group knowing I was a witch—and obviously this inner circle of the Moonshadow Coven was somehow aware of that too—I wasn't ready to confirm the rumors to just anyone who happened to look outside their home at just the right time.

Fortunately, in just the few minutes we'd been inside, several more porch lights had gone off, including Matt's, and some rooms inside houses had gone dark downstairs as ones upstairs turned on with people getting ready for bed.

"Got a bowl," Sarah said, walking back into the living room.

I moved to the front door, then placed my hand on the knob. "Ready?"

"You bet."

We headed outside and to my garden where, over the last week, several crystals had been cleansed by the earth. If the vibrations coming in through my bare feet told me anything, the crystals' energies were in sync with my yard. Gram had said this meant the protection they offered would encompass my entire property and not just my house.

I kneeled on the grass in front of my patch of dirt, thinking of the crystals I was about to dig up and the flowers I hoped to soon put here. A memory of Gram's voice rang through my head about intent and mindfulness, and I pushed aside the thoughts of colorful flowers springing from the ground. That wasn't what I was here for right now.

Crystals.

The day had been hot, but the dirt had cooled as the garden fell into shadow over the afternoon. It had rained yesterday, and beneath the dry surface, the dirt was still damp. I pulled back the soil, revealing a rose quartz sphere.

The next smaller sphere, a tiger's eye, came next. It felt deeper in the ground than I had remembered going. Maybe it had settled. It had rained. I wasn't sure how all of that worked.

The next few were revealed in a similar fashion, and eventually I'd recovered everything from the garden that we'd put there the week before.

Well, everything but one.

I spread my excavation out wider than I thought it had been when we first came out here just in case. It was soon obvious that hadn't been necessary. I didn't know a lot about dirt, but it felt different. Not in terms of energy, that was all the same, but the dirt that had been dug up last week was looser and softer than the compact stuff I was running into now.

"It's not here," I announced, straightening onto my knees.

"What's not?"

I pushed a stray strand of hair behind my ear. "One of the spheres. We're missing one."

"How can you be missing one?"

"I don't know, but I remember this one specifically because it was right before Gram and I talked about cellphone signals after she stopped me from burying the malachite. It was a grayish-black but see-through."

"The smoky quartz?"

"Yeah, that one."

"Well, where could it have gone?" She braced the bowl against her hip. "They don't sprout legs, and last I checked, your magic doesn't make things disappear."

"It would be news to me if it did." Then again when it

came to my magic, almost everything was news to me. "But to answer your question, I have no idea."

"And you're sure it was one you buried?"

"Positive." Possibilities floated through my mind as I filled the hole back in, then tamped the dirt back down. I tried to remember how this spot had looked when we came out here. It was dark, and I hadn't given it much notice. "Could it have gotten dug up?"

"By what, a squirrel?"

"I mean, maybe?" Although the crystal seemed bigger than what a squirrel could carry away.

"Or maybe a dog," Sarah said as if coming to the same realization. Dogs didn't regularly roam the neighborhood, but it happened occasionally. One in particular, Otis, was notorious for escaping his backyard. I'd helped a few times with trying to corral him back home. But what were the odds of him getting out, coming to my house, and digging up just that one stone without anyone noticing? I doubted it was him but didn't rule out the possibility of it being another dog.

I thought back to the screen door from somewhere nearby shutting right as we were walking back into the house that night. I'd written it off as someone letting their dog out. If that dog had seen what we were doing and taken an interest, then maybe it would have dug up the crystal, but no, we would have seen more evidence of that the next morning. The ground hadn't been messed with . . . unless they'd covered their tracks.

"Could the coven have had something to do with this? Someone's been watching me if they were able to make deliveries without me seeing. They would know the significance of all of this."

"No way. It's like you said. They know the significance of all of this. That's why they wouldn't dig up a crystal you were cleansing and charging. That would get their energy all over it. That's not something they'd do."

"I just don't know, Sarah. It was here and now it's not." Forgetting about the dirt all over my hands, I tightened my ponytail. Oh, well. I'd better get used to it if I was going to be doing this regularly as well as starting to garden.

"Wait, what about Ivy?"

"You think Ivy took it?" That possibility made more sense. And I didn't mind her having one of my crystals.

"If she saw it sticking out of the ground, sure. And it rained the other day, so maybe just enough dirt washed away from around it for it to catch her eye. What kid doesn't like shiny rocks? She may not have realized it was important to you."

"Well, she does know I'm a witch."

"She does? You told a seven-year-old before me?" I couldn't tell if the look of shock on her face was real or not.

"It was an in-the-moment decision up in the north woods after she helped me with what was going on up there. Don't worry. She's not going to tell anyone."

If Sarah could have, she would have crossed her arms. Instead, she was stuck holding the bowl of crystals. She raised an eyebrow at me. "How do you know that?"

I swiped my hands together to remove the remaining excess dirt from them, then stood. "We made her something special too. And one of her duties is to keep our secrets."

Her mouth tightened as she considered this, nodding slowly. "That's actually pretty smart. She's a good kid. I'm sure if you ask her about the smoky quartz, she'll give it back. She'll understand."

"Yeah." I thought of the small bag of rocks Gram had given me as a kid. "Maybe I can get her a set of polished stones that she can keep."

As we headed inside, that comment steered our conversation toward those large bins of tumbled rocks that we'd see in gift shops. Then Sarah said something about having gotten hers at the natural history museum on a field trip, and that turned into talking about our favorite trips in school. I'd been to the same museum as a kid. Everyone who grew up in the region went at least once with school. Fortunately, we wouldn't have to go quite so far as the museum to get some polished rocks and crystals. One of the gift shops on Main Street had them. I'd go tomorrow so I could get my crystal back from Ivy.

Sarah and I had veered completely off topic for the night, but we'd accomplished what we'd needed to. Besides, the tangent we went on was exactly what we needed to continue to get to know one another better.

The two of us weren't exactly what someone would picture if they'd been told to imagine a witch and her familiar. But as we sat down to have some tea after giving the crystals new homes around my house, I knew it was a picture I was proud to have in my home.

The next full moon is just around the corner, and the coven is waiting. Don't miss the continuation of Joanie's story in *Muffins and Mediums*.

WHAT'S NEXT?

The next full moon is just around the corner...

After being courted by the local coven, my anticipation over meeting others who could be like me builds. But that person is even closer than I think when someone comes into my bakery asking me for help in finding her grandmother. Or more specifically, her grandmother's ghost, who's gone missing.

Muffins and Mediums **is coming soon.**
Stay tuned for more of Heartwood Hollow's secrets.

Acknowledgments

Thank you to my family and friends for their continued support of this dream of mine. To Kahlan, my constant mini-editor, the clipboard is yours for another few weeks. To Rob, thank you for putting up with the crazy last-minute rush of publishing as always.

My continued thanks to the fabulous cozy mystery community I have found through social media and to the website 4thewords.com. I could not have finished this book without the alien event.

And finally, thank you to *you* for reading this book.

About the Author

Rosie Pease is a native Rhode Islander but has lived in Vermont, New York, and Ohio. She uses the places she's traveled to as inspiration for the settings of her cozy mysteries, pulling the theater from one, the cider mill from another, the river from another to create a fictitious town that feels familiar.

She collects Funko Pops of the Harry Potter, Hunger Games, Doctor Who, DC TV, and Marvel variety, with a few others thrown in for fun. Her desk is a mess, but she can find everything on it, so it works for her as long as things aren't falling onto the keyboard as she writes.

When she's not crafting cozy mysteries, she's playing with her daughter, hanging out with her husband, or being amused by her two crazy cats.

Come find Rosie online:
Website: https://rosiepease.com
Facebook, Instagram, Twitter, and Pinterest:
@WriteRosiePease

ALSO BY ROSIE PEASE

The Matchmaking Baker

Coffee and Calicos

Sweets and Santa

Mixing Up Magic

Cookies and Curses

Scones and Spells

Weddings and Witchcraft

Potluck and Powers

Muffins and Mediums

Purrfect Travel Companion

Catastrophe on the Road

Catastrophe in the Kitchen